THE APRIC

*Moonlight upon the Sea is dedicated to Amelia.
I sat for a solid fifteen minutes and tried to think of the person who deserved it the most, and it was you.*

You are an amazing friend. You uplift me when I'm down, no matter how depressed I get. You support the Apricity series no matter what happens. You have made this series into something beautiful and amazing with your art and without it, I truly feel like it would be less alive.

I am so excited to be taking this journey of friendship, sisterhood, and love with you.

I love you.

Book cover photo and character illustrations by Amelia L. Carter
www.meialoue.com

Novel content, book design, cover design, typesetting, and manuscript editing by Mariah L. Stevens
www.starlightwriting.com

This is a work of semi-autobiographical fiction. It was taken from multiple separate experiences in the author's life and compiled into one narrative.

Some characters, places, and incidents are from real pieces of the author's personal life. All names are fictitious. Some characters, places, and incidents either are the product of the author's imagination or are used fictitiously. Some resemblance to actual persons, living or dead, events, or locales is inevitable yet coincidental. Any musical band names mentioned are real.

First paperback edition April 2021
ISBN-13: 9798717032490 (paperback)

TRIGGER WARNINGS

If you choose to read this trigger warning page, unfortunately it will spoil a bit! So be mindful and aware before you read the warnings.

This trigger warning is a blanket warning for the entire Apricity series.

If you are a minor reading this book, please understand that it is an 18+ book, as is the entire Apricity series. The characters are age 19-20. They are not minors.

The Apricity series contains trigger warnings for:

Sexual assault/rape *(Book One – Chapter Eighteen: pg. 240-244. Do not skip page 245 and onward unless you want to miss an important plot point.)*

Emotional and mental abuse

Eating disorders

Toxic relationships

Mentions of racism/discussions about race

Religious themes and absence of faith *(specifically Christianity)*

Adult content warnings:

Marijuana and drug use

Sexual content

Foul language

Things the author ensures:

Author's personal experience with all content

Tasteful descriptions of content

The end goal of recovery *(no matter how toxic the relationship gets, the end goal is recovery. The point of the Apricity series is to show the dark side of trauma and why the only solution is recovery and medical help.)*

THIS BOOK SERIES IS WRITTEN FROM THE MALE CHARACTER'S POV FOR A SPECIFIC REASON

This is to showcase the eating disorder and the way it affects the people who exist outside of the eating disordered individual's experience. It showcases how eating disorders affect those around you, and what happens when someone takes it upon themselves to "fix" something that can only be healed through medical intervention and recovery. It has nothing to do with race or skin color, though those things as well as the "white savior trope" are tackled in this novel.

This is a graphic depiction of struggles that the author has faced, presented in a way that can help others seek the first step towards recovery. The author has written this story according to her personal experiences with rape/sexual assault, a 10-year long battle with Bulimia, and a 4-year long abusive relationship, however the narrative itself is done to tell a story for the characters.

For example, the author's sexual assaults were not under the same circumstances as the main character, however the author has still written completely accurate to physicality, emotional turmoil, trauma, and thoughts.

This novel as well as the Apricity Series is written by a Black author to provide representation and healing for other survivors of both sexual assault and eating disorders. While it does have an overarching plot, this series is meant to encourage taking the first step to recovery to save your life. And while the main character is also a Black woman, it is not a novel meant to exploit Black trauma.

The Apricity Series takes a pro-recovery stance.

There is no sugar-coating and there is no pretending that things like abuse, racism, and trauma do not exist.

If you complete reading of this novel and feel that a trigger warning is missing from the page, e-mail the author at starlightxwriting@gmail.com to notify her, and she will add it to subsequent novels in the series.

THE APRICITY SERIES

MOONLIGHT
upon the Sea

BOOK TWO

written by MARIAH LYNN STEVENS

illustrations by AMELIA LOUISE CARTER

CHAPTER ONE

October 2018

Ash feared the sea.

The waters, deep and pressing, spreading for miles. Stretching to the horizon, where the waves disappeared into the sky. Days where the sunlight glinted bright off the surface. Nights where the stars bathed it in gentle light. He imagined that if he were floating in the middle of the ocean underneath the moon, it would paint him in opalescence. He would look pretty while he drowned.

He feared the knowledge that something that big, that vast, that endless could pull him under and erase him.

Having feelings for Tayshia Cole was like drowning.

And he feared that.

October tripped over itself on its way to Halloween.

The rain continued unabated, pooling in the divots and potholes on the roads and drowning the grass outside. It got to the point where sometimes, Ash would wake to the sound of it and think the world was flooding.

It felt like his world had already gone under.

They'd never talked about the memory, choosing instead to speak as little as possible. There was a certain dynamic that had cropped up between the two and because of it, Ash wasn't quite sure how to act around her. It wasn't like they'd talked before but now, it was even more difficult. Tayshia didn't avoid him in the apartment, but she was so dead silent that it felt like the silence sucked the air out of his lungs when she was around.

Ash had stopped bothering her about her dishes, finding that it was best if he just cleaned them himself. Tayshia stopped yelling at him when he did, even though he saw her shooting him wary looks when he was arms-deep in soapy dishwater.

The routine didn't remain trapped inside the apartment.

In Myths & Legends, having her be so stone-faced made everything more difficult. They didn't sit next to one another but since she'd gotten along so well with Ji Hyun, she liked to sit next to her. And given that Ash and Ji Hyun sat at the same table every day, it was a bit awkward working together on classwork when Tayshia and Ash weren't talking.

The fact that she wouldn't let him in past the metaphorical wall she'd put up between them was the only reason why he hadn't beaten the living shit out of Kieran yet. He didn't need anything to make things worse and he knew how delicate the situation was. Once he got a chance to talk to her, Kieran was dead. Easy enough.

Until then, he settled for watching her like a hawk.

In the apartment, in the cafeteria, in class, in the hallways. No matter where they were, if they were in the same vicinity, Ash watched her. No one ever tried to come near her or bother her, however it made Ash feel useful to watch, just in case.

Kieran kept his distance at lunch, usually sticking to other tables or not showing up at all. He'd surround himself with other friends while Tayshia stuck to the same spot she always sat in. Usually, she was flanked by other students and friends. Sometimes Elijah sat with her, but that seemed to be only on the days where she ate a lot. He always brought her something.

Annoying.

Ash noticed things about her that he hadn't noticed before.

Aside from the bizarre way her eating habits swung from separating colors on her plate to eating everything in sight, she bounced her leg under the table. He saw it one day when no one sat across from her. On the days where she separated her food, she took measured bites, chewing slowly. On the days where she ate everything, she practically inhaled the food and left immediately after.

But she was safe, so long as he kept his eyes on her. That's what mattered to him right now.

As the weeks of October faded away and Halloween crept closer, Ash found that he hated how much she'd frozen him out. When he went to sleep at night, he still dreamed of her, but sometimes it felt like his subconscious went to war with the dreams. Like normal, unassuming dreams were having to fight off not only her daily play-by-plays every night but also the memories of her attack.

He just wished she would talk to him about it.

On Monday the 29th, he walked a few yards behind Tayshia in the hallway to Myths & Legends. She was walking slower than usual, hugging her books to her chest and staring at the ground. It was unlike her, but it seemed like she was tired. He wasn't surprised by that, as she'd been exercising in her bedroom every morning and night for the past four days straight.

He could hear her counting.

As she neared the door, he sped up and reached past her, crowding her as he held it open for her.

She looked up at him. "Huh? Oh... Thanks."

"Yeah."

She walked past him, her shoulder brushing his chest. He caught a whiff of her scent, finding familiarity in it that he hadn't noticed before. She wore a perfume that smelled like gardenias. It had a bold aroma, floral and woody.

Not that he needed that reminder right now.

When she got into class, instead of walking to her normal seat at their table towards the middle of the room, Tayshia took a seat in the far back corner table. She pulled out her materials like she usually did, but she looked pale. She'd taken her weave out recently, leaving her with her natural curls, which were kinky and spiraled out of the top of her head to her chest. Today, they were piled on top of her head. She wore a giant black hoodie, the sleeves nearly swallowing her fingers. She looked exhausted.

He didn't know whether or not he should tell her that she'd accidentally pulled *his* hoodie out of the dryer that morning.

Ash sat down in his normal seat beside Ji Hyun, fighting the urge to stare at Tayshia more than he probably should have. He knew it was creepy—that he wasn't even trying to be subtle—but his mind and body were in a tailspin right now. All he could think about was the memory. It was burned into his brain, a trauma in its own right, and it made him feel like he was falling apart.

He wanted to be there for her but she wouldn't let him, so all he could do was watch her.

"Hey," Ji Hyun said as she sank down into the seat beside him, dragging the word out in a sympathetic manner.

"Hey."

"Are you doing all right?"

"Yeah, I'm fine," he said, giving her a strange look. "Are you?"

"I'm great," she said, smiling. "It feels like it's been weeks since we've talked."

"What?" His head pulled back. "I have two classes with you and see you five days a week."

"Yeah, but I mean like, outside of school. Things are so weird with you right now. I can tell."

"They're not weird."

"Have you fixed things with Elijah?"

"I don't want to talk about Elijah," he replied. They hadn't spoken since the conversation in the hallway. Ash maintained that out of sheer loyalty, Elijah should not have gone into the nurse's office. Ash's stomach roiled with anger whenever he thought about it.

It seemed to be Elijah's sentiment that he owed Ash nothing.

"You seem distracted."

"I *am* distracted," he said, pulling out his notebook and pencil for the inevitable lecture that Miss Iqbal would be giving them when she arrived. "By you, right now, with your dramatics."

Fully expecting her to lash out at him, he was stunned when her response was to smirk.

"You're right. I shouldn't bother you with them. I *should* bother you with my theory, though."

"What theory?" he said, turning to narrow his eyes down at her.

"Oh, just your little crush." Ji Hyun rested her elbow on the table, propping her chin on her hand. With her pen, she scratched absentminded circles onto her notebook paper.

"I don't have a crush," he said. "What are you talking about?"

"Ash, come on." Ji Hyun rolled her eyes, grinning. "You can't think I'm that stupid."

"I do think you're stupid. I think you're stupid and blind."

"Or maybe you're just super bad at hiding the way you feel, dumbass. You ever think about that?" She gestured to the door with her pen. "Look—Miss Iqbal's here."

Miss Iqbal strode in with her curly black hair fluttering behind her, starting that day's lecture with something new. Since it was almost Halloween, she wanted to show them all some myths about ghosts from all over the world. Then, she wanted them all to talk to their table members about ghost stories they knew from Crystal Springs or from home. Ash felt relieved. Any day where there was no lecture was a good day in his opinion.

During the classwork portion of the period, Ash thought he was going to go nuts. Ji Hyun wouldn't stop smirking at him, even while they were sharing their stories. He was about ready to throttle her.

Miss Iqbal wandered from table to table, drifting to a stop in front of Tayshia's. She was by herself that day—no one had sat beside her. She stared absentmindedly at the tabletop, like she either didn't know no one was there or she was too tired to care.

"Hi, Tayshia," Miss Iqbal said, smiling down at her. "You didn't want to sit with Ash and Ji Hyun today?"

Tayshia slowly dragged her gaze up to meet the teacher's. She blinked, appearing puzzled.

"Mm—what? Oh. Oh, no. Not today."

"All right," Miss Iqbal said. "How come?"

Tayshia responded after a strange delay. "I forgot."

"Oh, okay." Miss Iqbal nodded slowly, but it was clear she was confused. "Well, I suppose it's all right for you to skip today's classwork. Are you well? Do you need to see Nurse Pri—"

"*No!*" Tayshia cried, her eyes widening. Her hands fidgeted in her lap. "I mean—no. No, I'm just tired."

"All right. Well, if you're not feeling well, feel free to go see her at any time during class." She started to turn, then stopped. "Did you ever get around to finishing up your essay on Irish fey? Why don't you take some time to work on that and turn it in to me at the end of class."

"Okay."

Ash and Ji Hyun exchanged glances.

"What's wrong with her?" Ji Hyun whispered. "I've been texting her like crazy, but she barely ever responds."

Ash shrugged. She'd relived what was most likely the worst night of her life.

Of course she was tired.

"Oh my gosh, I never told you!" Ji Hyun gasped, pulling Ash's attention to her. "Remember how I told you my grandparents wanted me to come visit?"

"In Korea? Yeah."

"Yes, so I forgot to tell you that I got my tickets already! My mom was..."

Ash sat and listened with half of his brain working as Ji Hyun launched into the whole story of how she was going to South Korea for Christmas, but all he could think about was Tayshia.

What was wrong with her?

In the last fifteen minutes or so of class, while everyone was buzzing with excitement to either go home or go to their next class, Tayshia got up and walked to Miss Iqbal's desk. She had a few sheets of notebook paper with her.

"It's just my rough draft," she said, her voice carrying to where Ash could hear. "I can take it home and type it if you want."

"You know what? That's okay," Miss Iqbal said, smiling up at Tayshia. "I'll take the rough draft as is and mark you full credit. Thank you, Tayshia. I hope you feel better, honey."

"Thank you," Tayshia said with a small, faint smile. Looking distracted, she turned and walked back, her gaze cast to the floor.

As she returned to her seat, Ash noticed that the way she was walking was a bit strange. It was almost like she was swaying, or listing towards the left...

Just like all those weeks ago, when she slammed into the table in the restaurant on her birthday, Tayshia held the heel of her palm to her temple and knocked into the corner of Ash's side of the table. Her feet caught on themselves and she pitched forward.

It was like second nature.

Ash's left arm shot out, wrapping around the front of her midsection. An *oof* escaped her lips as she fell into the crease, and he placed his right hand on the left side of her waist to stabilize her. Everyone was staring at them as though she'd just sprouted wings, but for a moment—as she looked at him from underneath her curly bangs with a mortified expression—it felt like they were the only two in the room.

"Good?" he murmured.

"I'm fine. Let go of me."

He did. She sprung upright lightning fast. Ash turned in his chair to watch her go back to her seat. The pitter-patter of her shoes against the floor provided the backdrop to Miss Iqbal's concern from the front of the room.

"I'm okay, Miss Iqbal," Tayshia said, and the chipper tone of her voice didn't seem to match the way her hands trembled.

Beside Ash, Ji Hyun cleared her throat.

"What?" he drawled. "What sort of guy would I be if I let her fall?"

"You wouldn't be Ash Robards," Ji Hyun said, and her tone was almost fearful. It drew Ash's gaze and when their eyes met, he was shocked to see that she looked worried. "You've always been the protective kind of guy when it calls for it."

"Uh, no. No, I haven't," Ash spluttered, on the verge of laughter. "Have you lost your mind?"

"The time you punched that kid for looking up my skirt at that party?"

"I was literally drunk. I had—"

Ji Hyun cut him off. "Remember Sophomore Year? At the skate park? That creepy guy? He said something to me about my chest. You shoved him."

"Nah, come on." He tilted his head back and slightly to the side, looking down his nose at her. "You're kidding. That's not being *protective*. That's just respect."

"You walked me to class every day for three weeks straight because I told you I thought I had a stalker."

"I did *not*—"

"If I set her up with Andre's weed dealer right now, what would you do? Like, if I texted him and said she was D-T-F, what would you do?"

Ash was torn between falsely claiming he and Tayshia were married, or simply passing away. He rearranged his bewildered facial expression into one that was as smooth as a painting.

"Nothing."

Ji Hyun reached for her phone, plucking it off of the table. She typed in the passcode, raising one eyebrow.

"Ji Hyun, I'm serious. Are you serious?"

"Bro, I'm dead serious." She opened the texting app.

A panic spiked inside of him—one that he couldn't place the origin of—and he fixed her with a ferocious, blazing glare.

"If you text him, I swear to God I'll fucking—"

"Why, Ash," Ji Hyun said, challenge woven in her voice. "That's awfully overprotective of you."

Around them, several students were getting up to leave early, Ash ignored them, knowing that to break eye contact with Ji Hyun was to admit defeat.

Ji Hyun smirked. "If you admit you feel protective over little Miss Tayshia Cole, then I won't text him. And you *know* he'd be all in on that."

"I don't like Tayshia."

"Did I *say* the word 'like' anywhere in that sentence?" Ji Hyun glowered. "I said *protective*."

"I fucking hate you, you know that?"

"Yes." Her smirk returned. "And I know you. I know how you hyper-focus and try to fix everything. You seem to think there's something in her that needs fixing. Now, admit it. It's fan behavior."

"Fine," he snarled, teeth gritted. "I'm keeping an eye on her. *Happy*?"

"Delighted," she said, setting her phone down. "But concerned."

"Stay concerned."

"Or you can tell me what's going on."

"All right," he said in a tone that dripped with sarcasm, "I will, if you tell me why you're so obsessed with me. I think I'd consider that fan behavior, too."

"Bye." She held up a hand in his face and turned to the front. "I'm done."

"Of course you're done."

"No," she said, raising her voice a bit. "No, I'm done. I'm not *obsessed* with you."

"Of *course* you're done. You always check out the minute I win."

"*No,* this has nothing to do with —"

"It has *everything* to do with — "

Just then, Miss Iqbal standing up from her desk to do a closing announcement silenced them both.

Ash tried his best to pay attention but he found it difficult. Ji Hyun seemed so sure that he at least cared about Tayshia enough to want to keep her safe. Which he did, after what they'd been through together.

So, yeah.

He was a little overprotective. He knew it was improbable for the man who attacked Tayshia to ever cross paths with her again, but it didn't stop him from feeling on edge. Sometimes, he wondered if maybe it would be easier to stop denying the fact that he'd had her on his mind in some way since that night in the amethyst caverns. If it might be easier to just embrace whatever it was that drew him to her. At least then, he wouldn't have to watch over her from afar.

He could just be there for her.

CHAPTER TWO

Ash's phone buzzed on the coffee table.

He sighed, pausing his game and setting the controller down. Leaning over, he ran one hand through his hair while he picked the phone up and looked at the screen. His stomach jolted.

It was another text from Ryo.

Hey again, kid. Third or fourth message now. I know it's tough, but you gotta face the things that scare you. Steven and I just wanna be there for you. We got holidays coming up and a room here for ya. You're family. – Ryo

This was horrible.

It was the worst message he could possibly have gotten.

He knew he was alone. He knew his family was dead and gone. Ash knew that unless he created a family of his own, he was going to be alone. Whether the Sunamuras wanted him in their life or not, he would always know that his family was gone. So, while Ryo's message was sent as a way to connect with him, it wasn't a message that Ash wanted to read.

It was a reminder.

Ash sank back into the couch with a heavy sigh, tilting his head back so that the base of his skull sunk into the top of the back cushions. Tayshia was gone, having left the house an hour or so ago saying she was going to a buffet with a friend. He didn't know why, but he felt as lonely now as he had in his cell.

He wished he could go back in time.

Running both hands up through his hair, he tangled his fingers in the strands. The grief inside of him threatened to overwhelm him, feeling like a deep, gaping hole in his chest. He took several shallow, shuddering breaths. His eyes stung.

What if he replied to Ryo and found out that he didn't actually care about him? What if the Sunamuras' intentions *were* true, but when he met up with them again, they didn't like the person he'd become?

God. How ashamed would his mother be if she were alive and saw what a useless loser that he was? He had this apartment for one year and the only reason why the leasing office had overlooked his felony was because he was in the pre-req program. But what happened after that?

What happened if he had nowhere to go not because he couldn't afford it, but because no one would approve him?

He was fucking *useless*.

Fuck, he thought as a wave of bottomless anguish washed over him for the first time in months. His leg bounced. He hadn't wept since jail. He didn't want to weep now, while he was in the fucking living room.

Ash gritted his teeth against the pain, which he felt inside his heart like an acute wrenching. He couldn't cry. It was a waste of time. It was a *waste* of *time*.

Don't fucking cry.
It's a waste of time.
It won't bring her back.

Ash's hands slid to cover his face, his head still tilted back on the couch. He broke down, sobbing so hard that it made his head hurt. It felt unbearable. Endless. Like an ocean tide ripping his feet out from underneath him and forcing him below the surface of his careful façade. It hurt to weep this way, to fall prey to the loss.

He wished he could bring her back.

Shifting, he prepared to lie down with the inevitable headache, but was stopped by a crinkling sound. He frowned.

What?

Ash moved again and realized that if he did it with a certain amount of body weight, it moved the cushions. Something was trapped between them and the back of the couch. Reaching in, he pulled whatever it was out.

"An empty chip bag?" he muttered, perplexed. "Why the Hell would she stick this down the couch?"

Setting the wrapper down, he reached into the couch again. He searched the back and in-between the cushions. The continued crinkling and crackling started to grate on his nerves as he pulled more wrappers out on both sides of the sectional, standing up so he could check the entire couch. Soon, he had a pile of wrappers on the coffee table.

It was all junk food—cookies, chips, crackers, candy. Sweet or savory, she didn't seem to have a preference. Every single package was empty. Tayshia had finished them off and stuffed them into the couch.

Why? And *when*?

A sound.

The front door swung open. Ash felt his heart leaping up into his chest. Quick as a flash, he used his free hand to wipe his cheeks. He stood up as Tayshia stepped into the apartment. The empty wrappers discarded stood out, shining under the light from the floor lamp and the paused game on the TV screen. Tayshia stopped dead in her tracks, eyeing the table with half-open, tired eyes.

"Care to explain why you're performing Satanic rituals to call ants to the house?" Ash said, roughening his voice to mask that he'd just been weeping.

"No." She walked closer to him and dropped her books and bag onto the coffee table. The wrappers crinkled and some fluttered to the carpet. When she straightened her back, she glared up at him. "Before you pop off—yes, I'm messy. We've established it. So, just move and I'll throw it all out."

Ash saw her bending to start gathering them, and he forgot himself and their circumstances. He started to move toward her to help. She glanced up, a flash of panic entering her eyes—something he never would have recognized had he not walked her memory—and she stumbled backward with her arms raised.

"I told you not to touch me," she hissed, eyes blazing. "You better back up."

"I wasn't going to touch you. I was just—look, I wasn't going to start in on you. I just wanted an explanation."

"Well, you're not going to get one!" she cried, her voice shrill and her eyes wild. She took a step back, her hands trembling at her sides. It seemed as though she couldn't look at either him or the wrappers. Like her shame was too great.

"Okay, but this is weird. I think you should explain to me why."

"I don't have time for this," she whispered, sounding like she was floating somewhere between anxiety and rage. She snatched up all of the wrappers, crumpling them together and storming to the trash can.

"You had time to stuff them in there," Ash said, crossing his arms. "Yet you don't have time to tell me why?"

"Just *shut up*, Ash!" she shrieked, slamming the trash can lid down and causing him to flinch back in astonishment. "Just shut up! Stop policing everything I do! I can't—" She made a frustrated sound through bared teeth, hands in fists as she stomped one foot. "—*take* it anymore! The dishes, the dishes. Every day, it's the dishes! It's the books, and the papers, and the trash in the couch, and the fact that I'm in the bathroom for too long! Can't you just leave me alone?!"

By the look on her face, the redness of her cheeks, and the way he could see her arms trembling, she was not in a right state of mind. And knowing what he knew about Paris—remembering how she'd fallen apart on the floor of that hotel room with the knowledge that her boyfriend had kept her phone from her with intent—he knew better than to let his anger control him at this moment.

"I can't, I can't, I can't."

Ash was aggressive and he was controlling and he was by no means perfect, but he never wanted to be angry with her again. God knew she had enough rage burning inside of her for the both of them.

"Take a fucking second, will you?"

Tayshia sucked in her breath and held it. Her hands were shaking so much that her fingers had curled. She didn't look okay.

She didn't look okay at all.

Ash took a cautious step toward her, his gaze bouncing back and forth between her frenzied eyes and clenched hands. He'd never been in this situation before and he didn't know exactly what to say. He just knew that whatever she said, he needed to counter it.

"Let out your breath," he said. "You're gonna get lightheaded."

"Why couldn't you just throw them away and not *say* anything?" was her reply, and it came out as a borderline sob. "Why did you have to be so mean about it?"

"Breathe."

Tayshia exhaled right as Ash inched closer to her. They were between the coffee table and the side of the sectional closest to the kitchen, and he could feel the heat of her body as he stopped right in front of her.

"I don't have time for this," she said under her breath, shaking her head. "I don't have time for this. I don't have time."

"You have time," he said, trying to keep his voice as soft as possible. With a slow, smooth pace, he lifted his hands to take both of hers in his own. As gentle as though she were made of glass, he wrapped his fingers around them, feeling how rigid they were in her panic.

She tried to pull away but he held tighter, his forefingers curving around the backs of her palms. His thumb dug into her pressure point, a place his mother had shown him to be calming during the times that he felt panicked after his father hit him. He wanted to soothe her.

Was he in denial? *Did* he like her? Or was this just a result of the dream?

"Calm down."

"I don't want to be calm." Her head shook from side to side as she gazed up at him imploringly. "I don't—"

"*Calm*," he murmured, raising his chin, "*down*."

"No! I don't—Ash—" She ripped her hands away, her anxiety rising in her eyes again. "*I don't want to be calm!* I told you to leave me *alone!*"

Before he could do or say anything else, she turned, walked away, and slammed the bathroom door shut.

Ash scowled, dropping his head back and scrubbing at his face with his hands. She was insufferable. She was a *nightmare.*

Why the *fuck* did she put food wrappers into the couch?!

☼☼☼

Every time he got a letter, Ash contemplated opening it.

The wooden chest on his dresser was starting to get full, the envelopes having to have their edges folded just to get the newest one in. They came around the same time each week, the paper of the envelope always stained with what Ash could only assume were tears.

It was the middle of October—a Friday—and here he stood, staring down at yet another one. His father's handwriting on the front had gotten worse, the normally solid lines looking wobbly and broken. The ink went from dark to light in an ombre pattern that seemed unintentional.

Maybe if he opened the newest one, he'd find out why.

Standing in front of his dresser, wooden chest open and letter in hand, Ash wanted to. He wanted to open it just to see. Just to *know.*

But he couldn't.

He couldn't because if he did, then he'd have to face down all of the other letters. He'd have to face down the fact that his father kept calling. The letters were Gabriel's metaphorical attempts to make sure Ash knew he still thought of him. That he was still his son even if Ash didn't want to call him his father.

If he read one of the letters, Ash would have to read them all and if he read them all, he'd hate himself.

He folded the edges of the envelope and tucked it into the chest, closing the lid and throwing the latch.

It was for the best.

Turning, he went out to the kitchen to make himself a snack. School had been stressful that day, with almost all of his teachers assigning mini essays for the weekend. He never had been much of a writer. Word counts were hard to hit when his thoughts were too loud to sort through.

He felt like he existed inside of a tornado.

As he waited for a bagel to toast, Ash tried not to think too much. He knew if he allowed himself to think, he'd focus on the fact that his father's birthday was in January. Ash was no longer in jail. He had no excuse if he chose not to visit Gabriel in prison. The letters going unanswered could be explained away by a wrong address.

But Ash had been released.

If he didn't go visit his father, then Gabriel would know it was on purpose. After losing his wife, the definitive nail in the coffin of his son's abandonment would destroy him. Ash knew that. It wasn't rocket science.

Gabriel would be devastated.

"Why do you look so angry?"

Ash looked up from the kitchen floor, his arms crossed over his chest as he leaned his hips back against the counter. He saw Tayshia entering the room from the hallway and to his surprise, she was wearing the hoop earrings he'd bought her.

Which, he supposed he shouldn't be too surprised because she wore them all the time. He just wasn't sure if she'd want to wear the things he'd bought her after their last encounter.

"Nah, I'm cool," he said, running a hand through his hair while resting the other on the edge of the counter by his hip. "How's your day?"

"It's fine." She went to the refrigerator and withdrew a can of the diet cola she'd asked him to buy via text. She popped the tab and then took a drink, staring at him while she did so. Then, she said, "Your shirt's ripped."

Ash glanced down at his blue-and-white-striped shirt. It had no collar, giving it a wider neckline that showed parts of his tattooed collarbones. "It's just how the shirt came."

"Oh."

He tilted his head to the side. "Your dress is cute."

"My dress?" She looked down at her lavender plaid dress, then gave him an inscrutable look. "Thanks."

This was the first conversation they'd had since her panic attack. In a strange way that Ash couldn't explain, it managed to be awkward while not *feeling* awkward. They hadn't spoken at all except over random text messages. Ash still couldn't look at her without thinking of Paris. The nightmare or memory, or whatever it was, was burned into his mind.

He bit his lower lip and looked down at her sternum, where he could see the crystal. It looked so small and unassuming.

Could it really be the thing that connected them together?

The bagel popped up from the toaster.

Ash pushed away from the counter and turned to grab a plate. He'd already retrieved the cream cheese from the fridge, so all he had to do was get a butter knife and start spreading.

Tayshia crossed behind him, the heavy thud of her combat boots against the linoleum alerting him.

"Wait, where are you going?" he asked.

She paused in the entrance of the hallway. "To my room. Why?"

"No," he said, gesturing at her with the knife. "I mean, you got your shoes on and shit. Where are you going?"

"Well, I'm going to a Halloween party with my friends. It's at Keely Daniels' house."

"It's only the fifteenth," he said, the scraping of the knife against the bagel seeming loud.

"Apparently she's back for the weekend from college and wanted to throw an early party. My friends said they were going, so I said I'd go with them." Tayshia's acrylics tapped against her soda can. "It's probably not your scene. It's just gonna be like, the sports kids and stuff."

16

"Parties?" Ash laughed as he tossed the knife into the sink for him to clean later. He took a large bite of his bagel, wiping cream cheese off of the corner of his mouth with the pad of his thumb. "Parties have always been my scene. Where do you think the best place to sell was back then? Football players pay. Including your little boyfriend, Kieran."

Tayshia's facial expression was disbelieving. "Kieran didn't do any drugs. There's no way. They do drug tests."

Ash held in another laugh. "If you think that they were testing any of their star players, you're delusional. The only thing Christ Rising has going for it is the football team."

"Um, *no*," she said, glaring at him, "I'm not stupid, Ash. I dated him for years. I know he got tested multiple times."

"I'm sure he did." Ash took another bite. "And I'm sure it's easy for the coaches to simply pretend he passed every single one."

Tayshia scowled. "I'm not interested in fighting with you. I'd literally rather die than hear you yelling at me right now."

"I'm not yelling."

"But you will yell because you always yell."

"No, I do *not* always yell."

"Yes, you do. The first chance you get, you're—" Tayshia cut herself off with a wave of her hand. "You know what? No. I'm not doing this. I need to go finish getting ready."

Ash stood there, fuming as he watched her disappear down the hallway.

They needed to talk about the dream. He knew that was why they were reverting back to the volatility that had existed in the apartment back in September. If they kept trying to bottle it up and ignore what they'd experienced, then it was only going to make things more toxic.

He finished his bagel and then washed the couple of dishes he'd dirtied. As he put the cream cheese back into the refrigerator, Tayshia came stomping back out wearing a coat over her dress. She set the half-empty soda can on the counter and breezed to the front door.

"You gonna throw that away?" he called angrily.

"Do it yourself."

The front door slammed shut.

It took every ounce of self-control Ash had in his body not to go out there after her. For a moment, he forgot about the dream and let his anger overwhelm him. But then, as fast as the tide came in, it washed back out. He took a deep breath.

She wasn't a bitch. She was in pain.

And so was he.

Ash went into his room. Right as he opened the door, he heard his phone buzzing on his bed where he'd left it. He jogged over to grab it, plopping down on the edge of the mattress amongst his messy blankets. It was a text from Elijah.

You up to party tonight?

Ash dropped his head back in exasperation. Things still hadn't gotten any better with Elijah and though he wanted to try and work things out, he didn't want to have to do it at a party full of people he hated.

Depends, Ash typed back. *Is it Keely's party?*

Yeah, the Halloween party. We don't have to dress up or anything. And you don't have to go if you don't want to. I just thought I'd ask.

Couldn't we just kick it here at my place? Ash grimaced as he typed. *Probably best if I'm nowhere near Kieran O'Connell right now.*

Why?

Ash froze. He wasn't sure how to explain that.

It wasn't like he could tell Elijah that he'd somehow found himself inside of Tayshia's body during a nightmare that was most likely a memory, and that in the nightmare-memory-thing, Kieran was a fucking prick.

And if he went to the party, would his temper keep itself in check? Ash had already disliked Kieran before the nightmare. If Ash heard him say one wrong thing, he wasn't so sure he'd be able to hold himself back. There were thousands of reasons for him to punch Kieran in the face, and exactly zero valid reasons why he shouldn't.

He's just an asshole, Ash replied. *And I hate him.*

Elijah replied with a laughing emoji and then typed, *Bro just come to the party. There's gonna be so many people there you probably won't even notice him.*

Ash rolled his eyes. *Fine. Come through and I'll meet you downstairs.*

Bet. Omw.

This was going to cause problems. Tayshia was going to be annoyed. She was going to think he was following her there.

Probably because he was.

CHAPTER THREE

Keely Daniels' house was huge.

Not like, mansion huge. But it was big. Big enough to provide ample space enough for a party. Ash had been to her two-story suburban home countless times, given that every time the sports teams wanted to throw a party, they did it at her house. Her parents were always traveling for work.

The music was loud, there were orange and purple string lights strung up, and Halloween decorations wherever Ash looked. Everyone stood in the hallways and rooms, red cups in hand and smiles on their faces. Ash received a few weird looks, as he'd only ever come to parties like these in the past to sell drugs, but he ignored them. His gaze scanned every face he passed, looking for Tayshia.

Because why else was he here?

Elijah and Ash went to the kitchen first, grabbing some drinks. Ash didn't really like the taste of alcohol but he took a shot anyway. Elijah was the designated driver, so he was the one who was going to be drinking soda all night.

"Do they have diet?" Elijah said as he rummaged through the cans on the counter.

"Why do you need diet soda?"

"I like the taste better. The sugary sodas do so much shit to your body. Ah, here—diet." Elijah opened it and took a drink, then smirked at him. "I thought you hated alcohol."

"I do," Ash said as he poured a second shot of tequila, "but I'm in a house full of people who hate me. I'm thinking I need it."

He tipped back the second shot, the burning pulling his brows together as his facial expression twisted. He coughed and shook his head out. Two was his limit, if not for the taste, for the fact that he would likely get tipsy off of those two.

"Nasty."

Elijah laughed. "I'll never understand you."

"It's for the best."

Ash grabbed a can of soda and led the way out of the kitchen. They passed a group of Senior girls as they went. The girls' conversation fell quiet as they walked by — another thing for Ash to ignore.

He wasn't sure if Crystal Springs was ever going to forget about what he and his father had done. He had a feeling that it was something that would follow him for the rest of his life if he didn't find the strength to leave. Not that he wanted to leave, necessarily. Crystal Springs was his home.

But no one wanted him here.

"So, how's things going?" Elijah asked, one hand in the pocket of his jeans and the other wrapped around his soda.

They'd found a corner in the crowded living room. It was far enough away from the second living room — which had the speakers — that the music was a bit less loud. No one was dancing in here, though the room was nearly packed to the walls.

And Tayshia was in the center.

She stood with a group of her friends, an assortment of girls and guys who all had drinks and were laughing. Ash noticed that she had no drink but that it didn't seem to deter her from smiling and laughing. It was almost strange to see her look so animated when at school, she floated about like a haunt. At home, she was moody and irritable.

But here she was, and she was alive.

"They're fine," Ash said, sipping his soda. "And you?"

Elijah shrugged. "Things are fine with me, I guess. My mom's the one who's struggling."

Ash frowned, tearing his gaze off of Tayshia's back. "What? What's wrong? Is she sick?"

"No, it's just finances. Things are always like, tight. Every month starts promising and then bam, we end up in shit halfway through the month."

"Fuck, that sucks, man." Ash's gaze slid back to Tayshia. She was pushing her hair behind her ear, speaking almost conspiratorially with her friend beside her. He recognized her from one of his pre-req classes but couldn't remember her name. "Did the bills go up?"

"No, they're just always stressful. I mean, my mom's a night nurse. She doesn't make that much."

Ash glanced at Elijah, but he was looking out at the crowd. "I'm sorry. That really sucks."

"Yeah." Elijah took a drink of his soda and then sighed. "I wish my dad would help but he's got the new wife, new kids, new house… You know how it is."

Tayshia and her friend were now talking to the guy to the left of her, all three of them laughing uproariously at something. The guy was like, Nick or Rick or something. Ash never was good with names. He remembered him from tenth grade Biology.

"I still can't believe he doesn't have to pay child support," Ash said. "It doesn't make any sense."

"Tell me about it," Elijah said. "It's like, he got to cheat on my mom and then just bounce. Now we're the ones suffering, while he gets to live this amazing life with this swanky new job. He's making so much money, dude."

"Weak."

"I mean, my mom is always overextending herself. She works way too many hours and they never pay her overtime. Look at what she did for you—she paid for your mom's stuff." Elijah threw up a hand. "That was like thousands for everything. Like, you paid for the headstone, which was great and everything. But for the spot in the cemetery and the—the whole thing? It was just a lot."

Why was Tayshia okay with this dude touching her like that? Why wasn't she snapping at him like she did with Ash? Why wasn't she pushing him away or standing up for herself?

"No, your mom's a saint, dude," Ash said. "She's a saint."

"Yeah, she really is." Elijah laughed. "Not like we can just ask for the money back from you, or anything."

"Yeah, that'd be kinda fucked," Ash said, distracted by the fact that the guy's hand was on Tayshia's upper back, rubbing up and down while he said something to her.

"It wasn't like you knew she had the life insurance paying out to you. I'm sure if you did, you would have sent my mom the money."

"Oh, of course. For real."

Ash wasn't exactly paying attention. He was more focused on the things that no one else could see. Ash *knew* Tayshia. She didn't like to be touched.

Something sinister and as hot as molten rock started to twist its way through his gut, spreading throughout his body in a way that made his teeth clench. His hand clenched around his soda, nearly squeezing the can.

Why was she letting Nick-Rick-what's-his-fuck touch her?

Tayshia reached behind her to gently push the guy's hand away, the two of them still chatting quite amiably. The guy didn't seem to be perturbed by it. In fact, it seemed to be making them both laugh. Ash could almost read her lips. It looked like she was flirtatiously telling him to stop.

"Anyway, I'm sure we'll be fine. My mom can always call the power company and postpone, or write a letter to the landlord. There's like, options and stuff. I don't wanna bore you with it. You don't have to worry about *any* of this stuff."

"Don't even worry about it, bruh, it's chill." Ash kept his eyes on the guy's hand. "You guys have it really rough, so I get it. You gotta vent."

"Well, it's just like… I mean, you probably never have to worry about being late on bills again." Elijah let out another laugh. "I can't even imagine what that's like. It must be hella nice."

"It's whatever."

As Tayshia turned back to face her friend, to say something to her, the guy grabbed her shoulder. He forced her back around, laughing as he did so. It was clear that the guy thought he was flirting. That he thought what he was doing was okay or warranted or wanted.

But Ash could see it on her face. A momentary slip of the mask. Her gaze snapping down to the guy's hand as it returned to her back, and then up to his face with wariness.

There was a flash.

A flash in Ash's memory, of a hand curving around Tayshia's shoulder. A hand, whipping her around and slamming her up against a brick wall. Ash, being trapped inside of her body, inside of a memory, inside of a nightmare, and feeling those bricks digging in deep.

"Hold my drink."

"What?" Elijah was slow to react. "Why?"

"Hold my *fucking* drink." Ash slammed his can into Elijah's chest, his eyes glued to the guy's hand as he started forward.

He'd made it two steps.

Two steps.

In that span of time, Tayshia had reached behind herself to push the guy's hand away. Two steps, and the guy had simply moved his hand to her opposite hip. As she stumbled against his side and looked up at him, Ash could see that her facial expression was no longer happy or alive or flirtatious.

And then Ash was there.

The crowd seemed to have parted for him as he made his way through, everyone staring as Ash grabbed the guy by the shoulder, spun him around, and pointed at him with two angry forefingers.

"Touch her again, and I knock your teeth out."

The guy's eyes widened in incredulity as he looked Ash up and down. "Are you kidding me? What the Hell is your problem?"

"I don't have a problem unless *we* have a problem," Ash said, gesturing between their chests. "And if you touch her again, then we have a definite fucking problem."

The guy scoffed and then, without another word, shoved Ash back by the shoulders. Stumbling back, Ash nearly slammed into Tayshia. Around them, everyone was watching, talking amongst themselves about Ash, speaking over the music about how unsurprised they were that he was acting like this.

Ash was known for his temper.

He'd always had a temper, ever since he was little. From tantrums as a toddler to destroying his room in elementary school, to getting into fights at lunch clear until he was eighteen, it was well-known in Crystal Springs that he wasn't someone to mess with if drama wasn't wanted. That temper had followed him to jail, where he'd been in so many fights that by the time he befriended the tattoo artist, every nurse on rotation in the infirmary knew his name, birthday, and favorite things.

It wasn't something that built within him, like with normal people who simply allowed their rage to build and build without ever letting it out. He wasn't the type to let things go. When Ash got angry, he acted on it immediately, without thinking about the consequences. It was more important to him that he get his point across.

At the moment, getting his point across to Nick with the knuckles of his left fist was extremely important.

Ash lunged forward with a snarl, aiming a left hook to the center of Nick's face that sent him reeling backward. Nick came back with a hook of his own, his fist connecting with Ash's cheek. Ash's rage grew and exploded outward through his body, pumping his adrenaline to new heights.

And then they were going at each other.

Fists were flying, teeth were gnashing. The crowd was moving out of their way. They were crashing into tables, knocking over home décor that was likely priceless. Ash was taller than Nick but thinner, so they were matched speed-to-strength. Nick could slam him into the wall so hard that he lost his breath. Ash could duck faster than Nick could blink, striking him under the jaw with sharp knuckles and more than enough vehemence for the both of them.

The last time Ash felt this angry, he was inside Tayshia's nightmare. He supposed he was overreacting a little bit. After all, it was just a hand on her shoulder, right?

Except that it wasn't just a hand. Because if it *was* just a hand, then her nightmare wouldn't have been what it was. Paris wouldn't have happened. If it was *just* a hand, then Tayshia's mask wouldn't have slipped. That fear wouldn't have been in her eyes when she looked up at Nick. That fear wouldn't exist within her at all.

And as he got Nick onto his back in the center of a crowd of jeering college students, punching him in the face again and again, all Ash could think about was the fact that Nick deserved this.

He'd touched Tayshia.

"Absolutely not! No the fuck you are not doing this in my parents' house!"

Keely came storming into the room, peeling the crowd apart as she did so. Her arms were stretched above her head as she clapped her hands loud enough to hurt eardrums. She looked livid. Her head shook from left to right.

Ash froze, blood dripping from where Nick's nails had caught him near the temple. His fist was reared back, stained with red from Nick's nose. He panted for breath, disoriented from how angry he was.

Elijah was beside him with his hands on Ash's arm, telling him it was okay and to get up. Tayshia was standing there, looking simultaneously shocked, furious, and horrified.

"Out, Ash. You need to leave. Elijah can stay, but you've gotta go."

Ash stood there, wiping blood from his own nose with the back of one tattooed hand.

"Ash, *now*," Tayshia snapped, glaring at him. "Come on."

To Ash's surprise, Tayshia turned and started pushing through the other partygoers. They all looked shocked, their eyebrows rising as she beckoned Ash after her. Ash looked down at Elijah.

"I'm gonna stay," Elijah said, kneeling beside Nick to help him sit up. He grimaced. "Probably for the best. Can you make it home?"

"Yeah," Ash said, voice monotone. He looked at Keely. "Sorry."

"Just go, you fucking asshole," came her reply. She was too busy focusing on Nick with concern in her eyes. "I don't even know why you came here."

That stung. Keely used to be his friend.

Ash turned and followed Tayshia, his face burning from the sheer amount of eyes that were on him, watching him. He liked to tell himself he was used to it but he didn't think he was. Knowing that there was hatred behind their gazes was enough to make his skin crawl.

Outside, they made their way down the cobblestone driveway and towards the gate. Tayshia was enraged—he could tell from the way she was walking with her arms crossed over her chest and her curls bouncing. Ash wasn't too happy himself but he didn't regret what he'd done.

Nick deserved it.

"You're probably ecstatic, aren't you?" Tayshia said when they were on the sidewalk, standing next to one of the many cars parked on the road. The music from the party was still audible, though faint and muffled. "Just Ash, doing whatever the fuck he wants, whenever the fuck he wants."

"Yeah, and? He touched you," Ash said, wiping his nose again. The blood stained the sleeve of his striped shirt.

She spun to face him, anger palpable in the air as she glowered up at him. "Except that Nick is my *friend*. You can't just beat the shit out of my friends!"

Ash took a step toward her. "So what you're saying is you wanted him to touch you?"

26

"I wanted—" She scowled and looked away for a second. "No, I don't like being touched. I've told you that. But he's my friend and I know he wouldn't hurt me. In any case, that doesn't give you the right to attack my friends!"

"Men should not put their hands on you."

"Men? Or just men who aren't you?"

"*Men should not put their fucking hands on you, Tayshia!*" he snarled. "What the Hell is wrong with you? You didn't want him to touch you. You didn't ask for him to touch you. And then he touches you and now you're *defending* him?"

"Okay, but you don't even know if I was in my feelings like that!" she yelled, waving her hands about in her anger. "You don't know. That's what I'm saying—you *don't know me like that*. So who are you to jump in and start running up on people to defend me when I was *fine*?!"

"I'm your friend, too."

"No, you're *not!*" she shrieked. "Not if you're gonna be attacking all of my other friends."

"This doesn't make any sense." Ash tangled his fingers in his hair, his anger and frustration shooting up to the stars. "I *saw* you. You pushed his hand away. When he grabbed you, you looked terrified. How are you so focused on the fact that I beat his ass? He *deserved* it!"

"I'm not worried about him touching me, or me being scared! It wasn't even like that! I'm worried about the fact that you're angry and violent and you *attacked* my *friend*!"

"You're telling me you're completely fine with the fact that he touched you, all because I fought him?"

"Yes."

Ash's shock rendered him speechless.

Tayshia was delusional. She was so delusional that she thought that it was more important to protect the men who harmed her than to admit they were treating her poorly. She was standing there, glaring up at him against his car while she fought for the right to keep Nick, the guy who'd just assaulted her safe.

That was fucked.

"I'm over here, trying to protect you," Ash said, pointing to himself with both of his hands, "and you're over there, letting people treat you like shit, and for *what*? For *what*, Tayshia?" He spread his arms. "So you can keep guys around you who don't give a fuck about you?"

Her gaze cut like twin daggers beneath the moonlight that shone high above them. "My friends care about me."

"*I* care about you." Ash crossed the remaining distance toward her, heedless of the fact that she was moving backward to get away from him. Heedless of the fact that her back had hit the side of a random car. He pressed against her, throwing aside decorum and reaching to push her hair behind one ear. He cupped the side of her face, a desperate look marring his features as he gazed down at her. "I'm the one that cares about you the way you deserve to be cared about. I'm the one that knows why no one — *no one* but me should be touching you."

Tayshia's face grew pinched for a moment and then, like lightning, her anger was back. With eyes like ice chips and a frown that covered up despair, she continued to glare at him.

"Then maybe you should have found it in your heart to care about me before."

"I did find it in my heart to care about you before. I just didn't have the strength to show it until after."

"Good to know my trauma brought you strength."

"Your trauma brought me nothing but pain."

They stared at one another, the silence aching like the space between each star in the sky. Aching like the eternal loneliness of the cosmos. Aching the way his heart did when he thought about the way she'd wept in that hotel room.

"It really happened, didn't it?" he asked, his voice a broken whisper. "It was real?"

She said nothing, choosing only to nod.

Ash's heart hurt. He tipped his head back, looking up at the sky for a moment as he struggled to control his desire to burst into tears. He knew he couldn't. It wasn't his memory. He didn't have the space to commandeer her pain.

He could only share it.

"And you know I was—"

She nodded, so he stopped. The confirmation was all that he needed.

"I attacked your friend because I can't stand the sight of anyone's hands on you," Ash said, the heel of his palm pressing to her jaw so he could tilt her face up. She watched him like she was

28

thirsty and she wanted to drink the sea. "Because I can't stand the sight of anyone touching you like that ever again."

"Why?"

"Because if I could have used my hands," he whispered, his nose brushing hers for a moment, "then that man would be dead."

He didn't need to explain which man. He could see it in her eyes that she already knew.

Tayshia squeezed her eyes shut and turned her face away. It slipped out of Ash's hold, her curls becoming tangled around his fingers, clenching to hold her in place.

His heart spasmed in his chest.

"Don't turn away from me, Tayshia. Don't run from this. This isn't something you can just ignore. You have to face it."

"I don't want to face it." Her right hand pressed flat to his chest. She seemed unable to decide if she should push him back or pull him closer. "I've already had to face it alone in my dreams for months now. I don't want to face it anymore."

"Then face me."

She looked up at him, perplexed.

"Face me," he whispered, finding the moonlight reflected in her brown eyes beautiful, "and we can dream together."

Her brows pulled together and then she pushed herself onto her toes, pressing her lips against his.

The moonlight above them. The faint music coming from the house. The quiet neighborhood. The warmth of her body. The anchor of his hand against her face.

It was like existed amongst the stars.

The way Tayshia kissed reminded Ash of what it felt like to swim in the ocean. The closer to the shore, the safer he was. But the further out to sea—the deeper his tongue delved, the further he pushed her into that realm of emotion—the more dangerous things became. The more he felt like willingly sinking to the bottom.

She didn't shy away from him like he expected her to. She surrendered to the waves and let him be the one to drown her.

Ash's lips were fluid as they parted to the slip of her tongue into his mouth. He sucked in his breath, inhaling her own, and moving with the rocking of her body away from the car. He kissed her as deeply and as honestly as he could, wishing that he could show her that he cared as much as he said he did. She kissed him with ten

times the fervor, like tidal waves rolling through their hearts and pulling them out to the horizon.

His other hand rose to cup her face, her precious face, and he wondered if she knew that ten years of apologizing to her for what he and his father had done would never make up for what they'd experienced in her nightmare.

No.

Her memory.

Because it was real. Everything she'd experienced was real. Paris was real.

And they were both in pain.

Ash pulled back, his lips brushing hers as he breathed, "You don't have to do anything alone ever again. You know that, right?"

She nodded, her eyes still closed. They kissed again, the slide of his hand to the front of her throat slow and sensual. His thumb caressed her skin the same gentle way his tongue glided against her own. He pulled back once again, his head tilted and nose nuzzling hers.

"You were so strong," he murmured, his lips pressing to the corner of her mouth. "But you don't have to be strong anymore. Not for me."

Tayshia went rigid.

"Stop. Stop, stop, stop." She held him away, one hand wrapped around her crystal and the other flat to his chest. She didn't look at him. "Stop doing that."

"Doing what?"

"All of it. Kissing me. Talking to me the way you do. Caring about me. Just stop."

Ash felt his heart sinking in his chest. He'd said too much. He'd overstepped.

"I'm sorry," he said, hanging his head and letting his hands hang at his sides. "I wasn't—"

"Stop reminding me of it, okay?" She extricated herself from his arms and walked a few feet away, wrapping her arms around herself. "If you know how it makes me feel, then why would you keep trying to make me talk about it? Why keep forcing me to relive it? Just because you were there for the nightmare doesn't mean it happened to you. It's not yours."

Ash clenched his hands into fists, glaring off to the left, towards the neighborhood.

She was right. No matter how horrifying it was for him to experience what he had, it was nothing compared to what Tayshia had endured. She'd burned in the firelight. He'd merely stood frozen in the shadows.

The trauma wasn't his.

"I know. And I'm sorry."

Tayshia watched him for a moment, the Fall breeze playing in her curls. She pushed them behind her ears and then crossed her arms over her chest.

"I'm going home."

"How are you gonna get there?" he asked, looking around.

"I'll walk. It's not that far."

That wasn't a lie. Their apartment complex was less than ten blocks away through suburbia. But the walk would take at least an hour.

"Come on," he sighed, pulling his phone out of his back pocket. "I can call a car or something."

"No, I want to walk. I like the moonlight."

Ash watched her walk down the sidewalk for a second before he called, "You can't just walk home alone!"

"Then walk me," she snapped without turning back around.

Ash jogged off after her, falling in-step as they passed beneath the branches of an oak tree. The wind rustled through the leaves, sending a calming chill down his spine. Beside him, Tayshia kept her distance and her arms crossed, her eyes forward.

He wished he could hold her hand.

CHAPTER FOUR

Ash avoided her on the 30th.

He shouldn't have. He knew he shouldn't have. He'd been trying to get her to a place where they could talk about the memory for weeks, so for him to just give up wasn't like him.

Except that it was.

It *was* in-character for him to give up on people. It was in-character for him to put way too much of himself and his energy into things, only to completely fail and burn out as soon as he reached the finish line. It was in-character for him to try and try and try with his father, only to end up in jail and then a year later, stuff his letters into a chest on his dresser.

The loneliness had become chronic in the way it pervaded his very existence. Like threads of shadow woven in amongst his countenance, he wore it like a cloak to shield himself from anything that could hurt him.

Because at his foundation, Ash knew that he was a creature of fear, and that the only reason why he put so much of himself into everything was because he was scared of what would happen if they failed. The reason why he threw his entire being into relationships with people around him was because he was scared of what would happen if they left. It was the same reason why he chose to follow his father into that ice cream shop.

He was a coward.

So, he avoided her. He kept his distance and alternated the times he left his bedroom so that he didn't have to look her in the eyes and admit that he was terrified. He was terrified of his emotions—of the way his dreams of her had influenced his life. How the dreams simultaneously made him feel more qualified to watch over her than anyone else, and less qualified because he'd watched her father bleed and hadn't done anything about it.

Avoiding her meant avoiding the answers to how he felt.

That day, Elijah approached Ash at lunch.

The two of them hadn't spoken in days. After the party, Elijah had proceeded to ignore his texts for almost a week. When Ash sent him a confrontational text about it, it devolved into a tense conversation about the fight outside the nurse's office. Ash knew there were people who disliked him for what he'd done, but having his best friend think less of him sucked.

It hurt.

When Ash looked up from his sandwich to see Elijah sitting down across from him, he raised an eyebrow. He viewed his friend in silence that was stoic, wondering what Elijah could possibly have to say to him after an entire month.

"Did you see the news?"

"Huh? No." Ash regarded him warily. "What was on it?"

"There's a huge rainstorm coming, wind, the whole shebang. I highly doubt anyone's going to be able to leave their houses. The power might even go out."

"Oh, shit," Ash said. "I had no idea. I mean, I knew it was gonna rain, but..."

"Were you doing anything?"

"For Halloween?" He shook his head. "Probably just chillin' at home. You?"

"I was gonna stay home and play video games, maybe stream it."

Ash nodded. They stared at one another. The awkwardness felt palpable.

"I... Well, I apologize," Elijah said, grimacing as he rubbed the back of his neck. "For what I—for everything I said."

"Oh, yeah?" Ash felt that palpable, present awkwardness stretching between them like a tense band. "Do you?"

"Yeah. I was cruel. Ignoring you after the party wasn't cool, either."

"It's chill," Ash said, shrugging one shoulder as he picked up his sandwich and took a bite. After he chewed, he said, "You were being honest, and honesty is key."

"Yeah, but there's honesty and then there's *honesty*. I literally eviscerated you."

"You eviscerated me." Ash rested his elbows on the table and laced his fingers together. He scrutinized Elijah. "But you were right. We're best friends but it's dumb to pretend like we can't have opinions of each other's choices."

34

"I mean, I get it. Your dad was terrifying, bro. But yeah — it's better for our friendship if we're honest."

"I'm trash," Ash said with another shrug. "What else is new?"

"Oh, shut up. You know you're not — "

"Just stop. If you feel like apologizing, cool. But let's not turn this into a therapy session. I'm eating."

The two boys held each other's gazes for a moment, engaging in a battle of wills and silence before Elijah conceded. He withered like burnt paper beneath Ash's fiery glare. His hands went up near his chest.

"Whatever you say, man. So, what have you been up to?"

They spent the majority of breakfast catching up. Elijah's life had been much less eventful than Ash's had been, and he seemed to be unaware of the fact that Ash was keeping his information close to the breast.

"... and I think I'll just write the essay on something architectural or something," Elijah was saying as he peeled his orange. "It's not like it's gonna be difficult. The last thing I want to do is write a fucking essay on Halloween when I'd rather be eating candy. You know what I mean?"

Ash just stared at him. "Elijah, when have I *ever* done homework on a holiday?"

"Never. Which is why I know you'll support me writing an essay on Wednesday that's due Thursday."

They exchanged glances. Elijah laughed. Ash hid a smirk behind another bite of his sandwich.

"So, how's things going with Tayshia?"

Ash sipped his soda, stifling the urge to cough as it nearly went down the wrong side of his throat.

"What the fuck are you talking about? There's no things to be going."

"Come on." Elijah popped an orange slice into his mouth and grinned. "Just admit you like her already. It hurts less."

"I don't like her."

"Lie."

Ash narrowed his eyes, casting a few surreptitious glances to the left and right. They had a bit of space between them and the rest of the students at the table, but it wasn't much. "Truth."

"You care about her. You care about what happens to her."

35

"I—" He paused. There was no harm in caring about her, was there? They were friends. They were friends, and friends cared what happened to one another. That was okay. "Yes. I care about her."

"Do you find her like, *annoying* to be around, or do you think she's easy to sit with? Like, could you—for a second, just imagine you're in a—a library or something. Could you sit and study with her, or would that bother you?"

"Inherently, yes it would bother me," Ash said. Under his breath, he added, "The air of annoying around her would become insufferable."

"So you wouldn't study with her?"

Ash looked him directly in the eyes. "If someone told me they'd slit my throat and murder me in my sleep, I would not study with Tayshia Cole."

"Harsh."

"The woman has slapped me in the face, Elijah."

"Ooh." Elijah's eyes went wide and he held the side of his fist over his mouth. "That's—that's not chill."

"Not chill at all."

"Well, do you think she's pretty?" Elijah's brown eyes glittered like crystals. "Because it's okay if you do. I mean, if you think she's pretty, there's nothing wrong with that. She's hot and she has a nice smile."

"Yeah, I guess she..." Ash trailed off, sandwich frozen halfway to his mouth.

Why did Elijah's questions feel like they were wrapped in barbed wire?

"Why are you looking at me like that?"

"You asshole," Ash said with a sneer. "I told you I don't like her. Why do you keep trying to get me to admit to something that isn't true?"

Elijah offered Ash a shrug as he tucked into his food. As he ate, Ash watched the way he seemed to keep pushing his wavy hair out of his eyes—his eyes, which he kept carefully averted from Ash's own. He looked uncomfortable.

Why did Elijah keep trying to get him to admit it? It held no bearing on his life.

Unless it did.

"Do *you* like her?" Ash asked.

"Huh?"

"What?"

"What'd you say?"

Ash scowled. "I know you're not going to pretend like you didn't hear me asking you."

"What? I didn't *hear* you!"

Yeah, right.

"Do you like her, Elijah?"

"No."

"Well, neither do I. And I'm gonna shave your fucking head if you don't drop the subject."

Ash's gaze slid to the right, moving on past Elijah's head and across the cafeteria. It landed on Tayshia at her usual table. She sat on one end of it, staring at the air in front of her face while she ate from a plate stacked high with chicken tenders, fries, cookies, and a few other sweets. Her curls were still in the same pile on her head that she'd worn yesterday — it looked like she hadn't bothered to take it out.

The amount of food didn't shock him anymore. Her appetite seemed to fluctuate between extremes every day.

Ash knew he was being suspicious just by insisting he didn't like Tayshia. He knew he did. They'd hooked up, for fuck's sake.

He just felt guilty about it.

☼☼☼

It was Halloween and it was already raining.

Elijah's claims about the news and the weather had been correct. Sometime in the middle of the night before, the skies opened up. Ocean winds blew in from the West, intensifying in their power as the hours went on. Ash woke to the howling, whipping sounds, and a text message from the school's notification system that school was cancelled until tomorrow, or until the winds had passed.

Ash tried to go back to sleep after that but it felt impossible.

Not when he could hear her counting.

He had officially lost control of his feelings and the situation. He had no clue what to do about the memory — no clue if it was even *real*. How was he supposed to approach her about something like that?

What right did he have to her memories, anyway?

Who was he to have even experienced that with her? Not that it was his fault, of course, but still. How violating would it feel to know that someone had seen your memory of an attack like that? It would be humiliating. She probably felt ashamed. He was *inside* of her mind, feeling everything that she felt for the entire duration. It was an extreme violation.

Fuck, he felt crazy thinking about all this.

How was it possible to watch other people's dreams and memories and nightmares? How was it possible that a fucking *rock* could connect him to her dreams? It didn't make any sense.

It was like magic.

Ash didn't bother changing out of his black joggers and navy V-neck, and he didn't bother taking care of his bedhead, either. He went out to the living room with his fleece blanket and pillow, taking up his normal spot on the couch and turning the TV and game console on. He pulled up a streaming service app so he could put on a random horror movie and pressed play. The volume of the movie warred with the wind and rain outside.

A few minutes later, Tayshia came strolling out of the hallway.

She wore a pair of leggings and another hoodie — this one actually belonging to her — and her curls were pulled up into a ponytail with the edges of her hairline swooped. The hoodie was a royal purple and her shoes were a pair of sneakers. In her ears were the silver hoop earrings he'd gotten her for her birthday. She held an umbrella in her hand.

God, he hated himself. She looked hella cute.

"I'm heading out," she said.

"Where?"

"My friend wants to go to that buffet. They got good breakfast, apparently."

"Again?" He gave her a surprised look. "Must be a good buffet."

"It is." She flashed him a faint smile. "I'll see you."

"Wait."

She stopped and looked back at him.

"Are you busy tonight? The storm is supposed to get worse and if the power doesn't go out, I'm watching horror movies all day." He bit his lower lip and studied her for a second. "If you wanted to chill when you get back."

"Oh, um... Sure," she said, and her tone was cautious. "I guess I could stop by the store and get some candy."

"Okay."

They watched each other and for a moment, all Ash could think about was going with her and holding her hand. Putting his arm around her. Keeping her safe.

"Anyway," she said. "Bye."

"Later."

The front door swung shut.

Ash got up to eat when lunchtime rolled around, unsurprised to see all the dishes she'd managed to stockpile while he was asleep. She'd recently started extending her eating habits to the nighttime, so Ash woke up most mornings to a full sink.

He didn't get angry anymore — he simply cleaned them.

Ash spent the majority of the day watching movies, wondering why Tayshia was gone for so long. Was she okay? What if she'd gotten hurt? He was being such a fucking simp, but he couldn't stop *thinking* about her.

One day, he was going to have to get her to talk about it. He didn't know what it was like to be her but he knew what it was like to be there. It had felt so real to him that there was no doubt in his mind it had happened. Magic, crystals, stars, whatever — it was real to him.

Maybe tonight, they'd reach some sort of breakthrough.

Around three in the afternoon, Tayshia finally walked in. She shook her umbrella out on the pavement outside before closing the front door and propping it against the wall. A plastic shopping bag swung on her wrist, full of colorful things.

"Jeez," Ash said, swathed in his blanket with only his head poking out. "Did you get lost?"

Tayshia looked at him and let out a small laugh. "I ended up going to my friend's house and hanging out for a while. Then I went and got candy."

"Nice," he said, feeling exhausted by the rain and his own thoughts. "I'm just finishing the last movie up, so... Horror movie marathon?"

She nodded. "Let me go put on my pajamas."

After dropping the plastic bag off on the kitchen counter, she practically skipped off to her room. Ash hadn't seen her in this good of a mood since...

Well, since the day they'd last hooked up.

Guilt rocketed through his body. He could still remember the way she'd panicked the first time. It all made sense now. She'd probably just wanted to feel normal and all he had done was remind her of her trauma. He hated the fact that he'd kissed her like that, letting his emotions and their volatile relationship get the best of him. He hated the fact that he'd treated her like any other hook-up, being rough with her and doing whatever he wanted without thinking about how she might feel.

Did that make him as bad as the man in Paris?

"I'm so excited," Tayshia said as she pranced back out into the room.

"Why?" Ash asked.

She had changed into his black hoodie, which surprised him. She'd also taken her leggings off and was wearing the hoodie as a makeshift dress. Her hair was down.

As she skidded into the kitchen, he saw her getting a large plastic bowl out of the cupboard and pouring the Halloween candy into it.

"Next to Christmas, Halloween is my favorite," she said.

"You do know that's my hoodie, right?" he said, trying and failing to keep himself from smirking.

"Huh?" She gasped, jaw dropping and eyes opening wide. "Oh, my gosh! I'm so sorry. I have literally been wearing this for like two days now. Do you want it back?"

"Nah, you can keep it," he said. "I just didn't know if you knew whose it was."

She beamed at him and he saw her teeth flash in the dimness of the kitchen, which was only lit by the window and the grey, stormy day. His heart skipped a beat.

"Sweet, because it's super comfy and I want it." She picked up the bowl and brought it out to the living room. As she sat down, she gasped. "Damn, I should have grabbed my blanket. Hold up."

"Ah, ah—" he said, snapping his fingers without looking away from the TV. "This is a queen size. We can share."

"With you?"

He shot her a sour look. "Yes, *with* me. What, you too scared to sit next to me?"

"Why are you asking *me* that? You're the one that's been avoiding me."

Tayshia stared at him as he pulled the fleece blanket from around him and held it up. Slowly, she walked over to him and sat down one cushion away, closer to the inner corner of the sectional. As she did, Ash felt a strange tingling spreading along the half of his body that was closest to hers.

She settled back against the cushions, pulled the blanket up to her neck, and pursed her lips.

"Well?" she said. "Put it on."

Ash obliged, picking the first installment in the series so they could watch it.

They watched the film in silence. Ash maintained the distance between them, finding that he felt strange. The choppy waters of anxiety that usually kept him on edge seemed to have quieted in her presence.

He found that he couldn't stop sneaking glances in her direction out of the corner of his eye. She looked tired — beleaguered, really — but in a generally good mood. Nothing about her countenance gave him any sort of indication as to her mental state regarding what happened in Paris, or what happened in her dream.

It was weird, sitting here, thinking about the fact that he literally walked her dreams every night and he'd just... Accepted it. He'd accepted it like it wasn't completely fucking bizarre. It was like magic, yet in a way, it didn't feel like it. If the legend of the hot springs was correct, then whatever was going on with them was tied to the crystals. And crystals, like everything else, came from the stars.

Wouldn't it be wild if we were written in them?

"These movies always make me laugh," Tayshia said with an amused tone when they were thirty minutes into the movie and half of the candy was already devoured by both of them. "Everything's always so dramatic, they're always trying to find out who the ghost or demon is, and everyone always *stays* in the house. I'd be outta there so fucking fast."

"Trust me on this," Ash said. "There would be no movie if they left the house."

"Well, *obviously*. I'm just saying, is all."

He looked over at her right as she looked up at him. His gaze flitted all over her face and then landed on her hairline.

"What is that thing you do with your hair? There, by your hairline. Is that intentional?"

"My — my edges?" She reached up as if to touch them, her hand appearing from the depths of the blanket. Then, she lowered it. "Yeah, I do it on purpose."

"Oh. Is that something people with curly hair do?"

She gave him a strange look. "It's something Black girls do. We lay them flat and shape them."

"Ah, okay. Why?"

"Because it's cute."

"Yeah, it looks good."

Wait.

Had he just said—

Fuck.

She side-eyed him. "Thank you."

Ash didn't want to talk through the movie, but he didn't want to sit in complete *silence* with her. It made things more awkward, and it made it more difficult for him to ignore the way he felt inside.

The curiosity was a mask.

"I, um—I like your tattoos," Tayshia said, the words tumbling out rushed and quiet. "If we're sharing compliments."

Ash's heart raced for reasons unknown to him. He supposed it was because he didn't get many compliments on them unless it was from Andre, or something. He arched an eyebrow down at her.

"Which ones?"

She frowned. "Is that supposed to be a joke?"

"Yeah," he said through a lopsided grin as his head turned and faced the TV screen again.

"Good, because you have like, 3500 of them."

"Yeah."

Silence prevailed, broken only by the screams and raucous symphony music in the movie. Tayshia cleared her throat.

"I guess I have a couple of favorites," she said. "I like the roses on the backs of your hands. And I like the waves and crescent moons on your forearms. I suppose—Well, I like the—the snakes on your collarbones. But honestly, I like them all. There's so many details in them that there's like, a lot to look at."

"You were staring at me?" he said, his voice coming out in an accidental purr of amusement. He hadn't meant it to, but for a moment, he'd forgotten he was talking to Tayshia.

It felt like he was flirting.

"Not on purpose!" she cried. "It was an accident."

"An accident."

"Yes," she said. It sounded like she was bordering on a whine. "It's hard not to look, Ash. Er—I mean, it's not like I'm looking because I *want* to. It's because it's right there in front of me. You know?"

"Don't pout," he said, glancing at her. "You'll get frown lines."

"I'm only twenty. I'm not gonna get *frown lines*." Another scowl. "Well, that's the last time I ever compliment your bitch-ass."

"Which is your top favorite?" he asked, forcing himself to sound nonchalant.

"What?"

"Which tattoo do you like the best?" He looked down at her, both of them coming to a silent mutual decision to stop watching the movie.

"The ones on your neck," she said, her gaze falling to his throat, where he knew both the neck tattoos and parts of his chest piece were visible. "The chains and the little roses. They're very... Well, the art is really beautiful. What does it represent?"

Ash took a moment to respond, finding that he'd accidentally been staring at the way her eyes seemed to look a rich umber in color from the growing storm outside. He had to think about his answer. He didn't want her to know what they represented, given that the tattoo was his emotional response to coping with his failure at the ice cream shop.

But the fact that it was her favorite tattoo of all the ones he had?

Hearing her say that made it feel more satisfying to have all the tattoos adorning his body, decorating it like ornaments on a Christmas tree. He sort of felt like they were... Worth it.

"The chains represent feeling strangled," he said, choosing his words as carefully as though he were plucking amethysts out of the wall. "And trapped—like I'm choking and can't move."

"And the roses?"

You. You. You.

"Just... The aesthetic," he lied, feeling heat rushing to his cheeks.

"Oh, okay," she said. "That's... Well, that's also really beautiful."

"Do you have any?"

"Any what? Any tattoos?" She let out a small laugh. "No. Not yet."

"Yet?" He perked up. "So you're not against them?"

"No, I'd get one or two. I have some in mind that I'd do, actually."

"Seriously?" Ash felt his mind whirling. "Are you being serious right now?"

"I mean, yeah," she said, appearing bemused. She shifted in her spot and it brought her a bit closer to him. He could feel the heat of her body underneath the blanket. "I would get one on my shoulder,

43

and then I want one on my forearm."

"Yeah, okay. Maybe one day, we could go to..."

He trailed off into a silence that ensued for a solid three seconds. What was he thinking? He and Tayshia going to get tattoos? It was absurd.

But then again, everything regarding her was absurd now.

"I mean, we could," Tayshia said. "We could... Yeah, we could go."

He stared at her.

"I'll be right back," she said. "Gotta go to the bathroom."

Ash merely nodded, glancing down at the half-empty candy bowl and wondering what else the night had in store for them.

CHAPTER FIVE

When Tayshia returned to the living room, Ash was in the kitchen making himself a snack.

"You want some of this?" he called after he heard the couch shifting. He turned to glance across the room at her, seeing her wrapping herself up in the blanket and lying down on her side with her head on his pillow.

"What's in it?" she asked, her voice catching. She cleared her throat and let out a cough. "Like I mean, what are you putting in it, and what are you cooking it in?"

His face twisted in confusion as he turned back to the stove. "It's just vegetables in olive oil. But like, with pepper and shit."

She was silent for a long second before she said, "No, I'm too tired."

It took Ash a second of chopping celery to realize what she'd said. "Too tired? What the fuck are you talking about? How are you too tired to eat?"

She didn't answer.

Even more perplexed, Ash spun to look at her.

She was asleep.

What the fuck? How could she have fallen asleep that fast?

When the food was done, he scooped it into a bowl and took it out to the living room. He stared at the couch for a second, debating. He could easily sit on the other side of it, far away from her. Or he could pull the blanket open and sit in the spot she was in before she took his. The way she was curled up on her side meant that he'd be near her rear, but if he kept a decent distance between them, he could respect her *and* stay inside the warmth of the blanket.

Decision made.

He pulled the blanket open and sat on the couch beneath it with his knees pulled up to his chest and Tayshia four or five inches from him. She inhaled deeply through her nose and settled deeper into the pillow, hugging it closer to her face.

As the second movie began to play, Ash took a bite of his food and glanced over at her. He gazed at her face, at the peacefulness he saw there, and he realized something.

Tayshia was beautiful. *Really* beautiful. And it wasn't just because she had striking features that he found attractive.

It was her resilience.

The way that she'd suffered through all that pain not even six months ago and she'd still come to school. She'd made the decision to keep going, to keep living, to keep breathing. She was the girl who wasn't afraid to offer herself up to spare unnecessary pain, whether it be her father's or her own.

Here she was, asleep with frown lines etched into her forehead that he wanted to smooth away, and she was beautiful.

Holding the bowl of steaming hot vegetables with one hand, he reached over with his other. His tattooed fingers brushed a stray curl out of her eyes, revealing her face again. He saw her eyes moving beneath flickering eyelids. Ash wondered what she was dreaming of this time.

What if the reason why she dreamed was to keep the memory at bay?

Tayshia jolted awake, her bleary gaze traveling back and forth between his fingers and his eyes.

"What happened?" she whispered. "Did I fall asleep?"

"For like two seconds."

"Damn. I don't even remember closing my eyes. It feels like I slept for ten hours."

Ash took a bite of his food, his heart pounding. Was she going to say anything about him touching her hair?

Tayshia watched the movie without lifting her head from the pillow. The storm had picked up outside, just barely loud enough for Ash to need to turn up the volume a couple notches on the TV. The movie was ten minutes in, the loud music already grating on his ears.

"I'd like to let the record state that I have had it with white people in horror movies," Tayshia said, her voice muffled from sleep. "All they ever do is wake up and choose violence. Every. Damn. Day."

"Fuck. You're not wrong."

When he glanced over at her, the smile still fading from his face, he was surprised to see her lips twitching. She turned her head for a moment, as quick as she could, and then a mask of haughtiness washed over her face.

"I love horror movies, but I'm telling you — all they have to do is move out of the house. And don't give me none of that *but the demon will follow them* shit. You think demons don't have better shit to do than follow these bitches around?"

Ash laughed, unable to stop the sound from bubbling out of his chest before it faded.

It was difficult to listen to her, cracking jokes and pretending. Pretending that August 17th had never happened. Pretending to be okay.

When he looked at her, it was hard for him not to see past the façade and remember the feelings of fear and helplessness that had spread through them both like wildfire. The hope when she tried to talk her way out of it, and the resignation when she realized she couldn't. The pain when she cried on the floor at the foot of the bed. The numbness when she showered. The catatonia before she finally fell asleep.

Tayshia was and always had been as strong as stone to him. He'd thought that in flame, she would be forged into diamond. But there they were — the cracks running throughout. She looked like a diamond on the outside but inside, he knew she had to be floating in a zirconian fog.

He at least understood that.

Though Ash had never been the emotional sort, he felt something gut-wrenching for her. Something he couldn't quite place. The best way he could think to explain it was having the desire to hold her hand and caress her skin, while also wanting to murder anyone who looked in her direction.

That terrified him.

Finishing up his food, he took it to the kitchen and stuck the bowl into the sink. As he turned around, he saw that Tayshia had gotten up and was heading toward the hall. He reached the walkway behind the couch right as she did.

She looked at him as her foot moved forward and then she blinked like she was dizzy. Letting out a gasp, she pitched forward.

Ash gave it no second thoughts. He reached out and caught her, one arm around her back with his hand gripping her right elbow. His other hand held her left forearm.

"What's wrong?" he murmured.

"I'm fine," she said, her voice seeming to become swallowed up by the room. "I just felt a little faint. Poor timing. You can—you can let go."

"Faint?" He didn't let go of her, finding that he felt weirdly complete to have her in his arms in any capacity. "You seem to feel faint a lot. Like, I've seen you looking fucked up at school. Fucked up and super tired."

"What? No, I... Can you just—you can let go now, okay?"

Ash narrowed his eyes, a new suspicion arising. "Why are you deflecting?"

"Deflecting? I'm not."

"Yes, you are. You literally passed out on the couch and now you just fell over. What is—"

"*Ash, let go of me!*" she cried, her voice echoing. The suddenness of her shrieking startled him, and he let go of her as though she'd caught fire. She glared up at him while she rubbed her fingers in anxious motions. "Don't touch me. Don't ever touch me unless I ask."

Ash wanted to die for the shame that burned in his heart. Of course she wouldn't want to be touched.

What the fuck was he thinking?

"It's my bad," he said, averting his eyes. "I'm sorry."

"It's fine."

She went down the hall to the bathroom.

Ash went back to the couch and took the spot that was his, right beside his pillow. He pulled one foot onto the couch, his knee against his chest as he dragged his hands through his hair in exasperation. He made several attempts to push back his negative feelings towards himself.

Fuck, all of this stress was starting to wear on him.

Bzzt. Bzzt. Bzzt.

Ash glanced up. It was a phone vibrating on the coffee table, and it wasn't his. It was Tayshia's. He glanced at the lock screen.

I don't see what the point is. I wasted my time. You wasted yours. I fucked Quinn. You fucked Ash. We can call it even. – Kieran.

It looked like a reply.

She was texting Kieran? Why the Hell would she want to text him? He'd cheated on her and after the things he'd seen in her memory, why on God's green Earth would she have any interest in speaking with him in *any* capacity again?

And why the fuck would she lie about something like sex after what she'd been through?

Tayshia walked back out, pulled the blanket open, and sat down beside Ash again. Her body pressed flush against him, a confusing contradiction to her little meltdown before she'd gone to the bathroom. Outside, tree branches were being whipped so violently by the windstorm that they were lashing against the windows and the sliding glass door to the balcony. Inside, only the TV provided noise.

Between Ash and Tayshia, it was dead silent.

"Are you mad at me?" Tayshia said after a while.

"Why would I have a reason to be mad at you?"

She studied him and then said, "I didn't mean to yell at you. I just freaked out."

"No, but you're used to getting yelled at." His gaze snapped down to hers, their faces less than a foot away from one another in the fading daylight. "You might actually miss it."

"Excuse me? What are you *talking* about?"

He scoffed and shook his head, pulling his other knee to his chest and folding his arms atop his kneecaps over the top of the blanket. "Or maybe it's just your cheating abusive ex that you miss."

"Abusive?" Tayshia raised her voice. "What the Hell are you *talking about*?"

Ash said nothing.

"Ash!" she cried. "What do you mean?!"

"Watch your mouth," he snapped in a taunting tone. "Wouldn't want you to lie."

Tayshia watched him for a moment and then her arm shot out of the blanket. She snatched her cell phone up and clicked the power button to light the screen. There was more silence after she read the notification on the screen.

"Just catching up?"

"Oh, my God." She ducked her head into her own knees and covered the back of her head with her arms. "Oh, my God. I'm so embarrassed."

"Are you trying to get me jumped? No, seriously. Are you *actually* trying to get me jumped by the entire fucking football team?"

"No, I'm not!" Tayshia cried, holding her phone in one hand and waving the other about. "I don't know why I lied. I just wanted to hurt his feelings because he hurt mine."

Ash glared down at her. "So you told him I fucked you?"

Her mouth opened and closed, several sounds leaving her throat that showed him he'd flustered her to speechlessness.

"But you hate him," she finally said, voice meek as she winced.

"I despise Kieran," he said. "You know that."

"I do know that."

"So, why are you asking?"

"I'm not asking anything. I didn't ask a question."

"What do you want from me?!" he snarled. "Do you want me to walk up to him and punch him in the face? Huh? You want me to smash his face into a wall until his nose bleeds? What the fuck? What the *fuck* do you *want*?"

A few seconds passed where she stared at him in astonishment and then without letting her breath out, she answered him.

"Yes."

He blinked. "What?"

She let out a scowl and looked at the TV. He heard her acrylic nail tapping against the screen of her phone, playing out the tune of her anxiety. "It's selfish of me, but yes. I do. It's so juvenile and stupid but that's what I want. I'm tired of thinking about the fact that the only reason why I wasn't good enough was because she would sleep with him and I wouldn't."

"Hey," Ash said, tone gentle. He thought about putting his arm around her, then thought better of it. "It's not stupid. Juvenile, yeah. But not stupid."

"I'm just..." She hung her head. "I'm tired of feeling like I'm the only one who can defend myself. It gets tiring. Constantly fighting for myself when sometimes I just want... I just want..."

"A tall boy with tattoos to beat your ex-boyfriend up?"

When she said nothing, choosing instead to glare resolutely at the television, Ash couldn't help it. His anger melted into mirth and he burst out laughing. She whirled on him, rising onto her knees on the couch with one hand on his shoulder and the other with her fist raised. He laughed harder, raising a defensive hand.

"Okay, okay!" he said. "I'm just fucking with you."

"Don't put it like that." She wrinkled her nose in a pout of irritation and then slid down until she was sitting with her legs curled underneath her, still facing him. "It's humiliating and sounds even more immature."

"But I'd do it," he said, lacing his fingers behind his head and leaning back against the couch. "If you asked."

It looked like she was fighting the urge to smile. "I doubt that. Risking your probation that way? You'd go straight to jail. Possibly get expelled on top of that."

Ash lowered his gaze, frowning as the light spirit in the air dwindled to nothing. It mingled with the churning waters inside of him and turned them into whirlpools of rage. His future when it came to his probation was uncertain. How he felt about Kieran was as certain as the sun coming up every day.

"It'd be worth it. He deserves it."

Tayshia started to say something, then seemed to change her mind. Without another word, she turned and resumed watching the movie. A quiet yet charged silence existed between them.

Ash didn't want the opportunity to get her to open up to pass. He needed to get *somewhere* with her on the path towards talking about the memory. It was impossible for him to erase that it had happened. He was never going to forget what he'd seen. What he'd *felt*.

Just because she wanted to play pretend didn't mean he could.

"So you want it done at school? Or you want me to pull up?"

"What? Don't be ridiculous. You can't *actually* attack Kieran."

"Yes, I can," he said, eyebrows shooting up. "Are you joking? I can do whatever the fuck I want."

"But the consequences are typically supposed to outweigh the desire, Ash."

"Typically," he said.

They held each other's gazes in yet another challenge.

"You're ridiculous," she said. "Do you live in a completely different dimension from the rest of us? You can't just do whatever you want. There are rules and there are cogs to the machine that fit together the way they're supposed to."

"Bruh." Ash breathed a laugh, then rubbed the stubble on his chin with his fingers. "I know how things work. I went to jail, so I *know*."

"Then what's the difference?"

"The difference is that I don't always give a fuck about the rules or the consequences or the *cogs in the machine*. In this particular situation, I *would* be willing to risk all of that just to smash his face into a fucking wall. I would, and the only reason why you don't want me to is because you're afraid of what people will think of you if they find out you were involved. The difference is that now, I have a reason not to care about the rules."

Tayshia lifted one brow and he went on.

"Kieran deserves my fist in his fucking face."

Both of Tayshia's hands went to the hem of the hoodie, where she gripped it and fidgeted with it. He saw her chew her lips, clearly unsure of what to say next.

"Has he spoken to you since you broke up?" he asked. "Like, in person? Not over text."

"No," she said. "And I never officially broke up with him. I just ghosted him the weekend of my birthday. Then I walked up to him at school and told him I knew he was cheating. He told me—" She looked away and then said, "He took it better than expected."

"What did he say?"

"Nothing. He just... Took it better than expected."

"What did he *say*?" Ash growled through his teeth.

"*Nothing*." Tayshia blinked, looking like she wanted to move away from him. "Just leave it alone. And don't say anything to him. I don't know why I even have to say that. Let it go."

Ash bit his lip and looked down into the shadows between the coffee table and the couch. He nodded to himself, on the verge of grabbing his car keys and driving into the storm to find the piece of shit. If the way he'd heard Kieran speak to her in the memory was any indication, he was sure it wasn't *nothing*. Kieran had probably had all sorts of fun, neat things to say to her.

Ash didn't like that.

"You do realize that you told him we fucked, right?"

She cringed. "I know."

"Weren't you worried I was gonna run into him at any point, and that I wouldn't know what the Hell he was talking about if he confronted me?"

"I was concerned, yeah. I just hoped you hated him enough to avoid him at all costs. I was banking on him being so angry that he just moved on with Quinn and never spoke to either of us again."

"Why'd you text him then?"

"Don't get excited. This reply came two weeks later."

"Why did you text him *at all*?"

Slowly, her mouth tipped down into a grimace. No words came forth.

"Were you trying to initiate something?" Ash said.

"... Maybe."

Ash's heart jumped in his chest. "Between who? You and I? Or you and him?"

"Both."

"And then *what*?"

Her grimace turned into a weak smile. "I assumed there would be an argument and the two of you would get into a fight. And then... A boy with tattoos would beat my ex-boyfriend up?"

Ash laughed.

He laughed, and he couldn't stop. He tilted his head back, holding the back of his hand over his mouth while the humor and absurdity of the situation overwhelmed him. As much as he did truly want to fuck Kieran's shit up, the thought of Tayshia plotting to manipulate Ash into being her personal street fighter?

It was hilarious.

"What?!" she cried. "He's terrified of you! I didn't think getting the fight to start would be the most difficult part. I figured the hardest part would be getting him to believe you cared about me enough to do it."

"How would this shit ensue?!" Ash said between laughs, his vision swimming with tears of mirth. "Was I supposed to just magically *know* you've been wandering around the apartment, orchestrating these fucking *plots*?!"

"Bruh, shut up!" she cried. "Damn! I would have told you eventually if I needed to, I just didn't need to yet."

"If you want me to kick his ass, just ask," he said. "Don't orchestrate plots to trick me into it. Honestly, it would take less than a question. A pointed look is all I'd need."

"I didn't want to do that—to *ask*. It feels wrong to even think about it." She hugged the blanket around her neck and pouted.

"But not wrong to create an entire plot to get *me* to do it?"

"Uh—" Another grimace and then a wince. "No?"

"Well, what the Hell were you thinking would get him worked up enough to want to throw down?! Just seeing my face?!"

She lifted her shoulders in a meek shrug. "I *said* it was juvenile and stupid."

"I'm a little hung up on the fact that you told him we slept together." Ash regarded her warily. "Why would you think he'd believe that?"

"Getting him to believe it was the second part of my—well, my plot."

Ash looked at the TV, watching the actors in the movie. He listened to the howling of the wind and the rain slamming down against the apartment roof as the gears in his mind continued to turn. Then, everything clicked into place, fitting neat and firm.

"I am not going to pretend to date you."

Tayshia sprung up onto her knees on the couch, her hands clasped in front of her.

"Ash, come on," she whined. "Please? We literally wouldn't have to do anything except *maybe* hold hands."

"No."

"Come *on*! It's just a hand hold. We've done way worse."

"No."

"Why not?!"

"Because you don't need to impress that piece of trash," he said, glaring up at her where she knelt. "It degrades you, degrades me, and gives him power over both of our lives. If you want me to beat the fuck out of him, I got you. But if you wanna do that juvenile fanfiction shit, you're gonna have to ask Elijah or something."

Tayshia was silent in the wake of his tirade until she said, "Maybe I will."

Something reared back inside of him, preparing to whip his anger into him like a lashing.

"Maybe you should."

He saw her chewing the inside of her cheek, her brows furrowed low over her eyes. Ash listened to the sound of his own heart as the thoughts trickled their way across her face like flickering shadows.

"I know it's stupid," she said, her voice lowering to a whisper as she sank down onto the couch again. "And I know it's childish. But he made me feel like nothing. And somehow, even though we don't get along, you don't make me feel that way. It's not about pissing him off or making him jealous. It's about showing him that just because he didn't see my worth, doesn't mean that other people don't."

Ash swallowed, his throat feeling dry. "What are you trying to say?"

"I'm saying that it's stupid. It *is* stupid."

"... This isn't about Kieran." When she shot him a sharp look, he knew he was treading on dangerous waters. "This is about the fact that you want to prove something to yourself—because you know

Kieran doesn't care. The thing is that *you* care. But the fact of that matter is that you won't even let me touch you. You just screamed at me over there to get me to take my hands off of you. So why the Hell would you think that you'd be able to pretend to be my girl?"

"That's not—it's not—I don't know how to explain it. I figured we would... I dunno... Ease into it? Try again?"

"Do you mean... Like reenact what we—in the hallway?"

"Yes."

CHAPTER SIX

"It's stupid, I know."

"No, it's not," Ash said. "It's not stupid to you, so it's not stupid to me."

After giving him an unreadable look, Tayshia got up and walked toward the hallway. She paused by the end of the couch, giving him one last lingering look before she disappeared into the darkness, leaving him with the sounds of the TV and the storm.

Ash watched her go, a statue on the couch with his elbows on his knees and hands in his hair. He hadn't forgotten the two times they'd hooked up. After the dream, he'd tried to, but not because he hadn't liked it.

Because he felt guilty.

Now that everything was different, he saw how wrong it was that he'd kissed her out of the blue. He hadn't even asked her. He'd just pinned her against the wall and taken what he wanted, even if he hadn't realized he wanted it. Swept up in hormones and anger, he'd reached into the void and ripped out the darkest parts of them both.

What if he'd caused her to cry the way she had in Paris?

What if he was just as bad as the man?

What if he was a monster?

As he made his way towards the hallway, he felt his heart sinking so low that it plummeted to the core of the Earth. He gazed into the shadows until his vision blurred and the faint light from the television looked hazy. His shoulders began to slump a bit.

Ash liked to think he had changed, but what if that didn't matter?

Am I no better than the men who hurt her? Am I no better than the attacker, or than Kieran?

"I wasn't thinking we would *actually* hook up again." Her voice pulled him out of his somber reverie as he stopped right in front of her. "I know I sucked but don't look so *sad* at the thought."

"You weren't bad at it, and I'm not sad," he said. *I'm just worried*

I hurt you before anyone else ever did.

"It's not as if any of it is new to you," she said with a harsh breath. "I *know* you were all over town with girls in high school."

"You're right," he said. "I was."

"And look—" Tayshia walked back to the spot on the wall, each step she took ringing in his heart. "—if we can manage this without me getting overwhelmed, then it means we..."

"Means we what?"

Could do it again?

She said nothing.

Ash ambled deeper into the hallway after her, his arms crossed over his chest. He tilted his head to the side, his hair falling across his eyes as she positioned herself with her back to the wall.

"Like I said. We just ease me into it." Her breathing hitched as though her lungs were being squeezed from the outside. "And maybe it will make me more comfortable."

"For what purpose, though?" he asked, shaking his head. "The purpose of proving something to Kieran, the purpose of proving something to yourself, or the purpose of proving something to me?"

"All three." She answered without missing a beat, her gaze cutting through the shadows to meet his. "I want to prove that I'm normal. That I can be just like everyone else. That I'm still..." She shook her head out, as though trying to rid herself of the end of the sentence. "It's better than you getting into a fight and thrown back in jail."

"You're so confident that I'd do it."

"Do what?"

He took a step closer to her. "Fight him for you."

"Wouldn't you?"

Ash moved forward again, putting their bodies within inches of one another. His heart rattled in his chest like it was trying to escape a cage. They were dancing around the subject of the dream, twirling circles around the base of the Eiffel Tower.

He looked her up and down.

"Yeah."

The back of her head brushed the wall as she tilted her chin up. "What else would you do for me?"

He ground his jaw. He couldn't tell her the truth. He couldn't tell her that at this point, the answer was *anything*.

"This," he said, gesturing to the situation with a nod of his head.

"Easing you into whatever it is you're wanting."

"Even if I said I wanted to go all the way?"

He opened his mouth to respond but saw the challenge there in her eyes. It sparked like lightning. It showed him that they really were dancing around the subject of Paris. That she knew that he'd been in her dream. She knew what he'd experienced.

She wasn't gonna be the first to admit it.

"You don't want to go all the way," he said. "You just want to know what it feels like to be the one who gets to decide."

The lightning fizzled. "I — Yes. Actually. That's exactly it. I know it's ridiculous, but I... I think I need this."

Ash unfolded his arms. He saw her eyes track the movements of his arms, scanning the tattoos that adorned them like she always did. Before, he didn't know if it was because she liked them. After their earlier conversation, he knew different.

He turned his head with a sigh, looking off down the dark hallway for a moment. His head rolled back towards her and he looked down the length of his nose at her, vision shrouded by his eyelashes.

"You need my consent?"

"Of course I do!" she cried, giving him a look that could wither roses. Then, the fire faded from her eyes and showed him the Winter that etched frost along her bones. Her voice lowered, as did her gaze. "Of course I do."

"What do you want me to do?"

"Huh?" He saw her shoulders jump, as though she hadn't expected him to ask the question. "Oh, just... Maybe if you tried touching me? Kieran never liked touching me. And I mean like, in normal places. Like, you know how in the movies when characters kiss, the guy will like, touch her face on her cheeks, or the side of her neck? He never did that. He didn't like holding my hand or touching my waist or touching any part of me. There was no affection, you know?"

Before Ash could talk, she spoke again.

"We messed around a few times. But I didn't want to. I felt pressured. And when we did, he didn't—" Her gaze darted up to Ash's face and then away again. "—it wasn't like with you. You *touched* me. Kieran was disgusted by me."

Ash pulled a face. That sounded awful. He couldn't imagine

being in a relationship with someone that was expected to end in marriage, and never experience any affection from the other person.

"That's actually really fucked up."

"Yeah, well." She shrugged. "I used to complain but he would just say I wasn't respecting his personal boundaries. So I gave up after a while. It's so embarrassing but I used to daydream about having a boyfriend who would just like—" Ash saw her cast a wistful look somewhere past his shoulder. "Touch my face or show me some affection."

Ash reached up and brushed his knuckles along the height of her cheekbone.

"Like that?"

She gazed up at him, her eyes wide in the dark as she let out a heavy breath. It was like a sigh but without the relief. Like he'd only managed to raise the bar of her anxiety.

"Yes. Like that."

Seeing her from this distance, he could see parts of her face that he hadn't noticed before within the shadows cast in the hallway. He could see the way her nostrils flared when she was frustrated, and the animated way her brows moved when something didn't work— like she was shocked it wasn't working for her because she was who she was. She didn't seem to want to touch him.

She wanted to be in control of him when *he* touched *her*.

"Can I touch you?" he asked, swallowing against the somewhat nervous way his throat was bobbing. He lifted his hands in slow, small increments.

"Yes, but..." she said and in the pause after her words, he felt it. They *both* knew that she was expecting him to follow along and figure out what was okay and wasn't okay, even though she didn't want to talk about any of it. "... Nothing *untoward*."

"What's your definition of *untoward*, Miss Vocabulary?"

"You know." A one-shoulder shrug.

Ash's face slackened into a deadpan expression and then he sighed.

Inside, his heart continued to beat in random patterns. His stomach had coiled into a tight knot that reminded him of the day he'd had to give his first speech in school. He could feel a storm whipping up inside his mind and body, with rumbling clouds of thunder and grey. It promised a hurricane with an unknown outcome.

Tayshia tilted her head back. It was so she could look into his eyes, or perhaps it was because it was awkward just staring at his throat above the neckline of his shirt. Whatever it was, it made Ash feel something like a shock to his system. It rolled up his spine, into his chest and down to his stomach, where it shifted into something completely different.

Something he recognized.

Ash's left forearm landed against the wall above her head. His right one slipped around her waist, dragging her up onto the tips of her toes and pressing her firmly against his body. She was warm in spite of how cold her skin was, and the juxtaposition of that and her cold palms pressing flat to his chest sent a chill through him. Before she saw it in his face, he dipped his mouth towards her left ear, effectively trapping her head between his raised arm and his lips.

"Is this too much?" he said, and his voice came out in a throaty whisper. His hand was flat on her lower back. He could feel the dip of her spine through the fabric of her top.

"No." She shifted, his arm keeping her from lowering back to the soles of her feet. "It's okay."

"You're so stiff," he said, pulling his head back far enough to look her in the eyes. "Relax."

"I'm not," she said, but she was.

"If you wanna do this, you're gonna have to relax," he said, trying to keep his voice calm in spite of the rapid beating of his heart. He hoped she couldn't feel it slamming against his chest.

"I know that," she whispered, and he saw a flicker of something familiar in her eyes. Something he'd felt when he was a passenger inside her mind, walking her haunted memory in Paris.

Fear.

"This is because it's me," he said, "and you don't trust me. I get it. But I have no intention of hurting you."

Her hands were still flat against his chest, pushing slightly as though she wanted to shove him away. He didn't move, knowing that she would say the words if she wanted him to.

He hoped.

"I know that, too," she said, sounding breathless. Her gaze was focused on his neck now. "I'm just—I'm sorry. I'm trying."

"What did I tell you before? Do not apologize to me," he said, biting the words out. "If you want me to move back, I will."

His hand slid along her back as he began to move, but she made a sound of protest. One of her hands clenched in his shirt while the other slid up to his shoulder and curved over the top of it. Still without looking at him, she spoke.

"It's not you. It's me." She took a deep breath, which he felt brushing the hollow of his throat. "It's me. I think I just need to get used to you being here, or something."

"We don't have to do this tonight. We don't have to do this at all, to be honest. We can go finish the movie and —"

"No!" she cried, voice shrill. "No. I want to do this. I *need* to be able to do this."

"Okay." Ash ducked down a little until he caught her gaze with his. "You're in control. Got it?"

"Yes."

"Yeah?"

"Yes, Ash."

"Good girl." Tayshia's eyes widened a fraction, never leaving his face as he stood upright again. He kept his arm on the wall and his hand against her back. "You're in control."

"I'll just get comfortable with you," she said. He could feel her body trembling. "I'll touch you now, okay?"

"Do whatever you want with me."

Still on tip-toe, Tayshia lifted her hand from his shoulder and reached for his face. He tried not to flinch when her fingertips brushed his jawline. Because in reality, Ash hadn't been touched like this since his mother died.

Not exactly what he wanted to think about right now.

She trailed her fingers down the side of his neck, raising pebbles on his flesh along the way down to the outer edge of the furthest rose on his neck. He could tell she was struggling to keep her breathing even, and he made sure not to move lest she spring up like a bird and fly away.

Even though his skin was sensitive, he forced himself to remain as unmoving as a mountain as her fingers traced every petal and link in the chains that were etched into his skin. Above his shirt, her touch drifted across his collarbone and down into the center of his chest where the V-shaped neckline of his tee shirt dipped. She traced everything she could see.

Girls had touched him before, but something felt different about this. It was there, lurking in the waters that existed within him. Ash was powerless to stop the shiver that rippled through his body.

Her gaze snapped upward.

"Sorry," he said, one corner of his mouth twitching.

Wariness passed over her face. "Stop it."

"Stop what?"

"Looking at me like that. Stop."

"Like what?"

"Like *that*. Like you—like you *see* me, or something. I don't like it."

"So you can touch me, but I can't look at you?"

She frowned, lines furrowing their way into her brow as she lowered her glare to his chest again.

"Why would you want to?"

Ash opened his mouth to reply but realized that he didn't know what to say. Everything he wanted to say was too earth-shattering. Too confusing. The words that were bouncing around his head were out of control, flung from the left side of the field. If he uttered them, he knew it would change things between them when he didn't even understand what they meant.

He wanted to tell her that she was the only girl he wanted to touch.

"If you want me to stop looking at you," he said under his breath, "then stop touching me."

She said nothing, looking only curious as her hand went back up again, along his pulse where she felt his stuttering heartbeat for a halting moment. Then it was on the move, fingers traveling the length of his jaw and brushing his earlobe. His eyelids fluttered shut in spite of himself.

Tayshia's fingers sunk into his hair.

His stomach twisted tighter and tighter, his chest feeling narrow and his diaphragm constricted. Her fingernails scraped along his scalp. They scratched up to the top of his head, sifting through the bleached strands of his hair, and back down to the base of the right side of his skull.

Ash's mind went completely blank.

"Holy *fuck*," he whispered as he nuzzled into her touch. "That feels good."

She scratched her fingers along his scalp in long, wide circular patterns. Ash was a puddle. He was turning *into* a puddle. He'd never felt anything so nice or so soothing.

So good.

His fingernails dug into her back a bit as he tried to keep control of himself—tried to remember that this wasn't just any other girl. This was Tayshia. This was a girl that had been through something he could never understand, even if he'd been present in her memory of it.

There was something about him that made her feel as if he was the one she could trust to ease her into whatever it was that she was trying to ease herself into.

If she didn't want to talk about the dream yet, he'd take this.

Ash relaxed and his head tipped forward, his cheek resting on top of her head. She stiffened up at first, but his hand sliding around to her other side, fully ensconcing her in a one-armed embrace seemed to assuage her. The tension left her body in waves as she lowered back to the soles of her feet and let her arms hang down at her sides. His right palm smoothed over the dip of her waistline, his left hand sliding into the curls at the back of her head.

Finally.

"It's all right," he breathed, as if it were second nature to comfort her. He couldn't stop seeing the hotel room with its blue décor. He closed his eyes and saw her curled up on the floor, sobbing the words *I can't* like they were a healing song. "I got you now. It's all right."

Tayshia turned her head to the side, resting it on his chest.

"Ash?"

"Yeah?"

"Tighter."

Ash obliged, tightening his arms around her. Tayshia let out another tremulous breath and sagged against him.

And he fucking held her.

He had never been the comforting, soothing type. He'd never been the sort of guy who liked to sit with girls while they cried. But there was something about Tayshia that had rent his heart in two when he heard her sob that first *I can't* that made him want to shed his skin for her. And even though the embrace was for her sake, Ash couldn't help but feel his own emotions rising to the surface.

The last person to hold him was his mother.

After a few minutes of silence, Tayshia spoke.

"Do you regret it?"

"Regret what?" he said, straightening up to look down at her.

"Hooking up with me." She wore a shy yet open expression on her face. "Do you regret it?"

"Some parts. I should have asked for your consent before I kissed you like that."

"Yes, you should have," she said, and it was her turn to lift her chin. Her hand slid up to his shoulder, her thumb brushing the base of his neck.

The coil inside Ash's stomach loosened a bit, his curiosity piqued.

"Are you saying you would have said no?"

"Not necessarily. But that's the point—how are you ever going to know the truth if you don't ask?" Her upper lip curled and she glowered at the carpet in the shadows. "You men and your inability to understand that most women will say yes if they like you. And if they don't, then you could always find a girl who does. There's no reason to take what isn't yours when there are people who would be happy to be with you, provided you're not a complete creeper. Maybe if men weren't so fucking forceful, thinking with their *dicks* all the time, then women wouldn't think they wanted to hurt them."

She grew more and more agitated. Her body stiffened up again, her teeth beginning to clench. Her fingers dug into his flesh. In her eyes, he saw her anger burning bright.

Ash leaned forward before he could stop himself, his lips brushing against her ear. She stopped in the middle of her sentence.

"And do you?" he asked, glancing off to the left, towards the living room where he could see the faint blue flickers of the still-playing movie.

"Do I what?"

"Do you think that I want to hurt you?"

"I don't know." She said it like an epiphany of her own.

Ash inhaled, deep within his chest. "If I would have asked you before I kissed you, what would you have said?"

"Does it matter?" Her breath tickled his neck. "It was weeks ago."

"Come on." He straightened again, pulling back to look at her and leaning his weight against his hand on the wall. Letting go of his hold on her waist, he reached up to trace the swirls of her edges along her hairline. He could feel the product there, the smooth crispness of the hair fascinating him. "I asked you a question."

"I don't *know.*"

"You would have said no?"

"No," she said, and then he felt her body go rigid once more. "I mean — that's a lie. That's a — it's a lie."

Ash's heart skipped a beat. "If I said to you, *can I kiss you?* If I looked you dead in the eyes and asked you that, would you have said yes or no?"

"I would have said no."

"And what about now?"

She looked terrified — absolutely *terrified* — and then she said, "I'd say yes."

Ash felt something cracking inside of him, splintering and shattering like glass. It drove him to bend down, where he planted a kiss to her lips that was way more heated than he meant it to be, yet nowhere near the temperature that he wanted. He continued to kiss her skin, up and down her throat, close to her jaw and then with his lips laid over her pounding pulse. He heard her trying to complete her sentence, starting words that fizzled into short breaths.

His right hand cupped the other side of her neck, fingers tickling the curly tufts of hair at the back of her scalp, brushing through the ones that hung down her back. His thumb pushed upward on her jaw, tilting her head so he could have better access as he tasted her flesh like it belonged to him. His tongue was soft, his lips gentle, but his teeth scraped with a ferocity that had her panting harshly into the sudden silence.

A storm inside of him swirled into an inferno of colors, so many that he couldn't name them all. His heart was singing. He felt like he was floating.

When his tongue found a sensitive spot near the junction of her shoulder and neck, she gasped. Rising up on tip-toe again, Tayshia's fingers fluttered along his tattooed skin, as if she had to feel the tattoos more time, and then went to the back of his head. Long fingernails massaged his scalp again, right in the depths of his hair, and he couldn't help it.

He moaned.

Ash pressed her so hard against the wall that she couldn't have stood flat on her feet if she wanted to. He intensified the press of his tongue and the caress of his lips. The breaths she was pushing into his ear turned to pants that bordered on whines.

"Yeah?" he practically whimpered between kisses to her throat. "That's good?"

Her response came right as he sucked a bruise into her pulse point. His right knee found its way between her thighs.

"Yeah," she whispered, whimpering and arching her back until her chest was tight to his. Her trembling increased as he felt her trying to rub her thighs together without being able to — they pressed to either side of his leg.

Ash's knee hit the wall right as she lowered to the soles of her feet, bringing her down onto his thigh. Her head fell back in a moan as she ground her hips down against him.

"Fuck." This felt like a tidal wave of unavoidable chemistry. His hands went to her hips, pulling her sharp and hard. His breath was harsh in her ear. "Is this okay? I'm going to rip your fucking clothes off. I can't *fucking* think."

Her answer was to moan again, her back arching as one of her hands dug its fingers into his thigh. She tilted her hips forward, the pace of their rocking slowing. It grew firmer and more targeted. It was as if she wanted to hold him in place while she got herself off.

God, she had one of the most sensitive, responsive bodies he'd ever felt.

His hand went to her breast.

"Is this okay?" he asked again between kisses to her pulse, his voice and heartbeat frantic. "If you want me to stop, then tell me it's not okay. Is it okay?"

"Yes," she moaned, breathless. "Only with you."

"Is this good for you? I mean, does it work?"

"Yeah," she said. She made a choked sound. "I'm really… Wet…"

"*Shit.*"

She blew his fucking mind.

Tayshia sucked in a sharp, halting breath when he moved his hand on her chest in massaging, gentle circles. Ash slammed his lips against hers. She gasped into the kiss, her entire body trembling. Ash's heart beat so hard that he was losing his breath, too.

"Are you gonna make yourself come, baby?" His voice was hoarse against her lips, his mind traversing nonexistent planes as he forgot himself. All he could think about was the fact that she was only wearing his hoodie and her underwear. "Gonna make yourself come for me?"

"Yes," she whined, her other hand leaving his hair so it could hold the other side of his thigh. His body pressed her even harder to the wall so all she could do was move her hips. Their tongues tangled as Ash tilted his head to the side and swallowed half of her desperate moans.

"Fuck, I love how sensitive you are," he said as he kissed down her throat again. He was barely thinking—just saying whatever words materialized in his head. "You're so perfect when you come for me like this. Come on—you're so close. Come on, sweet girl. I want you to get there."

"Huh?" Her fingers clenched around his thigh. "What did you—you call m-me?"

He ran the tip of his tongue up to her ear.

"I said I want you to fucking come, sweet girl."

The moment he pulled her earlobe into his mouth, Tayshia lost whatever faculties she'd maintained for the past five minutes. Her hips rolled and twisted, grinding against his thigh twice more before her climax washed over her. It was slow and deep, causing the back of her head to smack against the wall behind her as she groaned a long, low *fuck* out to the ceiling.

He had to stop. He needed to *stop* or he was gonna fuck her in the hallway.

And Tayshia didn't deserve that.

Ash threw himself back from her, staggering a couple of steps.

"I'm sorry," he said, his voice hoarse. His stomach was slow to untwist, and the blood even slower to return to the rest of his body. "Forgive me. I got carried away."

"It's okay," she panted out, a hand covering her neck where his mouth had been. She leaned back against the wall for support. Her curls were only half up at this point. "I think you left a mark, though. A lot of marks."

Ash pushed his fingers into his hair for a second, closing his eyes against the wild urge he had to grab her and pick up where they'd left off. He let out a strained breath.

"That's a good thing, isn't it?" he joked. "Something for Kieran to accidentally see."

"Stop."

"Huh? Stop what?" Panic bloomed in his chest and he took a step toward her. "Did I hurt you?"

"What? No! No, I..." She winced. "Stop saying *good*."

Ash raised his eyebrows.

Well.

"But thank you," she said. "I know you hate when I say that, but...

I still don't care if you do. "

"For what?"

"Thank you for asking for my consent."

She left, walking into her bedroom, and closing the door behind her.

☼☼☼

Ash woke up on the couch with the streaming app asking him if he was still watching.

After Tayshia had gone into her room, she hadn't come out for the rest of the evening. He'd returned to the couch to finish the movie marathon by himself but had fallen asleep during the third one in the franchise. He couldn't hear the sounds of the wind and rain anymore, showing him that the storm had passed. Checking his phone, he saw that it was almost one in the morning.

He went to the bathroom for a late shower, enjoying the way the warm water felt against his skin. He sighed and pressed his forehead against the tiles on the wall, feeling the tension in his body easing bit-by-bit. His eyelids falling shut, his mind spun back to the hallway and the shadows.

To the feeling of his arms around her, holding her tight against him. To the way he wished he could have held her like that in Paris, and how he wished he could have been there to handle the situation with Kieran before he'd ever gotten the chance to fuck her over as bad as he had. To the way she'd rested her head against his chest and let herself be held by someone she'd once considered a passive bystander to her father's near-death. To the way he could still feel her shaking in his embrace, and the way he wanted to do it one more time.

"Only with you."

How starved was he for affection?

When his shower was done, he stepped back into his joggers but chose not to put his shirt back on. He was going straight to bed so there was no point. After pushing his fingers through his hair and messing it up the way he liked it, he used the toilet.

As he lifted the lid up, he paused.

Why were there orange flecks under the rim?

Back in his room, Ash tossed and turned for a while, trying to quiet his spirit so he could drift off to the land of slumber. It was difficult when he could still feel the press of her body against his and hear the sounds she made ringing in his ears. He wondered if he would dream about her again.

Fuck. It was a nightmare trying to sleep when his mind was this full of consternation.

Lying on his stomach, he reached over onto his bedside table for his pipe. He was out of weed until he could get more from Andre so he was going to scrape it.

Not wanting to deal with the jarring brightness of turning the lights on, Ash grabbed the small bobby pin that he'd stolen from Ji Hyun ages ago and scooted over to the other side of his bed. He leaned sideways against the wall beside the window, shouldering it to keep himself upright. Pulling his knees to his bare chest, he used the light of the moon and stars to guide him as he spent the next twenty minutes scraping resin out of the bowl of the pipe. Once he had enough, he used the lighter to light it and began to smoke.

It tasted fucking awful but he wasn't complaining. He was bone-tired, his mind way too alive to get to sleep without something to help. Gazing out the window at the golf course behind the complex, he wondered when he would ever be able to sleep without dreaming again.

By the time the resin was gone, Ash was sufficiently high. It felt like the Earth was spinning slower and there was a pleasant feeling that had washed over his entire body. It was enough to lower his eyelids and infuse lethargy into his muscles.

Perfect.

He fell into bed after putting the paraphernalia away and closed his eyes.

Knock, knock, knock.

Ash sighed and rolled back over. He hadn't realized that he'd fallen asleep. He glanced at the clock on his bedside table, the moonlight falling across it from the window.

Now, he *knew* she was not knocking on his door at two in the morning.

He swung his legs until his feet were flat on the floor. Resting his elbows on his thighs, his mind spun from the deepness of his interrupted sleep. He rubbed his face with his hands and struggled to wake fully.

Knock, knock, knock.

"I'm coming!" he snapped in annoyance, standing up and muttering to himself. "Can't even put on a *fucking* shirt. I'm so *fucking*

Goddamn *tired*."

He ripped the door open and shouldered the doorframe with his arm outstretched. It was dark as pitch in the hallway, but the moonlight from his window cast blue into the shadows. Tayshia stood there, wearing oversized pajama pants and a large dark shirt with long sleeves. She was swimming in the clothes, looking quite the sight with her curly hair sticking up in several directions and her arms wrapped around a pillow. Her crystal seemed to glint where it rested on her chest.

Her gaze swept his destroyed hair, roved down to his shirtless torso, and then bounced back up to his face.

"Does your offer still stand?"

"Shit," he said, trying not to scowl through his yawn. He rubbed his eye. "*What* offer?"

She gave him a look that bordered on helpless. It took him a second to remember, and then he sighed.

"Get in here."

Ash watched as Tayshia padded into the room, ducking underneath his outstretched arm to do so. She stood halfway between the doorway and the bed with a strange expression on her face. Brows furrowed and lips frowning, eyes wide with trepidation. Like she was already regretting her decision.

Seeing Tayshia in his room again was just as startling now as it was the first time. She appeared small and beige under the moonlight, half bathed in shadows and seeming on the verge of toppling over. With her pillow and the way she kept biting her lip, he thought she looked kinda cute.

Ash walked past her, towards the bed. "You can take the bed. I'll take the floor."

"Okay," she said.

He grabbed one of the pillows from his bed and set it on the floor. Then, he reached for his fleece blanket.

"Wait!" she cried, her voice ringing in his ears. "Sorry — that was loud. Just wait. We can share."

"What?"

"We can share," she repeated. "You've got a full-sized bed and it's cold. Also, you're like, twenty feet tall. It doesn't make sense for you to be cramped on the floor."

"So logical," he said, picking his pillow back up. "Why?"

"Because I want to lay next to someone, Ash," she snapped,

stomping over. She ripped the comforter back, exposing the black satin sheets. Glaring at him, she plopped down onto the mattress. "Why do you always have to make everything so damn difficult? You're the one who told me if I had a nightmare, I could come in here!"

Ash felt old anger rising. It was like it was September and the dishes were dirty again.

"Well, forgive me if I don't believe you'd be wanting to sleep in a bed with a felon." He scraped his hair back. "I made the offer so you knew I was here—I didn't think you'd actually be comfortable enough to."

"Why wouldn't I be comfortable?" she said through clenched teeth as she laid back beside the window and curled onto her side. "There's nothing for me to be uncomfortable about."

He sensed the tension pulling taut and he closed his mouth. He'd strayed too close to the memory—to the nightmare. The one he knew she was avoiding.

Paris.

Fuck if he didn't wish he had somewhere he could put his memory of it away for a while.

Ash climbed back into bed, pulling his half of the comforter over himself and lying facing the bedroom. He closed his eyes. The silence was awkward, but he supposed it wasn't as bad as it could have been.

At least she didn't seem scared.

"You're not gonna put a shirt on?"

"Nah, why would I? It's my room, bitch," He propped himself on his elbow so he could fluff his pillow, and then laid back down. "Besides—you said you liked my tattoos. There's plenty to look at on my back."

"Yes, *bitch*, your entirely unique dragon tattoo with wings that span your shoulder blades," she said, her voice dripping with sarcasm. "Intermingled with flames and thorns. How original."

"What's that supposed to mean?" he asked, feeling a distinct urge to roll over and kick her leg with his foot.

"It's just that your tattoos aren't as original as you think." She let out a haughty sniff. "Every guy with tattoos has a dragon, an anchor, a skull, a rose, a—"

"Yeah, yeah." He scowled.

"Bold of you to assume, however, that I'd want to look at them."

73

"You seem to have no issue looking at any of the others."

"That's because they're on the front of you, headass!" she snapped. "Where the Hell else am I supposed to look?!"

Ash was powerless to stop the chuckle that slipped past his lips. "You're feisty as fuck at night."

"Shut up!"

"Why are you always such a bitch?"

"Why are you—" She cut herself off, likely realizing that he wasn't actually doing anything wrong. "Why don't you just get over it?"

"I will."

"Fine."

"Already am."

"*Okay.*"

"Okay."

"I said *okay.*"

Ash bit his tongue hard enough to silence himself. Tayshia was acting like a brat. It was so unlike the sort of person he thought she'd be, yet so much like her that it could only be described as a darker part of herself. He could handle it.

He could handle her.

They laid there for a while, his irritation running so high that he didn't have the energy to put focus on the fact that he was lying in bed next to her. It existed so far outside of the realm of absurdity that it felt like a dream in and of itself. Like his consciousness was trying to float outside of his body so it could catch a glimpse of what they looked like as a pair.

"I was ashamed."

He shifted, his eyelids feeling heavy as they dragged upward. He'd been halfway to slumber, but something in the quiet of her voice had yanked him back into waking.

"*Mm*—what?" he mumbled.

"I was ashamed," Tayshia whispered, "and that's why I haven't talked to you about it yet."

"About what?" Ash rolled onto his back and turned his head toward her kinky curls in the moonlight. She hadn't turned around. "Talked to me about what?"

"The dream. Or the memory. Whatever it was." She was silent for a second, and then she said, "No one knows what happened, and I hadn't planned on telling anyone. Having someone—having *anyone* see it is humiliating. Especially you."

Ash's mind snapped to attention. He felt his hands begin to tremble from an emotion he didn't understand. It was something like nerves but not quite. He had so many questions.

Did she know about all the dreams he'd been having of her? Did she know his mind drifted to hers at night? Did she think it was the crystals, too? As soon as he thought of the amethyst, he thought of his half of it, which he hadn't even taken off for his shower. He felt the gem, warm against his chest.

He didn't want to fuck this up.

"You have nothing to be ashamed of," he said in a soft voice. "All right?"

She didn't respond. Instead, he saw her curl into a tighter ball beneath the comforter.

His heart wrenched, remembering what it had felt like to be inside of her mind while she laid awake and stared at the hotel room's wallpaper. How much she had despaired, how her anguish wove its way through her veins. There'd been no reprieve until the moment she closed her eyes.

Ash wanted her to know that he was there. He wanted her to know he was there so he could fix it, even if she was pretending not to be broken.

"We can talk about it when you're ready," he said.

"*If.*"

"If."

He turned to face the room.

As he started to drift off once again, he felt the mattress shifting. He cracked one eye open right as Tayshia rolled over. She scooted closer, until her forehead was pressed against the dragon's head between his bare shoulder blades. He held his breath, feeling his skin prickling with every exhalation that brushed against it.

When she burrowed her face into his skin, her nose and lips smoothing across sensitive flesh, he felt his mind begin to whirl. He couldn't see them but he could feel them—the churning waters of edged confusion. The ocean that seemed to draw him towards her.

She placed a tentative hand on the wing of the dragon, her palm and fingers tracing the outline of its scales and claws. It felt like his veins were on fire, burning him from the inside out. But even as he burned, he felt his muscles relaxing into the bed, like her touch could carry him across the sky on a cloud.

Tayshia's fingernails moved, arching down to trace the inked flames and thorn-covered branches that were embedded in his skin. She traced his ribs, pausing only when he took in a sharp breath.

"Should I stop?"

"No," he breathed, his voice somewhat gravelly from his exhaustion. He couldn't open his eyes even a fraction. "That feels good."

"It does?"

"Mm."

Ash's eyelids fluttered and his toes curled into the softness of the sheets. He felt relaxed. Soothed, like when his mother would draw on his back as a child. It was comforting and gut-wrenching, all at once.

She resumed her tracing, only her forehead touching him so she could watch her finger travel down to the lowest part of his spine and back up. He felt her fingers touching each and every vertebrae. Sleep drew closer.

"When."

"What?" he murmured.

"*When* I'm ready."

She traced the tattoo until he fell asleep.

CHAPTER SEVEN

The stars were silver.

They always were in Ash's dreams. Ever since he was a kid, the stars in his dreams were silver, and the sky was whatever color his mind seemed to think mattered the most. It didn't matter what he was doing in the dream — whether playing medieval knight or flying on the back of a dragon — the sky was always the color that made him the happiest.

But when Ash opened his eyes and saw a lavender sky and silver cosmos, he wasn't happy. He was confused.

He hadn't been inside one of his own dreams in months.

Sitting up, he saw sprawling hills, distant mountains, and white flowers. Gardenias littering the grass that were drifting back and forth with the wind, bathed in faint silvery moonlight. The mountains were tipped in snow, but it wasn't cold on the hill he sat atop. When he got to his feet, in the distance to the left he could see the ocean stretching the length of the horizon. He glanced to the right and saw more hills and fields of thick, lush grass covered in glowing white flowers.

Ash.

Well, this was odd. He'd been watching Tayshia's dreams for so long that he'd forgotten what it was like to have one of his own.

Tayshia's dreams were always memories. Pieces of her experiences with the people around her each day. They could be arbitrary, like studying in her bedroom or doing cornrow braids in her hair. Or they could be a little more exciting, like the time that Tayshia and her friends had driven to Seattle for a shopping trip right after graduation.

The only thing that was certain was that they were flashes. Never her entire day — only the things that felt safe to see.

Ash's dreams were more whimsical, which was in sharp contrast to the way he felt when he was awake. He dreamed of things like flying, doing magical things, or sitting and watching the sunset. Peaceful things that didn't cause him fear or concern. He was always alone, with no other humans or civilization nearby, and that was something he'd always liked.

It felt almost alien to be inside his own head for a change.

Ash.

He decided to head down the hill towards the white flowers.

Ash always had liked flowers. Especially gardenias. They were his mother's favorites, and they were the only thing he missed about his home. The only part of Gabriel that Ash liked. At any given time, fresh gardenias could be found in every windowsill, on every shelf, and in every vase just for the family.

At least, until his father fell apart.

Kneeling down, he plucked a flower out of the ground with a quiet snap. Eyelids fluttering shut, he inhaled the scent of the flower in his hand and a sense of calm washed over him. Perhaps he would take the flower to the seashore. It would feel like his mother was there with him, watching the water crash along the sand. They used to go to the Oregon coast sometimes, but not as much as they should have. His mother loved it.

Standing, he turned and headed west across the field.

ASH!

Ash nearly leapt out of his skin, the hairs on the back of his neck standing up. He whirled around to look behind him.

Tayshia.

She was here.

"Can you hear me?" she said.

Ash stared down at her. She wore the same pajamas she'd been wearing when she came into his room that night and the breeze was playing with her curls. There was a strange curiosity in her eyes that didn't match the fearful frown on her lips. Around her neck was the crystal.

"I guess you can't," she said. "But you can see me."

"No, I —" He cleared his throat, the sound of his voice a little jarring. His dreams were usually devoid of words. "I can hear you. Can you hear me?"

She nodded. "Is this a memory?"

"No, it's —" His brow furrowed. "Tayshia, the sky is purple and the stars are silver. Come on."

"Well, I didn't notice!" she said, throwing her hands up into the air. "I was a little busy wondering how the Hell I got into your dream!"

Ash bit his lower lip, reaching up with his free hand to touch his crystal.

Was now the perfect time to tell her? He wanted to. He was just scared what she would think. Months of walking her dreams, watching her life unfold and progress, and he'd never said a thing to her.

If he was ever going to win her trust, he needed to start somewhere.

"Well, given that I've been watching your dreams for four-and-a-half months now, I'm not as surprised to see you as I probably should be," he

said. "I'm trying to figure out what's different."

Her jaw dropped. "You've been doing what?"

Ash twirled the flower stem vertically between his forefinger and thumb, grimacing. "Dreamwalking in your dreams for four-and-a-half months?"

She was speechless, eyes wide underneath the eerie lavender light from above. He didn't blame her, knowing how shocked he'd been the first time he dreamed of her — his nineteenth birthday. Right after putting the necklace on. A few moments passed by and then Tayshia held her hands to her cheeks.

"You didn't see that dream I had the weekend I moved in, did you?"

Ash's face contorted with his confusion. "Wait — what?"

"The dream. In September, the dream!" She leapt forward and grabbed his wrists. Her eyes were wild. "The one I had about you! Did you see that dream?!"

"No. You don't dream like... Well, like this. You dream about your day."

"No, I don't. I dream like normal."

Ash frowned and said, "Then why can't I see them?"

"I dunno." She shrugged her shoulders. "I'm a little freaked out here. I'm standing inside your dream, talking to you and — wait, you said I dream about my day?"

"It's usually memories," he said. "Glimpses of points in your life. They've been chronological, too."

"That's so weird. Why would you see my memories, but not my dreams?"

"Maybe it's harder to see them because they're blocked by something?" he suggested, careful not to bring up Paris. "Maybe you have to let me in."

"How am I supposed to let you in when I have no idea what the fuck is going on? I mean..." She laughed, but it was mirthless and out of clear nervousness. "Being here means that the legends at the caverns are true. And if that's the case, not only is it weird, but we're also soulmates...? That's so far outta pocket that we are nowhere near the clothing article, okay?"

"Okay, chill. Just because we've never heard of it doesn't mean it's not real. I mean, the legends had to come from somewhere, right?"

"So, what do we do?"

"We could research it? What other option do we have?"

Tayshia's frowned deepened and she looked down at her crystal, lifting it up to inspect it.

"So... Do you think it could be the crystals?"

"The only times I've seen your memories were when I was wearing the crystal," Ash said. "So, yeah."

"I've literally never taken this off," she said. "Never once. I shower with it on. Maybe it only works when we're both wearing it?"

"But this is the first time you've been inside my head," he said. "And I've only been able to see your memories. If I have never been able to see your dreams, and you have never been able to see my memories or my dreams until right now, tonight, then what's going on? Like, what are the requirements?"

Tayshia chewed the inside of her cheek for a long moment, then said, "Guess we're gonna have to do some research. Crystal Springs is old – there has to be something somewhere in town."

They stared at one another. Ash thought she was taking this whole thing rather well, given that it was basically the same thing as finding out magic existed. Then again, he'd been coping fine himself. He had barely questioned the dreams – he'd simply embraced them.

The dreams made him feel less alone.

"Wait," he said, a smirk slow to spread across his lips. "You dreamed about me?"

She grimaced. "It doesn't matter – you didn't see it, so it's for the best."

"Now I wanna know what it was. What did you dream about?"

"Nothing," she said, her voice taking on a bit of a whine as she gave him a scathing look. "And I'm not telling you, so you're just gonna have to accept it."

"You hated me when you moved in," he said, still smirking. "What could you possibly have dreamed about?"

"I'm not telling you." Her cheeks flared red.

"But I wanna know."

"Cry about it."

Ash opened his mouth to protest but stopped himself. His brow furrowed and he lowered his gaze in thought.

"It wasn't a nightmare, was it?"

"Ash, you're a terrifying person," she said, clasping her hands behind her back, "and I can't pretend you didn't terrify me back then. But was it a nightmare? Yeah, no. Not a nightmare."

"At least you haven't deluded yourself into thinking I'm a good person," he said with a small laugh.

"No, I haven't deluded myself. But I don't think you're a bad person."

His heart skipped a beat. What was that supposed to mean?

Ash held his hand out, and she took the proffered gardenia from him. She stood there, barefoot in the grass with the fingers of both hands clutching the stem. He watched her lift the petals to her nose so she could smell it.

If she didn't think he was a bad person, what was it about him that she knew to be true?

80

"You're forgetting that I stood there and watched your dad bleed out. So, don't convince yourself that I'm in any way heroic," he said. "I would absolutely have stood there while he died. Back then, I mean."

Tayshia's brow furrowed. "Are you saying that to scare me away from being your friend, or because it's true?"

"Both," he whispered, looking over her head, past her at the mountains.

"But, you're different now," she said with an air of finality that told him there was nothing he could say to change her mind. "I think if it happened again tomorrow, you'd make the right choice."

Ash could feel the blood rushing up to his cheeks, trying to force him into blushing. He ran his fingers through his hair to distract himself from it.

"I tell you I've been in your dreams for months and you're more interested in the fact that I've changed, but not in why I was in your head in the first place?"

She pressed her lips into a flat line, still gazing down at the gardenia. He could tell she was thinking, so he remained quiet, choosing to listen to the wind rustling through the flowers until she spoke again.

"I am curious as to why but I think there's an explanation. There's always an explanation. It just might take a bit of research."

"You are way too calm," he said, slipping his hands into the pockets of his joggers. His dream had chosen to keep him clad in his pajamas, too. He felt the breeze against his shirtless torso. "And so am I. Why are we both so fucking calm about this?"

"You've been walking my dreams and my memories for months," Tayshia said, still looking at the gardenia, "and I never noticed. But now, I'm here inside of your dream. That means we have a connection of some sort, we just don't know what it could be. There's no point in panicking about something we don't know anything about."

Ash watched her, wondering if the reason why she was so calm was because she didn't want to be lonely anymore, either.

Tayshia tucked the gardenia in place behind her ear. The flower added a bit of light to her face, making her look pretty in a way that Ash found himself unable to look away from. But before he could think of what to say, she shoved past him.

"Where are you off to?"

"To sit by the water. We might as well embrace this shit, instead of standing around waiting to wake up. Come on — it's not that far."

Ash fell in-step beside her and they walked across the grass towards the seashore. The closer they got, the heavier the air felt. Its salty scent grew thicker and headier, a sense of peace settling over him in a way that made his lips curve into a soft smile. He wondered what it would be like to sit by the sea with Tayshia in reality.

He could feel that something had shifted between them, too. He wasn't sure if it was on Tayshia's part or his own, but it didn't feel like he was traversing a thousand mile-high wall any longer. Something felt inevitable between them, like the passage of time. Whatever was going to happen was going to happen, but he didn't think he'd be seeing it happen without Tayshia.

In a strange way, it was exciting.

"I think," Tayshia said as their feet crossed from grass to thick, cool sand, "that we'll have to research it when we wake up."

"Right when we wake up?" He chuckled.

She stumbled in the shifting grains. Ash's hand shot out to wrap around her own. To his surprise, she squeezed it and held on while they made their way closer to the water. Her words continued.

"No, we have class, idiot. But I'm going to get started as soon as I can and once we both have free time, we should go to a bookstore."

"Do you think the answer will be there?"

"No." She slipped again and he pulled on her hand, keeping her upright. "At the least, it'll be a good start. Either it has something to do with stars or we're soulmates. Which is just ridiculous."

Tayshia Cole and Ash Robards soulmates?

Their laughter ripped through their guts, causing them to double over. Tears of mirth gathered in Ash's eyes. She wiped her own away.

"It's probably the stars," Tayshia said, still laughing. "Because the alternative is just — "

"Wild."

"Exactly."

She was still stifling hysterical giggles as they found a massive piece of driftwood to sit on. Ash kept hold of her hand to assist her in sitting, and then he sat down next to her. Resting his elbows on his knees, he wrapped one hand around the opposite wrist and gazed out to sea.

"This is weird," she said.

"Yeah."

"Like, really weird. I'm in your dream, talking to you. And in real life, I'm just... Asleep next to you."

"Yeah."

They sat and watched the waves kiss the shore for what felt like hours. The soft sounds mingling with the somewhat forceful whip of the oceanside wind offered a strangely familiar sconce within which to exist. It wasn't uncomfortable, perhaps because this was Ash's dream and he was in control.

He knew that nothing could happen here that he didn't want to happen. No one could hurt them.

Ash wondered what would happen when they woke up.

"Is it all right if we're friends?" Her voice was quiet, swallowed by the immensity of the sea.

"Yeah," he said in a voice that was just as soft. He tried to glance down at her but instead got a face full of curls. His heart was racing, and he couldn't place the reason why. "We're friends."

Ash felt Tayshia tracing the outlines of the waves he'd gotten tattooed on the outer part of his forearm. In spite of the sensitivity of his skin, there was a tension in the air that kept Ash frozen. He feared that if he moved, it would shatter.

"Ash, I..."

"Hm?"

"Earlier, when you asked me what I would say if you asked me if you could kiss me, I wasn't clear enough. Do you remember?"

His heart nearly tore its way out of his chest. He forced himself to stay as calm and still as possible. Of course he remembered, but he wasn't going to destroy any sort of moment they were having with sarcasm.

"Yeah."

"I should have been clearer."

"Okay," he murmured, watching the waves on the choppy sea with intensity. "And what would you have said?"

"I think I would have said — I mean, I'd like to think I would have said yes." Her fingers moved down his forearm. "I haven't exactly kissed many guys, but I think it's all right with you."

"But you were avoiding me."

"No," she countered, "you were avoiding me."

"Well, you slapped me."

"And you screamed at me for the dishes multiple times." She lifted her head, her arm remaining linked with his and her hand curving over his fingers on his wrist. A glare was affixed to her face. "We all have stupid things we get angry over."

"Having a clean kitchen is not stupid. It's basic human decency."

"Because you're the expert on basic human decency. Not you, the boy who went out of his way to be a jerk to me just because I followed the rules. I know you're not the one saying that to me."

Annoyance broiled in the heat of his stomach. "Not the girl who was despised by me telling me she wants me to kiss her."

"Not the guy pretending he doesn't want to kiss me by way of *deflection," she snapped.*

"Not you pretending like you're the one in control of this dream."

"Not you acting like I'm not."

Ash looked at her with scorching hot anger for two seconds before he felt the desire rising inside of his body. It drowned everything else he felt out, the anger fading into a firestorm of lust. The way she was looking at him, like she wanted to throttle him until he died, was quite possibly the most attractive thing he'd ever seen.

Maybe he'd just gone crazy.

He surged forward, dipping his head down to press his lips against hers. It was just for a moment, because he didn't want to mistake her comments for consent if they weren't, and then he pulled back. Her lips were as soft as gardenia petals.

"There," she said, her voice quivering. "It wasn't so bad, was it?"

"Nah," he said. "But what was it for? Practice for Kieran's sake?"

"No. It was for me."

Tayshia laid her head on his shoulder. Ash's lips twisted up into a half of a smile as he looked out to sea again.

He knew when they woke up, they'd have to discuss the fact that she'd been in his dream like this. They'd also have to figure out why he'd been dreaming of her for so long. Eventually, they'd have to talk about Paris. But the rest?

The rest could stay here in his dreams, witnessed by the sea.

CHAPTER EIGHT

November 2018

"I'll drive you to school."

Tayshia stopped at the front door, one hand on the doorknob and the other wrapped around the strap of her messenger bag. She turned, her pleated miniskirt flaring out around her as she did. Her eyes were alight from beneath her wild curls.

"Deadass? I hate the shuttle bus."

Ash nodded, in the process of rolling a joint at the coffee table. He wore his typical skinny jeans and a hoodie, the sleeves pushed up as he leaned over with his elbows on his thighs. "We should talk about—"

"The fact that the legend of Crystal Springs Cavern is in some way real because I can enter your dreams and you can enter mine?"

"Yeah." He shot her a look. "That."

"I agree. We should discuss it and figure out what we're gonna do. I mean, we can't... Uh, we can't..."

His eyes met hers as he licked the paper to seal the joint. Her words faltered for some reason unknown to him and she remained silent as he put the joint in his mouth and lit it. He watched her as he inhaled, letting the smoke fill his lungs before he released it in a hazy cloud around his face.

Tayshia cleared her throat before continuing. "We can't just let it go without figuring out why it's happening. It's crazy—unreal, really—but it's happening. There's answers somewhere."

"Mm," he said, his voice humming in his chest as he studied her and smoked.

Ash wondered how she could wear a skirt and a crop top at the start of November like that without a coat. Outside, he could hear the rain pattering against the roof of the apartment building, like the footsteps of elves running back and forth. She was going to freeze or get soaked. Maybe both.

A flush to her cheeks, Tayshia walked over to the couch, plopping down to sit on one of the cushions. Ash saw that not only did she have a pair of high-heeled combat boots on, but she was also wearing her crystal. The jewel stood out against the backdrop of her black crop top. She pursed her lips, a judgmental expression on her face.

"You can't go to school without getting high first?" she asked.

"No," he said in a monotone, exhaling a cloud of smoke. "I can't go to school without getting completely fucking blazed."

"And there's a difference?"

"Yeah." He shot a casual glance in her direction. "You wanna come over here and try it?"

"*No,*" she said, her words whipping quick and snappish from her throat. "I'm cool with most things, but I have no intentions of ever trying weed."

"Not very Christian of you to try most things, is it?"

"Boy, shut up," she said, tsking. "Just hurry up."

She sat there in silence, her gaze tracking the movements of his hand as he periodically brought the joint to his lips to take a drag. Since she was watching, he decided to show off a bit, blowing smoke rings and doing interesting things with the clouds using his fingers. She seemed fascinated by it all.

Sufficiently high, Ash went to his room to grab his backpack, wallet, keys, and his black windbreaker. In the living room, he held the jacket out to her.

"What's this for?" she asked, staring at it as though it offended her.

"If you're not wearing a coat for the sake of fashion, then at least take my jacket. You won't have to sacrifice your style."

"Is that a joke?" she asked with an incredulous expression.

"It's like sixty degrees outside today," he said. "So, no."

She stared at him.

"We have literally hooked up three times now," he said. "You can wear my damn jacket."

Slowly, she reached out and took it from him. Setting her bag on the floor for a moment, she slipped it on. It was huge indeed, the sleeves drowning her hands and the hem of the jacket nearly covering her pink-and-lavender plaid skirt.

"It's too big," she said, pouting.

Ash said nothing, reaching forward with one hand to pull the hood on. He patted the top of her head, his hand lingering, curving around the top of her skull. She stared up at him, her eyes studying the planes of his face as though she were trying to decipher a hidden message. He gazed down at her, unable to see anything other than her lips. They'd gotten swollen when he kissed them last night.

They always did.

But he felt selfish for it, knowing what had happened to her. Everything was in a different perspective now. The hook up would have been normal if she were just a girl he met at a party, but she wasn't. She was a girl who had a connection to him that somehow enabled him to enter her dreams. And when he did, it brought him to a nightmare. A nightmare that had forced him to experience the most traumatic, painful night of her life. A night that no one deserved to experience.

"Let's go," Tayshia said, her voice tremulous as she ducked out from underneath his arm and went around him. She yanked the front door open, letting in the cool air and the scent of the rainfall. "I don't wanna be late for breakfast. I'm hungry."

Weird.

Her dirty breakfast dishes were in the sink.

☼☼☼

"So, what do you think?"

Ash watched the scenery going by outside his windshield as they hurtled down the highway that led up the mountain. Outside of Tayshia's window, the forest stretched down the side of the mountain and out for miles into the distance. There were more hills and rocky areas, but the mountain they were currently driving up was definitely the king of them all. Everything was green, lush and dark as the rain poured down around them. The sound of the water on the road as it splashed against the car's wheels could probably be heard if his music weren't so loud.

"Ash."

He said nothing, focused on the road.

"Ash!" Tayshia, whose elbow was on the windowsill and knees were pulled to her chest with her feet in the seat, glared over at him. "Turn the music down and maybe you can hear me!"

"No." He yawned, relaxing back in the seat with one hand on the wheel and his other hand in his lap. The raucous screaming, heavy electric guitars, and thrashing drums soothed him. "I heard you."

"Then why aren't you answering me?"

"Because I'm fucking high, Smart One," he drawled, rolling his head to look at her from beneath his hood. "And what do you want me to say? I don't have any idea what's going on."

"Well, you have to have *some* thoughts about it. You're the one who was in *my* dreams for months. Don't you think it's weird that I wasn't in yours until recently?"

Ash shrugged. "I don't know. Maybe it has something to do with the way we feel. Like, if we like or hate each other. Maybe you deciding you didn't hate me anymore made it so you could get in, or whatever."

"I—" She cut herself off, her brow furrowing. "Actually. That's a good theory. Maybe letting your guard down is part of it, and if we both have our guards down, it's like a... Like a pathway between our minds."

"*Do* you still hate me?"

"Undetermined."

"I'll take the dreams as proof then," he said, smirking in her direction without taking his eyes off of the road and the other cars.

The music played uncontested for a solid thirty seconds before Tayshia spoke again.

"You don't hate me, do you?"

"Nah. Never did."

"Oh. Okay."

Ash glanced at her. "That bother you?"

"No," she said, her tone a bit wistful as she stared out the windshield. "It's just confusing."

"Which part?"

She was quiet for a long time, seeming to choose her words as carefully as though she were picking berries in an orchard.

"I don't understand how you could not hate me, but still have been content to stand there and watch my dad die. I know you went to jail and that you're... Different now, but it still makes me wonder how you could be okay with it, even back then. And it makes me nervous."

His heart wrenched in his chest, causing his hand to tighten on the lower curve of the wheel. He gritted his teeth against his guilt, averting his gaze to his window as though it could offer him reprieve from the tension.

"You don't have to be nervous around me," he said, turning his head to look down at her. "I would never hurt you."

"I don't know."

That hurt.

"So, what do you want to do?" he asked. "About the caverns."

"Oh, I don't know..." Tayshia sighed. "Maybe we could talk to Miss Iqbal about it? I mean, if anyone's going to know something about the caverns, it's gonna be her, right?"

Ash nodded. That was true. Miss Iqbal was the teacher of the Myths & Legends class, so it stood to reason that she would be the person to go to regarding the caverns. They couldn't tell her specifically what was going on, but they could glean something from her through asking the right questions.

When they got to the school, they parked close to the staircase up to the entrance doors. As they headed up the steps behind the crowd of students who were coming from the parking lot—the ones who didn't live in the dorms—Tayshia stumbled.

Ash wasn't sure how it happened. He only saw her go pitching forward. Thinking quick on his feet, he turned and swung his arm around. She slammed into it with an *oof*, her hands clutching his forearm as he pulled her upright. Several other students sent them wary looks, but Ash ignored them.

Something was wrong.

"You're the epitome of a fanfiction protagonist at this point."

"Huh?" Tayshia closed her eyes, shaking her head. When she opened them, they seemed a bit unfocused. "I'm okay. I'm fine. Just got dizzy all-of-a-sudden."

"Shit. Do you need to go to the nurse's?"

"No," she said, immediately forcing herself to stand up straight. "I'm okay. Let's just get to Miss Iqbal's classroom. I'm really hungry."

Ash pulled a perplexed face and followed her up the staircase. He kept his hand on her lower back just in case she got dizzy again. He didn't need her face-planting it on the concrete, or swaying backward and going tumbling down.

In Miss Iqbal's room, they were fortunate.

She'd been about to leave to go to grab breakfast in the teacher's lounge. They were able to catch her right as she was locking the classroom door behind her. She took them into the room so they could talk, perching on the edge of her desk while Tayshia and Ash leaned against a table.

"We're just wondering if you know anything about the legend of the hot springs inside Crystal Springs Caverns," Tayshia said. "It's for the final project this term — the one you said we had to do research for."

"Ah, believe it or not, but I haven't had a student choose the caverns the entire time I've been teaching," Miss Iqbal said, grinning. "I love that you're taking an interest in the things we have at home. Have either of you been there?"

"Yeah, we went there," Ash said, exchanging glances with Tayshia. "What do you know about it?"

"Well, I don't know as much as I probably should, to be honest," Miss Iqbal said, crossing her arms over her chest and shrugging her shoulders. "What I do know is that the legend's been around for as long as I've lived here, and I've been here since I was born. It's something well-known by older members of the community. As to the origins, I'm unsure. It could very well be something made up, or it could be something that has nothing to do with the area."

"Nothing to do with the area?" Tayshia asked, sounding curious.

"It could have nothing to do with the springs or the caverns themselves — it could just be word-of-mouth. Which, you remember we talked about when we were discussing ancient lore earlier this term. It's a good example."

"Do you know if anyone has ever mentioned experiencing any strange dreams after going into the hot springs?"

Miss Iqbal's brow furrowed. "I'm not sure what you mean, Tayshia. The hot springs have been off limits to civilians for a long time now. I think since I was little. "

"Oh... Well," said Tayshia. Ash could see her trying not to look at him. "It's just a rumor we heard, that if you go into the hot springs, you'll have weird dreams. We just wanna explore every lead. Maybe it has something to do with the fact that the caverns are full of amethysts...?"

"I do know that crystals can encourage those sorts of things," Miss Iqbal said. "Especially amethysts. You could try going to Moonbeams & Things in town and check out their book section?"

Ash had never heard of it, but Tayshia seemed to have. She nodded with enthusiasm, looking up at Ash.

"Tayshia, you okay, honey?" Miss Iqbal peered at her. "You look a little ashen."

Ash's head whipped to the right, down to look at Tayshia with concern. Her facial expression appeared surprised, but somewhere dancing in the meadows of her eyes, he saw faeries of fear.

"I'm fine," she said, and her smile was tight. "I just felt a bit dizzy today. I, uh—fell on the stairs. It was a whole fiasco."

"Hm. Well, make sure you go to Nurse Pritchard's if you're feeling under the weather."

"Okay, we will!" Tayshia grabbed Ash's hand and dragged him out to the hall. "See you later today, Miss Iqbal!"

Ash allowed himself to be pulled down and around the corner. The moment they were out of sight, regardless of the fact that he saw some of the high school students at their lockers, he yanked on her to whip her around to face him. She cried out and flew forward, her palms braced against his chest. The momentum caused the hood of his jacket to fall off of her head as she craned her neck.

He glared down at her.

"What's going on?"

"What?" She started to pull back, but Ash was too strong. "Nothing! *Nothing!*"

"If it's nothing, then why do you look so terrified?"

"Because you won't let go of me, headass," she snapped, and then her hands curled tight in the fabric of his hoodie. She shoved him backward so suddenly that he nearly tripped, almost careening into a locker. "Don't trap me in the hallway and then ask me why I look scared!"

She... She pushed me.

Ash saw crimson, like a flare going off in his mind.

He slammed her up against the nearest locker, one hand pinning her left shoulder while the other pointed an angry finger in her face.

"Stop fucking hitting me."

"Then stop manhandling me," she shot back.

A group of pre-req students traipsed by, talking about their breakfasts, and they slowed their pace. An assortment of boys and girls that they'd gone to school with for years, they seemed shocked as they caught sight of the compromising position. The rumors were already brewing in their eyes.

Ash and Tayshia were playing with fire.

"You can keep walking," Ash said to the students, his tone threatening. He felt Tayshia struggling against his hold, but he ignored it. "*Now.*"

The students lingered, appearing uncomfortable. One of them—a raven-haired girl name Nicole—frowned, clutching her College Geography textbook tighter to her chest. She took a step closer.

"Are you guys friends?" she said, and she sounded revolted.

That pissed Ash off. Tayshia was the one who completely flipped her lid and shoved him.

But no. Just like at Keely's party, *he* was the felon.

"Just *go,* Nicole!" Tayshia said, sagging against the lockers beneath Ash's grip. "It's not your business."

Nicole's facial expression contorted into one of indignance. She scowled and spat out, "You're such a whore, Tayshia. No wonder Kieran left you. The last thing you are is a Godly woman."

Okay, *that* pissed Ash off, too.

Remembering the things Kieran had said to Tayshia in her memory, coupled with the hypocrisy of him cheating on her, and now finding out he was telling the Christian students that Tayshia was a *whore*? He was about to start seeing red again. Tayshia was absolutely having a tantrum moment right now, but she wasn't his whore. A woman didn't have to be *Godly* to have worth, either.

Tayshia had value purely because she existed.

The students stormed off after Nicole, disappearing down the hall. At the lockers, the younger students were sharing whispers as the rumors already began to trickle outward. As soon as everyone was gone, Ash turned his attention on Tayshia again. She looked like she was hovering between rage and devastation.

"Look at me," he said, using his knuckle to force her chin upward.

She did, but she was pouting.

"You *don't,*" Ash whispered, his gaze flickering back and forth between her eyes, "push me. Do you understand me?"

"Then stop grabbing me all the time," she hissed. "I'm not yours to trap or grab or hold."

As she started to walk past him, he glared up at the ceiling and pushed her back by the shoulder again. The lockers rattled.

"Hey," he said gently. "Wait a sec."

"What? *What* do you want?" She looked annoyed. Exasperated. Done. "*What,* Ash?"

"You're not a whore. Don't listen to them. Anything that Kieran says is bullshit, and we both know it. He's trash."

She glared off to the right.

When a tear escaped the confines of her lower lashes, he felt his chest spasming. Concern flooded through his earlier anger. He was quick to wipe it away, fingers brushing across her cheek.

"Knock it off," he said, lowering his voice. "Don't let those people get to you. You're stronger than that."

"Why should I have to be?" she snapped, sniffling. "Why do I have to be strong all the time?"

"You don't," he said. "I've seen you at the fucking bottom, and you were still strong as fuck. But you don't have to be that strong person around me."

She froze, staring up at him in horror. Before he could fully grasp the consequences of what he'd just said, she wrenched herself away from him. Realizing, he opened his mouth to apologize, running a hand through his hair.

Tayshia's hand went up, fingers splayed and palm vertical.

"Don't talk to me," she said, voice flat. "Back up and go to class."

"*Wait*, all right? I'm—"

"I don't wanna hear it," she said, eyes blazing. "Just go to class and I'll see you later. After school, I'll meet you in the parking lot and we'll go to that shop. Okay?"

"Yeah. I'll meet you by the steps."

"Good."

With one last glare, she spun and stomped off. The *click-clack* of her heels against the floor echoed behind her, ringing in the emptiness of Ash's heart. All he could think about was Paris.

He pushed it all to the back of his mind, where those fearful faeries danced.

CHAPTER NINE

"Well, that didn't tell us anything."

Ash said nothing. He felt so terrible over bringing up the memory earlier that day that he'd barely spoken a word the entire car ride to Moonbeams & Things. He knew better than to do it, but he wanted to talk about it so badly that he kept forgetting she didn't want to.

It wasn't his place. He needed to remind himself of that every day until it sunk in.

In the store, which was covered wall-to-wall in all sorts of interesting things, Tayshia hadn't found anything that could be of use. The store clerk had directed them to an author who had written a book entirely on amethysts that could be found at any major bookstore or online. Tayshia liked hard copies of books, so she decided they'd go to the bookstore another time.

They'd left the store empty-handed and were now driving down the road, trying to figure out where to eat. Ash had suggested every fast food place known to mankind, but she wasn't interested in any of them. His patience had already disintegrated.

"Let's just get something to cook," she eventually said. "Because I'm not like, craving fast food, you know?"

"Are you sure? It'd be easier—"

"Yes, I'm sure," she said. "Let's just go to the store."

"All right. If you want."

They pulled into the store parking lot and got out. It wasn't raining, but the smell of the past rainfall lingered in the air as they strolled to the doors. Tayshia fell behind several times, the rapid clicking of her heels as she continued to run to try and catch up nearly sending him careening into space with how hilarious it was.

"Maybe if you weren't a fucking *tree*," she grumbled as they entered the store. She was breathless from exertion. "And here you are, laughing."

"My bad," he said, still grinning. "It's just funny."

"My height is not humorous."

"You're not even short." He took the red basket from her and held it, giving her a once-over. She looked cute, still wearing his windbreaker with the sleeves covering her fingers and the hem of her skirt peeking out from beneath it. "You're five-foot-eight."

"Then why are you laughing at me?"

"Because it's cute watching you try to keep up just because you chose to wear heels, Smart One."

She rolled her eyes and looked at some of the things on the racks in the Juniors section. He could tell she was embarrassed by the way she was trying to breathe heavily through her nose so she didn't pant. Ash didn't know why she had such a hard time keeping up, but he wasn't going to make fun of her for it anymore. He knew his legs were long and he *did* walk sort-of fast.

"Here," he said, holding his hand out. "So you don't fall behind."

"I'mma smack that hand out the air," she said, glaring at him.

"Your funeral."

When he pulled ahead a third time, she seemed to give up on her stubbornness. With a loud scowl, she slipped her hand into his, lightly intertwining their fingers as though she didn't want to. In fact, she wouldn't let their palms touch. But when he tried to pull away, she curled her fingers tight until they touched the back of his palm to stop him.

He raised one eyebrow in her direction.

"Cry about it," she said in a mocking tone. "Can we just get the food and go?"

"Yes, Queen," he said in an equally mocking tone. Before she could retort—or smack him—he dragged her down the aisle.

They held hands while they made their way to the grocery section. Ash found he rather liked the way he could tug her this way and that, and that if he did it with just a tiny bit more force, her heels caused her to bump into his side. It was entirely selfish. Hearing the occasional *Ash, knock it the Hell off* was worth it.

After gathering up some chicken and other things to cook, they made their way down the center aisle to get to the registers. The store was crowded but Tayshia didn't seem to mind the fact that they were holding hands where anyone in town could see them. Sometimes, he wondered if she realized how much he was hated in Crystal Springs.

Did she not realize how it looked, the fact that he'd gone to *jail* for holding up the ice cream store where her father had gotten shot?

Ash almost let go of her but when they got into a line, she reached to hold the other side of his hand. With it cradled between both of hers, he didn't dare ruin the moment. An emotion danced across her face, one that filled him with curiosity.

"You good?"

"Yeah." Tayshia stepped closer before glancing around at all of the people. "I just got a lot of anxiety. I don't like crowds. Like, I'm fine at school because I know most everyone or I've seen them around. But crowds in town just freak me out."

"Well, it's almost our turn. Just two people to go."

"I know," she said, glancing around one more time before she stared at the ground.

"You'll be all right. I got you."

"Oh, stop," she said, but her cheeks were flushed red. "Everything you do is so dramatic and extra."

"You look pretty under this lighting," he said through a mischievous grin.

"*Stop*. Good God. Stop playing."

Ash's gaze slid toward the front of the store, across from their aisle. He did a double-take, his heart skipping a beat and his nerves causing his stomach to do a little drop.

At first, he'd thought they just looked familiar. Upon the second glance, he realized who it was that was standing in the aisle diagonal from theirs, waiting in line to check out.

Kieran and Quinn.

Quinn spotted them first, her jaw dropping and eyes popping. Her ebony hair shifted over her shoulders as she turned to nudge Kieran, who looked over at Ash.

And then they were staring right at them.

Ash remembered the lie Tayshia had texted to Kieran to try and make him jealous. And even though he thought it was juvenile, it was difficult to remember that when he saw Kieran's reaction. The dark look that shadowed his face was enough to urge Ash into petty territory.

"Hey," Ash murmured so no one but her could hear.

She was looking at the candy, still gripping his hand in a double vice. "What?"

"Come here, sweet girl."

Gaze locked with Kieran's glowering one, Ash reached for Tayshia with his free hand. His fingers brushed her jawline, causing her to startle. He lifted her face upward.

Eyelids fluttering shut, Ash leaned down, tilted his head a bit, and pressed a searing kiss to her lips. Her shock was palpable, present in the way her body went stiff at first. But then she relaxed, her hands tightening to squeeze his hand between both of hers as she applied the same amount of pressure, kissing him back.

His heart sang.

As he pulled back and looked into her eyes, into those shimmering hazel irises, he wasn't sure it was false or fake or feigned. He didn't care about the fact that she had at one point wanted to pretend to be dating just to make her ex envious. Ash really didn't need an excuse to kiss her.

He wanted to.

Ash kissed her again, lips lingering against hers with the hope that she understood that it was real. When they broke apart, a smirk played about his lips.

"What were those for?" she asked, breathless.

He thought about telling her he'd seen Kieran. He contemplated telling her it was because of Quinn.

But he was selfish.

"Because I wanted to."

Kieran and Quinn were gone before they reached their register. Ash paid for everything, having to let go of Tayshia's hand so he could take his wallet out of his back pocket and swipe. She grabbed his hand again the second she could and held it all the way back to the car. And on the drive home, her hand snaked onto the center console to hold his *again*.

She didn't tell him to turn the music down.

After working together to cook the chicken, vegetables, and garlic bread they'd gotten, Tayshia sat down beside him on the couch.

Ash tensed. She didn't often sit next to him. The sectional was huge. Typically, he sat on the side that faced the TV; she sat on the side that faced the sliding glass door. This was the first time they'd not only sat down to eat in the living room, but had also made food together.

They ate in silence while watching the TV, Tayshia getting up to go to the bathroom afterward. When she came back, she curled up on the couch beside him, her feet facing him and her head on a couch pillow in the corner of the sectional.

She fell asleep within seconds.

Ash didn't know what to make of this. Except for Halloween, she *always* sat far away from him. The fact that she was sitting—no, *lying*—beside him on the couch? It was so domestic.

He wished she were sleeping with her head on his chest.

Later, when night fell, Ash grew too sleepy to keep watching shows. He got up, taking their empty plates to the kitchen sink and deciding to do the dishes the following day. Then, he went back to the couch to wake Tayshia.

"Hey." He started to shake her, then thought better of it. Instead, he touched her face, pushing a stray curl out of the way. She jolted awake, just as he expected she would, looking around in terror. "It's just me."

She stared at him.

"You should get to bed," he murmured. "We got school tomorrow."

"Okay," she said, sitting up. Her curls had flattened on the side she'd been asleep on, tangling and squishing together from the pressure. She looked half-asleep. "What time is it?"

"Time for sleep," he said, absentmindedly reaching over to tug on the ends of her curls until they fell down again.

Tayshia watched him, her gaze dancing up and down his face as he fixed her hair.

The tension increased, wrapping around Ash's lungs until it grew difficult for him to catch his breath. He remembered what it felt like to kiss her in the store, right in front of everyone. Right in front of Kieran and Quinn. How soft her lips felt, how soft they always were. How it felt like dancing with one foot in the flames, playing with the way the fire burned.

It was dark in the room.

"Well, good night," Tayshia said.

Ash sat there for a moment after she left, his heart still pounding.

☼☼☼

A knock at his door fifteen minutes later brought Ash out of bed.

He crossed his arms over his bare chest and shouldered the door frame. A smirk graced his features as he gazed down at Tayshia. She wore an oversized shirt and baggy pajama pants and her curls were pulled up into her satin bonnet. He was happy to see her crystal on its silver chain, clasped around her neck where it belonged.

"Well, well. Can't sleep without me?"

"Put a damn shirt on," she said with a scowl, shoving past him into his dorm room.

Ash looked down at himself, at the tattoos that littered his skin like a series of intricate paintings and his crystal hanging onto his chest. Dragging his hand backward through his hair, he turned to face her while kicking the door shut behind him. He wandered over to his dresser, where he rummaged for a clean shirt.

Tayshia sat down on the edge of his bed, dropping her head into her hands. Ash paused on his way back to the bed, feeling a tiny nagging in the back of his mind.

"Too bad today wasn't successful," he said in a nonchalant tone, sinking down onto the side of the bed he always slept on. He felt like the right half of his body was prickling, the hairs standing at attention and reaching toward her. "When did you wanna go to the bookstore?"

"Tomorrow. After school."

"Okay. And what about earlier—you falling over? Are you feeling any better?"

"Just—" Her voice sounded thick. Beleaguered. Exhausted. "Just drop it. I don't want to talk about it."

"Okay," he said. "Then at least tell me what's going on with you. Because you're not usually like this."

"And you're the expert on all things Tayshia?" she cried, lifting her head from her hands. Ash glanced at them, the opalescent moonlight casting him enough light to see that they were trembling. "Shit, Ash! Just leave me alone!"

His hackles rose. "You're in my fucking room, and you want *me* to leave *you* alone?"

"*Leave me alone!*" she screamed, her voice echoing. "Please, okay? I just want you to leave me alone."

In the thick, tense silence, Ash felt calm settling over him, pulling him forward to rest his elbows on his thighs. He laced his fingers and stared at the floor, contemplating what to do. He didn't like being angry with her.

There was clearly something wrong.

"I'm just so sick of this," Tayshia said.

"Sick of what?" he replied, sitting up straight. "Sick of me?"

"I'm sick of the pressure. It feels like everyone wants me to be a certain way or act a certain way. And then when I do, I'm annoying and nobody likes me. No one likes me, my parents are mad at me, and my—" Tayshia let out an incredulous, mirthless laugh. "It's unreal. My life is unreal. I just hate my..."

She trailed off.

"Your life?" He turned to look at her but her back was to him. He didn't know what she was talking about. It seemed like something had happened.

"Myself."

Her voice was a whisper, cracking like it was choked off in her throat. His heart skipped a beat. He recognized that tone.

Tayshia was going to cry.

Ash stood up and walked around the bed. He knelt down beside her, positioning himself into a crouch. He placed his right hand on the mattress beside her and his other hand on his thigh, giving her enough distance so she wouldn't feel like he was crowding her.

She looked forlorn. Lips curling down into a pout, eyes downcast, shoulders slumped with dejection. In that giant shirt, she seemed frail.

"Why?"

"I don't know how to explain it."

"Try."

"I don't want to, Ash," she whined, her voice trembling. "Please? I just want to sleep. I'm... I'm *tired*, and I can't even sleep for twenty minutes without... Ever since having to relive it, I just can't stop *dreaming* about it. It was in the past. I had put it somewhere else inside me. Somewhere else where I could forget it happened and I— I—I just—"

She was hyperventilating now, taking in more breaths than she was letting out. He could see her legs shaking, one of them bouncing in agitation.

Ash felt his heart and stomach twisting together into one mass. In the next two seconds, he was sitting beside her on the bed. He placed his hand on her back.

"Hey. It's okay. We can sleep."

One more inhalation and then he saw her close her eyes. Tayshia took a deep breath and let it out. A tear escaped her lashes. Her chin and mouth quivered.

"I had a routine," she said in a high-pitched voice, tears

continuing to roll unchecked down her cheeks. "I had a routine where any time I felt those feelings come back up—those reminders—I could get rid of them quickly. But now, I can't. No matter how hard I try, I can't forget it again. I want to go back to that day and do it all over. I wish I would have kept my mouth shut. I just wish I wouldn't have stood up for myself with Kieran. Maybe he wouldn't have taken my phone."

Ash's brow furrowed and his heart raced, hovering between hatred for the man and anguish for her.

"It's not your—"

"I just want to sleep," she said, cutting him off. "I just want to *sleep*."

She broke apart like a fallen porcelain doll, her pieces lying shattered on the floor. Sobs ripped through her, gut-wrenching in the way they made her entire body shake with violence. It was the same sort of weeping that he'd heard in her memory, when she was on the floor at the foot of the bed in Paris, desperate for reprieve.

Ash didn't think about it. He didn't think about their past, or whether or not he was going to scare her or make things awkward. He thought about nothing.

Nothing except her.

He wrapped his arms around her, one hand curving around the silk of her bonnet at the back of her head. The other arm curled fully from shoulder to shoulder, pressing her against his side until she turned her face into his chest and wailed into his shirt.

"Come here," he murmured. "Come here, to me."

She curled her legs up and across his lap. Her hands wrapped themselves in the fabric of his shirt, pulling until he thought she might tear it if he tried to put any space between them. She clung to him as though they were in that blue hotel room and she just needed someone to hold her.

"Try to breathe," he said when her weeping began to sound somewhat strangled.

"I c-can't," she gasped between sobs, her tears slick on his skin. "I c-can't b-b-breathe. I d-d-don't w-want to."

Ash tightened his hold on her, remembering Halloween night and how she'd asked him to hold her tighter. She felt so small in his arms and he didn't know if it was because she was so broken and he was the only thing holding her pieces together, or if it was because she really was that fragile.

Tayshia Cole wasn't supposed to be fragile, but he supposed that type of thinking was what had caused her so much stress.

Slowly, her breathing began to return to normal as she inhaled and exhaled through her continued weeping.

"You're doing it, see?" he crooned, his fingers stroking down the nape of her neck to try and calm her. *Anything* to make her feel better. He didn't want her to faint. "You're breathing. It's okay."

He held her while she cried for the next few minutes, ignorant of how tired he'd been when she'd first came to his bedroom. Eventually, her sobs quieted to catatonia and the occasional sniffle. Even then, he continued to hold her.

"Do you wanna maybe lay down?" he asked, keeping his voice low. He dipped his head down a bit so he could look at her face, which was cast in shadows due to Ash blocking the moonlight from the window. "We can get some sleep."

She nodded, her eyes closed.

Ash thought for a moment about the best way to move them both, settling upon hooking one arm beneath her knees. He lifted her, surprised when there was hardly any resistance, and turned to set her down. Once she was lying down, he cast one more glance at her face. Her eyes were open now, half-lidded and puffy. Tears kept falling, rolling slow and sporadic from her eyes to her jaw. She looked swollen and somehow more beautiful to him than he'd ever thought anyone could be.

That disturbed him.

He went back to his side of the bed and climbed in, pulling the coverlet up over the both of them. Lying down, he had just started to roll to face the room when she surprised him by moving until she was pressed to his side.

"Did you want me to—"

"Yes," she whispered, and then her fingers twisted in his shirt by his abdomen.

Swallowing against his sudden urge to blush, he faced her and slung his arm over her. He curved it around her back.

"More."

After some hesitation, he slid his other arm between her body and the mattress and gathered her up against him. It felt nice, having her so close, and he imagined it felt nice for her to be embraced.

"Your head's not even on the pillow," he said.

"I don't care."

He felt her burrowing closer, her nose brushing his neck.

"Fine," he said. "Now, we sleep."

She didn't reply, so he let his eyelids flutter shut. Ash didn't think he'd ever felt more at peace, which was strange given that it was Tayshia he was full-on cuddling in his bed. And for a moment, his life flashed before his mind's eyes. A life where he went to sleep in his bed with Tayshia in his arms every night, safe from anything and anyone who could hurt her.

Neither of them would be alone.

CHAPTER
TEN

"We're in the clearing again."

Ash turned to see Tayshia sitting next to him on the hill. She had a gardenia in her hand, plucked fresh from the flowers by her feet. She wore a black dress made of chiffon with thin straps and a tight waist.

His eyes lingered on her chest, but not her breasts. Her chest bone. The ridges were so prominent.

What the Hell?

"How did you change your clothes?" he said. "Last time, you had the same pajamas on."

"It's a dream," she said, her lips curling up into a smile that didn't quite match the sobbing, weeping mess that had fallen asleep in his arms. "I figured we could do anything we wanted — so I imagined myself the way I wanted to look, and then it worked."

He tore his gaze away from her chest and let it rove the rest of her torso. Her collarbones were just as sharp, straining against thin skin as though they wanted to escape. Her neck was long and narrow and her arms looked skeletal.

She wanted *to look like this?*

Ash looked off to the left, towards the sea beneath a lavender sky studded with silver stars. Something hurt in his chest, deep in the depths where his heart resided. Realization began to creep in, slow and steady.

He didn't want to fit the pieces together. He didn't want to believe that what had killed his mother might be affecting Tayshia.

No.

It was just a dream.

Just because she dreamed of looking this way, didn't mean it was reality. He could imagine himself looking however he wanted, too. It was just her imagination.

He hoped.

"So, what do you want to do?" she said, sounding excited as she got to her feet.

Ash followed suit, seeing that he was in the joggers he always fell asleep in. He pursed his lips and closed his eyes, deciding to try what Tayshia had done and change his clothing. When he opened them again, he was wearing a pair of black jeans and a black crewneck.

"See? I told you," she said. "It's that easy. Now we match!"

He lifted one eyebrow. "Matching outfits? You're one of those girls."

"Me? Well..." She tilted her head to the side, tapping her chin with the gardenia in her other hand. "I guess I could be. I haven't ever really gotten the chance to explore that kind-of stuff."

"What kind? The fluff of teenage relationships?"

"And romance." She sniffed the flower, and a distant look crossed her face. "I've only had one boyfriend and Kieran just wasn't romantic. I don't know what it's like to have affection or gifts or dates that I don't have to ask my dad for money for, or to be told I'm beautiful."

"Kieran's rich. Why would you have to ask your dad for money?"

"He was stingy. He said if we were gonna be married, then we needed to get used to not going out all the time. Never mind the fact that we barely did in the first place. We dated for years, but every date we went on was on my dad's dime. I thought it was weird that he never asked his parents. Shoot, I wouldn't be surprised if he was taking Quinn out and paying for her."

Ash sneered. Even in dreams, he hated Kieran.

"I'm not surprised that he was terrible at that. Women deserve nice things — remember that."

"I haven't forgotten."

He glanced off into the distance and then back at her again.

"Good."

"And if it were up to me," she went on, "I think matching outfits would be cute. If I had a boyfriend and he took me out to a — like, a dinner date in Portland, it'd be so nice. And if he brought me flowers. I — well, I think that would be pretty cool."

Ash could see himself doing all of that for her. Happily, without ever feeling embarrassed by outfits that matched. And he could imagine her smile, too, the way it would sparkle in her eyes because she was finally being treated right.

He was fucked.

"Well, we're matching right now," he said. "And we can do whatever we want."

She lowered the flower and looked up at him with wide eyes. "What?"

Ash leaned down and gathered up ten or so gardenias. He arranged them into a makeshift bouquet and handed them to her with a bit of a smirk. The expression on her face was one of shock.

"Flowers," he said. "And I don't know if dinner in a dream is the best idea, so if you could do anything you want right now, what would it be?"

"What would you do?"

He answered without missing a beat because it was the same thing he'd always dreamed about since he was a kid.

"Flying on the back of a dragon."

"It's a no for me." She shook her head. "Absolutely not. Heights terrify me. I had a horrible experience when I was a kid involving my dad's failed attempt at a treehouse."

Ash opened his mouth to ask her for details but thought better of it. He didn't want to bring her mood back down. If this dream became another nightmare for her, then he'd never forgive himself.

He already had the sounds of her sobs burned into his memory.

"I would decorate a Christmas tree," she said.

"Why am I not surprised? All this talk about gifts..."

"I love Christmas," she said, pouting.

"I am not a fan of it." He held his hands up. "But fine — if that's what you want to do, then that's what we're gonna do."

Tayshia smiled and it lit up her entire face. With her standing there, curls loose about her upper body, clad in that dress with a bouquet of gardenias in her hands?

He would have said yes to anything.

"Okay, close your eyes."

She did so. The fact that she trusted him enough to close her eyes within seconds — it did something unexplainable to him.

His fists curled at his sides as he closed his eyes, too. "Think about the living room."

"All right," she said.

"Good. Now, open."

They both opened their eyes and just like that, they were in the living room of their apartment. It was fully decorated for Christmas with all manner of red-and-green décor, sparkling gold and glittering silvers, more lights than Ash had ever seen before. It was like a combination of the tidy little Christmases his family had, and whatever extravagant holidays the Cole family experienced. The lights were on, flickering and twinkling. Outside the sliding glass door and balcony beyond, the pitch darkness of the sky was broken by thousands of stars. The tree in the corner by the entertainment center stood devoid of decorations, waiting. At the foot of it was a box full of ornaments that Ash's dreamscape had provided.

Tayshia darted over with a gasp of delight, falling to her knees beside the box. She began sifting through the ornaments, separating the orbs from the more unique ones on the carpet.

Ash slipped his hands into his pockets and sauntered over, perching on the arm of the couch closest to the glass door.

"Someone's eager."

"I told you — I love Christmas," she said, her smile big and bright. "I was always the one who decorated the tree, and my parents would sit on the couch and watch me. My dad would help with the higher branches, of course, so that's what you can do. I'll do the bottom half."

"Oh, I'm decorating it with you?" He took his hands out of his pockets and pushed his sleeves up to his elbows, revealing his tattoos.

"Well, of course," she said, giving him a look. "Did you think I wanted you to watch me? Come on!"

Ash stared at her, feeling his heart racing faster. That smile was a dream in and of itself. It felt like he hadn't seen it in days. Weeks. Months.

It felt like he hadn't seen it since before he went to jail.

They spent the next few minutes in silence, hanging the ornaments on the branches in alternating patterns. Ash found that he liked the feeling of placing them, standing back and looking at his handiwork, then rearranging it all to make the colors look more balanced. He'd never gotten to do this at home, as his father was so controlling that he insisted he do it himself.

Ash wondered what it would have been like to grow up in a family like Tayshia's.

"I like it," she said. "It's coming along, don't you think?"

"Yeah," he said with a half of a smile. He placed a gingerbread man ornament on the tree, feeling amused. None of this was real, yet it felt like it was. It was weird. "You know we're going to have to do this in real life, too. Christmas is in two months."

"I know," she said as she hung a candy cane ornament on a lower branch and admired it. "I mean, I'll probably go home for Christmas, but I wanna put a tree up in the apartment so I can look at it."

Ash placed a couple of silver orbs in different spots so they wouldn't look too close together. He supposed this wasn't so bad. It wouldn't be too difficult to do it in the apartment in the waking world.

"I could help you, you know," he said. "You don't have to like — like, do it on your own, or anything."

She looked up at him from her place on her knees on the floor. She hung a red glittering orb without looking, the twinkling of the lights on the tree flickering across her face.

"Really?"

He shrugged.

"All right," she said. "Have you ever decorated a tree of your own before?"

"Nah," he said, hanging another orb. "We celebrated Christmas, but for

us, it was my dad's thing. He did everything — decorations, lights, gift wrapping. He just wanted to be in control. I don't think I've ever had a Christmas list."

"Never had a Christmas list?!" Tayshia grabbed an ornament and stood up to hand it to him. She watched him start decorating the highest branches. "I'm so sorry."

"Yeah, well." Another shrug. "My dad liked to believe he knew what we wanted. He did all right, except for the year he got me extra drugs to sell. It's ridiculous."

"Um, ew."

"Yeah."

Ash hung some more ornaments.

"You and Ji Hyun dated, right?" she said. "In Freshman Year?"

"Oh, yeah," he said. "But we were better as friends. Why do you ask?"

"I'm just wondering if she ever got you anything off of one of your Christmas lists. I mean, found family is still family, right? That way when your actual family fucks up..."

"Yeah, Ji Hyun is not a gift-giver." Ash snorted. "She's the girl expecting you to bring her a gift to your birthday party."

"You're so mean," Tayshia said with a laugh. "When we wake up, I'm telling her what you said."

"Go ahead. She won't disagree with you. But she's not a bad person." He sighed and ran his hand through his hair, resting his palm against the back of his head for a second. "That role belongs to me for my friend group, unfortunately."

"You don't think you've changed?" Tayshia knelt down by the box and resumed hanging ornaments on her level of the tree. "Since that day?"

Ash was silent for a long moment as he sifted through his thoughts and feelings. Yes, he'd walked into that shop when he could have gone for help. But the fact that he'd harbored the guilt since the sun set on that day granted him some reprieve from thinking he was the worst person in the world. He thought his father held that crown.

However, Ash was by no means perfect. He'd made choices that had gotten people hurt.

Which crown did he wear?

"There's no excuse for what I did," Ash said, crouching down to sift through the ornament box. There was a pretty gold star with intricate designs etched into the surface. He picked it up, feeling the cool metal against his fingers. "I've done some shitty things and pretending I haven't would make me just as bad as my dad."

Tayshia looked down at him, her hands frozen in the process of fluffing a branch. She tilted her head to the side, scrutinizing him.

"Don't compare yourself to anyone," she said, "because I think that's something I've learned this year. I've had to like, really stop and think about what's actually wrong with me, and what I'm perceiving to be wrong with me. To ask myself, am I the same person that I see in the mirror? It's been difficult, but I've gotten a lot of clarity about myself and other people."

Picking up the star, Ash stood up and placed it on top of the tree.

"And what are the details of this clarity you've received?" he asked, stepping back to admire the full effect of the ornaments, lights, and the star.

Tayshia came to stand beside him. "I've come to see that just because you call someone a friend, doesn't mean you really know them. Sometimes, the people you think you love can hurt you." She looked up at him and smiled. "And the people you think you don't know can actually turn out to be really awesome if you just get to know them."

His gaze traversed the planes of her face.

"Yeah?"

"Uh-huh."

They stood and viewed the tree for a while. The darkness around them, broken by warm twinkling lights and the faint scent of pine — made Ash feel like he was at home. He wanted to sit down on the couch and watch the tree sparkle until they woke up.

"Sometimes, I wish I could go back and do things differently," Tayshia said, her voice as soft as snowfall.

"So do I," Ash said, looking down at her again. "Maybe I'd see if I could get my parents to decorate at least one tree together like this."

"I'd go all the way back," she whispered. "Back to the day I first met Kieran. I'd unmeet him. I'd refuse to go to the same church as him entirely, and then I'd see what it was like to live in my world without ever becoming a part of his. I wouldn't have to do anything except be me."

"What?" he said, laughing slightly as he touched her elbow and turned her to face him. "You don't have to be anything other than yourself. Who is telling you that you have to be somebody else?"

She said nothing, not looking at him. Frustrated, Ash gripped her chin in a gentle hand and tilted her face upward.

"Who is telling you to be something you're not?"

"Everyone," she mumbled. "The world chose a role for me when I was born and I've been struggling to fit into that mold ever since. I'm not small enough to..." Her brow furrowed, lines appearing there as her hands came up to wrap around his wrists. "That's a hypothetical — I mean, I'm saying there's a mold that the world wants me to fit into, that I simply don't fit.

And it's gotten to the point where I'd rather unmeet everyone than keep trying to figure out how to make them all happy. I'm just so tired."

Ash realized that what she was saying was probably one of her darkest secrets. If any of her family or friends heard her say that she'd go back to a time where they weren't in her life so she could unmeet them, he didn't think they'd be too happy about it.

And he understood that sometimes, the pressures of life made you want things that were unheard of. When he was selling for Gabriel and Ricky, the stress had gotten so bad sometimes that he'd contemplated suicide if only to gain some reprieve. He'd been tired, too.

But what Tayshia had endured in Paris was much worse than anything Ash had been through.

"I'm sorry," he said, and he meant it. Because they were inside a dream and there was no one watching. No one to hold him accountable except the person the apology was owed to. "There's a lot of things I've done wrong. A lot of wrong choices. But if there's one person who doesn't expect anything out of you, it's me. You don't have to do or say or be anything other than yourself. Not that I'm on your list of people to impress, but... When you can't handle it anymore and you just need a break? You can come to me."

Tayshia pulled her face out of his grasp. He saw her gaze washing over the roses on his neck, nestled amongst the chains of his past. Slowly, she lifted a hand. Her finger traced the outline of one rose. He gritted his teeth to hold back the urge to shiver.

"Sometimes, I forget that I'm not the only one who's hurting," she said in a soft voice. "Do you miss her?"

"Miss who?"

"Your mother."

His heart wrenched and his fingers twitched at his sides.

Of course he did. More than anything. He missed her so badly that it hurt. He had no one to talk to about it.

"Obviously," he muttered. "I'd be a cold man if I didn't, don't you think?"

"I don't know," she said, her fingers trailing down his arm and along his wrist. She turned it so his palm was facing hers. Her fingers twined with his, her skin feeling much warmer in this dream than it did in real life. "I just want you to know that I'm here, too, if you ever need someone to hold you."

Another skip of his heartbeat.

"Yeah?"

She nodded, scrutinizing the way their hands fit together, the contrast *of his ink-decorated fingers stark against the back of her palm.*

"There's no reason why you should have to carry your burdens and mine."

"Hm," he said, humming in response. He couldn't stop looking at her face and the way the lights played off of it. When had she gotten so fucking beautiful?

And why couldn't Kieran see it?

Tayshia smiled, and it was everything. "I'm really glad we became friends, Ash. I just wish things could be this easy when we're awake."

"They can be," he said. "Come here."

Ash tugged on her hand. It caught her by surprise, forcing her to stumble forward and fall against his chest. Before he could think too hard on it, he wrapped his arms around her.

"We can hold each other whenever we want?" She lifted her hands, hesitating with them hovering over the back of his ribcage. "Whenever I want?"

"Yeah. Of course."

"Just like this?"

She slid her arms around his waist and locked them in place.

"Mh-hm," Ash turned his head to look at the tree. "Just like this."

"You have changed, Ash." Her fingers clutched at his back. "And it's a really, really good thing."

They watched the tree. Watched the lights twinkle on and off and the ornaments sparkle. Watched the peace exist in front of them as though nothing bad had ever or could ever happen to them again.

Ash felt content.

CHAPTER ELEVEN

Ash woke to the sound of rain, expecting Tayshia to be gone.

To his surprise, she was still lying in his bed. They were in the same position they'd fallen asleep in. His arms were wrapped around her, the fingers of one hand tangled in her curls. Her bonnet was on the pillow behind her head. Her face was pressed into the junction of his neck and shoulder and one of her legs was tucked in-between his as her hands gripped his shirt.

Lying there in a sleepy haze for a moment, Ash tried to separate reality from the dreamscape they'd created.

He remembered decorating the tree together and talking, remembered getting to know her on a level that he hadn't expected nor planned on. In the dream, it had felt so vivid and real. The lights twinkling on the tree, the feeling of his arm around her shoulders.

It felt like a distant memory.

The reality was the weight of Tayshia on his arm and the heat of her body pressed against his. She was something real that he could touch and feel, whether he was asleep or awake.

He liked reality better.

Tayshia woke a short time later with a start, her body going rigid.

"You snore, you know," he said.

There was a moment before she relaxed into him again, not moving her position. "Thanks for telling me. And what?"

"And what... What?"

"What about it?"

"Feisty when you get up, too, I see," he said, his voice hoarse. He shifted, relaxing further into her.

"Did we wake up late? What time is it?"

"I haven't the slightest clue."

He groaned in protest as she extricated herself from his arms and sat up so she could see the clock behind him. Her hair was a disaster—a beautiful one.

Tayshia gazed down into his half-shut eyes.

"We're halfway into the day."

"Like, it's noon?"

"No, I mean the *day*. Like, the *school day*. It's past lunch. How did we sleep so late?!"

"Shame," he said, smirking. "Let's just stay home."

"I don't skip school, Ash," she replied, glowering at him. "I'm *me*."

"Well, now you do."

She scowled and threw the covers aside, splintering his warmth with cold air. With more grumbling, he took the covers and pulled them up to his neck. He watched as she walked around the bed.

"You're a bad influence on me," she said, sounding annoyed. "But we're not going to sit around and do nothing. Let's go to the bookstore."

"The bookstore?" Begrudgingly, he sat up, his hair in his eyes. "What for?"

"You may be happy accepting something unexplainable for four-and-whatever months, but I am not. I need to know what's going on between us and why we're able to walk in each other's dreams. The fact that we can interact like we did the last couple of times is just..." She placed her hand to her temple and drew it away. "It blows my mind. Hurry up and get dressed. I don't have time for this. Let's go, let's go, little boy."

Ash stifled a laugh as she grabbed a pair of his skinny jeans from the floor and tossed them at him. He caught them right as she pulled multiple dresser drawers open. In the next few seconds, a fresh pair of boxers and a black pullover were on the bed with him as well. Shocked that she was just going through his drawers like that, he was slow to react when he saw her inspecting the wooden chest on top of it with curiosity.

The one he'd been throwing his father's letters into every week since he got out of jail.

"What's inside here?" she asked.

Her fingers unlatched the bronze clasp.

Ash's heart leapt into his chest. He tossed aside the covers and rushed across the room to get to her. Standing behind her, he curved one hand around the front edge of the dresser and the other hand around her wrist to stop her, boxing her in. She looked up at him, her hair brushing against his chest.

"What are you hiding? More drugs?"

"No," he said. "Do you need to know every little thing about me?"

"It's just a chest, Ash," she quipped. "And I've asked you hardly anything about yourself, so don't act like I'm some nosy bitch trying to insert herself into your life. You know things about me that no one else does."

"And that's your choice to let me know those things," he said, tightening his hand when she tried to move.

"Not all of it was," she said, holding his gaze with a spark of vehemence in her eyes. "You know that."

Guilt colored him pale as he realized what he'd just said. His words were only half-true. Some things he knew about her because she'd told him. He only knew about Paris by accident.

Still.

His father was off-limits.

"Please," he whispered, averting his eyes. "Leave this one alone."

"All right," she said in an icy tone. This time when she pulled on her hand, he let her. "But next time you wanna know my business, you can stay wanting to know."

He moved aside as she walked away from the dresser. Without looking at him again, she left the room.

Ash hurried to dress, glancing over at the chest. There was no desire inside of Ash to read any of them, but something about knowing the letters were coming had given him a strange sense of comfort.

He knew he was being overdramatic about them. They were probably mundane play-by-plays of Gabriel's daily life in prison—not his undying apologies for being a horrid father.

When his shoes were on and his cologne had been sprayed, Ash headed out to the living room. Tayshia was there, sitting on the arm of the couch. She'd gotten dressed, too—into another pair of leggings and the knit hoodie he'd bought her for her birthday. Her curls were pulled up into two buns again, spiraling pieces hanging down haphazardly around her face. She was staring at the blank television screen in a listless manner, shoulders slumped with what looked like exhaustion or dejection.

"Still tired?"

"Huh?" She jumped to her feet, whirling to look at him at the entrance to the hallway. He was shrugging into his jacket. "Y-Yeah, a little bit."

"So, what are we going to the bookstore for?"

"To try and find whatever we couldn't find at Moonbeams & Things," she said. "Books on crystals, dreams, caverns. I dunno. Anything."

"You know," he said, slipping his hands into the back pockets of his jeans, "it's entirely possible that there's no answers. You prepared for that?"

"Yes, obviously." She tucked a loose curl behind her ear. "I'm aware that things like magic aren't technically real. At least, not to society."

"You don't consider dreamwalking magic?"

"I do, to an extent," she said. "It's the same thing as astral projection. Is it real? Yeah, I think it is. Is it magic? Not necessarily, because magic *isn't* real."

"You say that like you've astral projected before." Ash had no idea what astral projection even was.

"I haven't. But I think there are some things that just seem real to me. Anything that seems like it could just come from another dimension makes sense to me. Like aliens."

"You been watching too much *Ancient Aliens* then."

"Ash. It's not like this is speculation. You've been in my dreams. I've been in yours. I just don't think it's magic."

"Then what do you think it is?"

She frowned, looking down at the floor in thought.

"I think it's astronomical. And no, I don't have any reason why I think that. I just do."

Ash shrugged. He supposed they'd find out. Or they wouldn't. Either way, a theory was better than nothing but questions.

"Well, let's get going," Tayshia said, heading toward the door.

"Did you wanna go grab some lunch since we missed breakfast?" he asked, keys jangling in his hand.

"Me? Oh. No, I ate while you were changing."

"Really?" he asked, eyebrows shooting up in surprise. "That quickly? Shit, I was only in my room for five minutes. You changed *and* ate an entire meal?"

"No, I—well, I mean, I had an apple."

"I didn't buy any apples last time I went to the store. I bought—

"

"Sorry, God. My bad. It was an orange." She patted her forehead and laughed. "Completely said the wrong fruit."

He saw her begin fidgeting with her fingernails, and he was reminded of the way she'd looked in his dream. The way her skin seemed to stretch thinly over her bones. How she'd imagined herself to look like a shadow, a ghost of who she was. His gaze swept her body.

Tayshia was lying. He knew it in his bones that she was.

And it was because she was lying and because of his mother's past that he knew there was a right way to go about this and a wrong way. It wasn't his business until it was. And while he didn't know the details of Tayshia's issue — if that were in case, the problem — he knew that she had a temper.

He had to finesse her to get to the bottom of it.

"After the bookstore," he said, moving forward again, "let's go to Gianni's. My treat."

"For what reason?" she asked as they headed down to the parking lot. The rain's weight was intermittent. "Early Christmas?"

"Sure, yeah."

"Okay," she said. "But—"

She stopped, pulling her phone out of the pocket of her hoodie. A troubled expression crossed her face when she looked down at it. Ash opened the driver's side door, hesitating before he sat down in the car. When she slid into the passenger's side, it was clear she was upset about something.

"You good?" he asked. "Did someone from the school call because you skipped?"

"Shut up. I'm not *that* much of a goody two-shoes. Damn." She side-eyed him. "Anyway, it's nothing. Just stupid bullshit with the Kieran situation."

"What did he do *this* time?" Ash turned the car on and put it in drive. Then, his hand went to the back of Tayshia's seat so he could turn to look out the back windshield. "Or was it Quinn who texted *about* him?"

"Quinn and I don't talk anymore," Tayshia said, putting on her seatbelt. She sighed. "It was Kieran."

Ash's stomach flipped over and he gave Tayshia a sharp look. "Why?"

"Nothing, just..." Another sigh, followed by a shake of her head.

"It's not a big deal anymore. It would have bothered me a while ago, but now I just don't care."

"What did he say?"

Tayshia was quiet.

Ash glanced down, seeing her holding her phone on her thigh. Her leg was bouncing, a blatant indicator for her anxiety. Whatever Kieran had said, it was *not* nothing. A sudden flare of anger rose up within him, red-hot and unbearable.

"I'm gonna snatch that fucking phone up if you don't tell me what he said," Ash snarled, his hands gripping the wheel tightly. "What the *fuck* did he say to you?"

"Why do you have to be so nasty when you're trying to get your way, Ash?!" Tayshia cried. "He called me a whore last night, all right? I have no idea why. Just texted me out of nowhere to call me a whore, and then he texted me just now to tell me he always knew I'd turn out to be a waste of time. It's not like it's anything I haven't heard from him before."

Ash's anger immediately flew out into the nether, replaced by his guilt.

It was his fault. Because Ash had kissed her in the checkout lane. He'd kissed her for his own selfish reasons, *knowing* Kieran and Quinn were there.

Why hadn't he assumed that Tayshia would get a text?

"Block him," Ash said through gritted teeth. "Literally just block that thundercunt."

Tayshia picked up her phone. She seemed hesitant.

"Block him," Ash said, raising his voice in an indignant manner. "Before I get pissed off."

"*Okay*! God, you are *so rude*."

The silence was tense as her thumb flew across the screen.

"There. Blocked *and* deleted. Happy?"

"I'm ecstatic." And he was. He was smirking, too.

More silence punctuated by Tayshia's scowling. Ash looked over at her and their eyes met.

"I'm gonna beat the living shit out of him if he talks to you again," he said. "I hope you realize that."

"Bold of you to assume I'd tell you if he did," she shot back.

"Okay. Anyway, I'm going to beat the living *shit* out of him if he talks to you again."

She scowled again, throwing her gaze up to the ceiling of the car and her empty hand into the air.

"Well, hot damn. I guess I'll just step aside while Mr. Felonious Assault takes care of business for me."

"I *will*. I *will* take care of it. I'm already taking care of you, Miss Broke-Ass."

"Don't you use that against me. Just because you're flush with cash—" She rubbed the fingers of her left hand together as she gave him a sour look. "—doesn't mean you're all that and bag of chips."

"I *am* all that and a bag of chips. The good kind."

"Oh, fuck off. Are you gonna shank him, too?"

"Depends. Would you like me to shank him? It can be arranged."

"The fact that you'd do it if I said yes is the problem, headass."

"And yet I don't hear you saying no." Ash's eyebrows shot up as he pulled up to the red light. "You want me to shank him old school? Like, with a sharpened toothbrush?"

"Knock it off."

"I can really, *really* fuck him up, though."

"Shut up, Ash."

"I can make him cry. You want me to make him cry for you, baby?"

"*Shut up, Ash!*" She whirled around to glare at him. "And wipe that *smirk* off your face. I'm not your *baby*."

"Yes, you are," he joked, reaching over to grab her chin and shake her head a bit. "And you're so cute when you're annoyed, too."

She smacked his hand away. He reached for her again, still smirking as she slapped at his hand a second time in annoyance.

They looked at each other.

And burst out laughing.

Ash covered his mouth with the back of his palm as he turned the wheel with one hand, trying not to laugh so hard that he drove off of the road. Tayshia giggled like a madwoman, tears of amusement filling her eyes as she struggled to contain her mirth.

They pulled into the parking lot of the shopping center.

"All right, you can shank him," she said, the *click* of her seatbelt loud in the space of the small car. "But you ain't gettin' no rewards, so don't ask."

Ash parked the car, nonchalant as he unbuckled his seatbelt, turned, and grabbed her chin again. He dragged her across the center console until her lips crashed against his. He wasn't thinking clearly and didn't really care to. It wasn't like a kiss made them boyfriend and girlfriend, or anything.

He just liked feeling like she was his from time-to-time.

At first, Tayshia started to pull back, her lips parting so she could inhale and prepare to berate him. But when his other hand slid up the side of her neck to hook beneath her ear, the soft grazing of his touch turned the inhalation to a sigh. His tongue was anything but tentative as he kissed down into her mouth with every intention of reaping rewards he certainly wasn't owed. His other hand held her in place so he could devour her like they weren't sitting in his car in the middle of the half-empty parking lot.

She tasted good.

"You—" she managed to breathe before he cut her off.

"Mm-hm."

"But—"

"Shh."

Ash slanted his head, becoming carried away by the thrill of kissing her like this when it felt so forbidden. He was the reason why they'd even been arguing. His own selfishness when kissing her in front of her ex had caused said ex to send her those nasty texts. Kissing her like this, debating pulling her into his lap so he could feel her against him, truly did feel like a reward.

He had no intentions of murdering Kieran O'Connell.

They could play pretend, though.

Ash pulled back, watching her eyelids drag open until she was looking up into his eyes. She looked somewhat delirious—like she was two seconds away from passing out. Her tongue darted out to wet her lips, her chest heaving as she panted for breath. The look in her eyes was as close to hungry as he'd ever seen her get.

"I didn't ask for a reward," he said, grinning down at her. "But I don't do anything for free."

It took a second but then she was smacking his hand away again. She was laughing through it and for some reason, it made Ash's heart feel lighter.

Tayshia had such a pretty smile.

"I hate you," she said.

"No, you don't."

She studied him as though she were trying to figure out what was off about him. Then, she surged forward to place another kiss on his lips. When they broke apart, she gave him a scathing look and got out of the car.

Ash took a second to catch his breath.

✧✧✧

The bookstore was mostly empty, save for one greying woman at one of the front registers.

"Let's start with the Occult section," Tayshia said, peering around at all the shelves and sections. "Look for anything you see that might have to do with dreams or the astral plane. That's the best place to start, and maybe we'll have a good direction after some reading."

"Where'd you get the *astral plane* from?" he asked in a low tone as they walked through the neat, organized shelves. "Like, what made you think of that? What even is it?"

"Basically, astral projecting is where when you're asleep, your soul leaves your body and walks the Earth. It can go anywhere, see anything within seconds. I'm wondering if dreamwalking might be something similar."

"Ah. Except that doesn't explain why I was able to do it for months without you noticing, only to suddenly have you come into *my* dreams and have conversations with me."

"Exactly," she said, sneaking a glance up at him that she averted the moment his eyes met hers. "That's why I said it was different from astral projection. Duh."

"Well." His lips curved up. "*Excuse me*, Miss Robards. I'd forgotten that you were the teacher."

"When it comes to research," she said, taking a right and entering the beginning of the Occult section, "I'm *always* the teacher."

"Confidence is key."

"*Intelligence* is key."

They began to sift through books, fingers grazing spines on opposite sides of the walkway. Ash looked for subjects that might apply, as well as the two she'd specifically told him to search for. He wasn't sure they were going to find what they were looking for, but he had hope that they could at least figure out a starting point to jump off of.

"Are you saying I'm unintelligent?" he shot back.

"Don't be stupid. You're the most intelligent guy I know." Her tone was a parental coo. "And I know I'm right. I'm intelligent."

"You're lying."

"The funny thing," she said, standing on tip-toe to try and grab a

122

book that was just out of her reach, "is that I'm not. You actually *are* the most intelligent guy I know."

"The funny thing—" he mocked, reaching up past her fingertips to pluck the book off of the shelf. He leaned down and handed it to her, his mouth near her ear. "—is that for someone who claims to be intelligent, you sure like to make yourself look too dumb to ask for help."

"Shut up," she snapped, looking at the cover of the book—*Understanding the Astral Plane*. "I'm not even short. And catch me asking a man for help? Absolutely not." She paused. "Okay, maybe you're different. I guess I wouldn't mind asking *you* for help. But you're not complete trash. I feel safe with you."

Something about her words caused him to stop dead in his tracks. He had his fingers pressed to the spine of one book, reading and rereading the title over and over until he realized he wasn't absorbing anything. Shock reverberated through him, straight to his core. He turned to look down at her, right as she approached his side to show him another book.

"You feel safe with me?"

Her cheeks tinged darker, a rose color amongst the bronze of her skin as she cleared her throat. "I—I guess so. Yes. Do I have reason not to feel that way?"

Ash was awestruck.

After weeks of her avoiding him, multiple arguments, and only two nights and dreams, she felt safe with him? She'd said it before, but he figured after the Paris dream and how violated she'd felt by having to relive it, she wouldn't feel safe around him anymore.

After everything he'd done—and everything he hadn't—she felt *safe*? With *him*?

"How?"

"I don't know." She looked up from the white pages of the book and did a double-take, seeing the serious expression in his eyes. "Ash—I don't *know*, okay? I just do."

"That's not an answer," he said, feeling a spike of panic inside of his chest.

What if he'd accidentally lulled her into a false sense of security?

What if she was just blind to what a horrible person he actually was?

What if she was deluding herself into forgetting every horrible choice he'd made?

"Why is this so important to you?" she asked, her face contorting with irritation. "Is there something you think I shouldn't trust?"

No.

Yes.

Everything.

Nothing.

"I feel safe with you for reasons unknown to me," she said when he didn't reply, "and I decided not to question it. There's so few people I feel that way around that when I realized I trusted you, I just accepted it. I don't have the energy to fight it anymore."

He followed her through the store. She stopped in the Astrology section and began to peruse.

Ash's words were a chaotic jumble inside his mind, each one clamoring to be amongst the ones he chose.

Tayshia pulled another book off of the shelf and in a casual tone, asked, "Does that bother you? Having someone like me feel safe with you?"

"Someone like you? What do you—"

"A *whore*."

"I don't give a flying fuck about what Kieran thinks of you," he said, trying to keep his voice down so the few people in the large store didn't hear their words echoing. "You're *not* a whore."

She stopped and with a sigh, turned to look up at him. "I know that. Or at least, I *thought* I did. But now I'm rethinking. Kieran cheated on me and my first thought was to hook up with someone. So, maybe he's right."

Stunned, Ash could only stare at her as she continued her tirade.

"But you seem so shocked that I would trust you. Are you not presenting yourself as someone trustworthy? Are you pretending to be someone you're not to get something out of me? I wasn't worried, but now I am. Maybe I *shouldn't* be—"

He cut her off, feeling more panicked the angrier she sounded. "I'm just... Confused. And I'm terrified. I'm not—people don't trust me. *Good* people don't trust me."

"What reason would you have to be scared?"

He placed his hands on the shelf in front of him and hung his head, struggling to force the words out. Then, he slowly met her gaze.

"What if I hurt you?"

The hardness in her face softened, melting like snowfall. She hugged the two books she'd grabbed close to her chest.

"I don't think you will," she murmured. "So don't say it like it'll happen."

Ash didn't know how to explain how terrified he was of hurting her after what happened in Paris. He had no words to explain to her how witnessing that experience had irrevocably changed him, and how the nights she'd slept in his bed were the first times he'd slept soundly since.

He lifted his hand, reaching towards her face.

Tayshia's eyes went wide and she gasped. He dropped his hand, anxiety pulsing through his veins. She reached onto the shelf that had been above his shoulder and pulled down a book.

"*Connected to the Stars — Star Signs and Their Compatibility*," she said, reading the title aloud. She turned the book over so she could read the back. "Did you find anything?"

"No," he said. "I was too busy arguing with you."

She gave him a chastising look and then turned to go towards a table. "Take another look, and then come to me over there when you're done."

Ash wandered through the books for a few minutes, grabbing anything that looked appropriate. His mind was whirling.

What the Hell was wrong with him? Why would he *say* something like that to her? It wasn't attractive, or funny, or soft, or kind to tell her he was terrified of hurting her. If he was so honored by her trust, why would he try to break it immediately after she told him he had it?

At the table, Tayshia was nose-deep in the book about star signs, so he didn't say anything to her. He pulled the chair out beside hers and began to read the book he'd found, another book about the astral plane. He tried his best to focus, his eyes glossing over the passages without absorbing much of anything.

What was he even doing? Why was he here, sitting and pretending to be friends with her? He was a horrible person. A bad person. He *knew* what had happened to her, yet he'd still kissed more times than he deserved. He'd still hooked up with her. He'd still kissed her in the dream.

Why couldn't he stop *pressuring* her?

He was no better than the man in Paris.

"Oh... My... God!"

He heard Tayshia's exclamation but he couldn't seem to focus. It felt like the stormy waters inside of him had begun to churn with a vengeance. Except now, the water seemed to have a direction, as though Poseidon had taken His hand and used it to shove the ocean in Ash's direction. As though He wanted the tidal wave to drown him and only him.

He felt like he couldn't breathe.

"Ash, are you all right?"

He looked at her, unable to speak for his overwhelming anxiety.

"Why do you look so freaked out?" Tayshia reached toward him, towards his face. "Are you—"

"Don't." His hand snapped up like a bolt of lightning, snatching her wrist out of the air. "You shouldn't touch me. We shouldn't be here, doing this. We shouldn't be near one another."

"What are you talking about?" A fearful glance was cast towards his grip on her. He wondered if she was second-guessing that trust now. "Why are you holding me so tightly?"

"Have you ever stopped to think about it?" he hissed, his heart slamming in his chest as the waters rose higher, nearly up to his throat. "Just stop and *think*. It's *me* we're talking about here. I'm *Ash fucking Robards.* I'm the guy who robbed a fucking ice cream shop with *children* inside of it. I'm the reason why your dad got shot. I'm not a *good* guy. I'm not the person you should trust. If I hadn't let my dad do whatever he wanted for years, then *none* of it would have happened. If I hadn't made the wrong choices, then—"

"Ash, please!" she interjected, the fear in her eyes intensifying with her ire. She tried to pull her hand back again. "Let go of my *fucking* hand!"

As though her skin had caught fire, he let go of her. She scrambled to her feet and away from the table, chest heaving as she looked upon him in bewilderment. Ash felt his stomach churning, the ocean still raging inside of him.

"I'm so fucking sorry," he breathed, staring at his trembling hands. "I was freaking out. I'm freaked out."

"I was trying to tell you," she said, shaking as she pointed at the book. "I found something in that book. What is *wrong* with you?"

"I don't know. I don't *fucking* know." He placed his elbows on the table and hung his head between his hands. He hated himself. This was just like with Ryo and the texts Ash had ignored. Gabriel and the letters. Elijah and their arguments.

Why was Ash trying to sabotage everything he had left?

"I think," Tayshia said, taking cautious steps back to the table, "and I could be wrong, but... I think we're connected."

"What, like our star signs are compatible?"

"No. I think we're *actually* connected. I think we got into those hot springs and it did something. Started something. I don't know. Then, when we pulled that amethyst out of the wall and broke it, I think it completed whatever it was."

"What do you mean?"

"If I were to call it anything, I'd call it a star connection."

CHAPTER TWELVE

Ash wondered if she'd gone crazy.

"A star connection? What do you *mean* star connection? What is a *star connection?*"

"Stop saying star connection! And don't yell at me," Tayshia snapped, and then she marched back over. "This part here says that *'star connections are something that no one can create or destroy — they are found in nature and written in the cosmos themselves.'*" She looked at him, eyes wide. "It means that a star connection is something that occurs at birth, or inherently. It's just myth, but this author is saying they believe that you *can* have a soulmate, and that it's tied to the stars."

"How does that even work?" He held two fingers to his right temple, massaging it against the sudden headache. "How does someone even get connected to a star?"

"It's metaphorical, I think. Not that I'm an expert on pseudoscience. Basically, I think it's a linking of your fate to a star to influence it. Like with horoscopes — to keep track of the good or bad things that happen to someone. This person doesn't say how because it's impossible to know, like religion or whether or not aliens exist. It's not a linking that's done by anyone. It's just something that is...?"

"I'm not following."

She let out an exasperated sound.

"Okay, listen. We're assigned a star sign according to where the sun was when we were born. For me, the sun was in Virgo, therefore *I* am a Virgo. And you're —"

"June 14th. Gemini."

"Right. So, with our horoscopes, we can determine our fate — like that upcoming day, or using an almanac to like, see where we're going in the future."

"But like you said — pseudoscience." He crossed his arms over his chest. "Not real."

"But," she went on, beginning to pace back and forth near the chairs, "our star signs are assigned at birth by chance. It's not like we pick our birthdays, you know? But if you look at the legend of the caverns, it says that if you stand in the water with your soulmate, then you'll be together forever. That implies you're already connected before you ever get into the water."

"Okay," Ash said slowly.

"If that's the case, then does that mean if you never go into the hot springs, you'll live your life with the chance of never crossing paths with your soulmate? Does that means there's other hot springs with the same benefits? And what about the people who don't get into the springs?"

"It's not that deep. It's not real, so I don't think it matters but maybe soulmates aren't like a *everyone has one* sorta thing. Maybe only certain people do and when those certain people get into that specific hot springs, something connects them? I dunno."

Tayshia said, "No, what I'm saying is that I think something *does* happen. I think when you pulled the crystal out of the wall—which was *after* we got out of the water—it did something. Because we broke it and kept them. The hole in the ceiling, where we could see Centaurus? I think it has something to do with that."

Ash looked up in thought.

"You're saying that... You think that people who get into the hot springs... And then pull an amethyst out of the wall and break it end up connected... Because the constellation Centaurus is above the cave. And that none of this would be possible unless you... And I..." He gestured between them with his finger and raised his eyebrows. "Are soulmates?"

"Yes."

"Because magic is real."

"No. I don't think it's magic. I think it's deeper than that."

"Deeper than magic?"

"Older."

He pulled a confused facial expression.

Tayshia sat back down in the chair to read aloud from the book, her leg bouncing as the words tumbled from her lips in a rush.

"'*The prime example of this type of connection can be found in Greek mythology. According to Plato, humans were born with four arms, four legs, and two faces. Dual beings. Because Zeus was fearful of how powerful they could become, he split them in half and condemned them to an eternal hunt. This separation ties two halves of the same whole together until they die.'* Until they *die*, Ash. And if we come from the stars — like, if all of life comes from the stars — then it makes sense that the stars would have the power to bring us back together if we got separated. The power of two stars, coming together to intertwine their destinies." She stared at him, looking almost terrified. "Soulmates."

"But where are you connecting that to the constellations?" Ash gave her a bewildered look. "That just sounds like typical Greek mythology. It's also not real."

"Let me finish!" she said, breathless as she continued to read. "*'An individual may not ever cross paths with the person who is their other half but will feel incomplete until such a time as they do. They will wander the Earth for all eternity, searching and never finding. This is what Zeus wished. But there are some gods who did not wish for humans to suffer unnecessarily. Their constellations watch over us to this day, guiding, encouraging, and connecting. For more, see the book...'* And then it lists a book about constellations and their origins, specifically Cassiopeia, Andromeda, and Perseus. It's not about the Greek mythology. It's about the constellations."

"None of those are Centaurus."

"I know." She met his eyes, chewing on her lower lip.

"Yeah, we need that fucking book."

"I know."

"How do we get it?"

"I'll ask the lady at the counter," she said, closing the book. "Maybe she can order it."

This was fucking insane.

They were just accepting this, weren't they?

Ash knew they had to. They'd lose their minds if they didn't. Because without this explanation — or at least, this possibility of an answer — they would never understand why they could walk each other's dreams.

He would never know why she felt like home.

"If this is true," he said in a soft voice, scrutinizing her, "then it would explain the way I feel about you."

"I know." She lowered her head as though she felt contrite, or he'd caught her breaking the law. "Me, too."

Ash's heart skipped a beat as he tried to remain calm. It was one thing to discuss the star connections in theory given that he'd thought he was the only one feeling anything. But if she was also feeling something for him, then that made it all the more real.

Which was terrifying.

"For—" He cleared his throat, leaning back in the chair and letting his hands rest between his legs. He was trying to appear nonchalant when in reality, he felt like panicking. "For how long?"

"I guess..." Her mouth twisted to the side. "I guess since the day I found out about Kieran. Specifically, when you gave me the birthday gifts. It's the first time I've ever gotten a gift from a guy and you did such a good job, it was like you knew me. And I thought it was weird because... Well, I kinda felt like I knew you, too. And then after that, I didn't hate you as much."

He couldn't help but let out a short laugh. "You could have fooled me."

"I just have a short temper these days," she muttered, playing with her crystal around her neck. She looked into his eyes again. "And I didn't know what it meant. I just accepted it."

"But the dreams. The first time for you was the time before last, wasn't it?"

"Yes," she said. "And you were able to see me and talk to me. Yet you were in my dreams for months and I didn't know."

"Do you think it had something to do with the memory?"

She froze. Within an instant, Ash felt regret chilling his blood. They hadn't talked about it yet. He didn't know if they were ever going to.

"My bad. For real," he said, sitting up straight. "I'm so sor—"

"So, I'm not sure what the crystals mean in regard to all of this," Tayshia said quickly, gathering the book to her chest, "but I think we'll know more once we get that book. Maybe not an answer, but we'll know something."

She went to speak to the lady at the cash register while Ash took it upon himself to put the books they'd picked up away. When he was alone in the shelves, he let out a deep, heavy breath.

Tayshia Cole and Ash Robards.

Soulmates.

☼☼☼

"Fuck."

Ash felt annoyed as he took off his jacket. He pushed the sleeves of his grey shirt up to his elbows, revealing his tattooed forearms.

They were at Gianni's, eating dinner before walking home. The waiter had gone to get their drinks.

"What?" Tayshia asked, tearing her gaze off of the menu. She looked at his arms, her eyes lingering for a few moments. "What's the matter?"

"It's Nurse Pritchard," he said, and then he glanced across the restaurant, where he could see the nurse with her husband. She was glaring at him. "Every time I see her, she looks at me like she thinks I'm going to whip out my strap in the damn establishment."

Tayshia snorted. Ash sent her a sharp look. She covered her mouth, her eyes twinkling.

"No, I'm sorry. It's just—That's funny. Your strap in the damn establishment."

"Oh, it's funny, is it?" he snarled. "Which part?"

"The part where you let everyone think you're this scary felon who just got out of jail," she said, stifling a giggle. "It's just funny. You're not anywhere near as scary as you look, and you don't have a gun."

"I *look* scary?"

"Ash, shut up." Her expression was deadpan. "You're covered almost from head to toe in tattoos. It's not normal, boo."

"And who are you to tell me what's *normal*? Little Miss Stuffs-Wrappers-in-Couch."

The color drained from her face right as Nurse Pritchard walked by on her way to the restroom. Yet *another* wary glance was cast in Ash's direction, this time focused on his exposed tattoos. It felt like her gaze burned with the fires of mistrust and disappointment.

Pritchard looked at Tayshia and then like lightning, a real, genuine smile spread across her face.

"And how's your weekend going, you two?" she asked, her voice like liquid gold as she wandered closer and placed a hand on Tayshia's back. "It's been raining quite a bit. I hope it didn't get ruined by having to stay indoors."

Tayshia looked as taken aback as Ash felt by her switch in attitude.

"It's going good," Tayshia told her. "We just did some wandering, so it wasn't too bad."

"Oh, good," she said, her tone merry. "Well, it's gearing up to be quite a rainy November, so don't be surprised if you see more grey days like this."

"We won't," Ash said.

Nurse Pritchard's eyes tightened as she forced a smile. She bustled off toward the bathroom hallway. Ash glanced around, seeing that the restaurant was fairly empty for a Saturday.

After the waiter dropped their sodas off and took their orders, they fell back into their conversation.

"See?" Tayshia eventually said, crossing her arms and giving him a smug grin. "I told you that you'd changed. Even Nurse Pritchard can see it."

"Yeah, well... Tch. Took her long enough."

"Well, you've gotta be realistic," Tayshia said. "You know who you are, and *I* know who you are now. But for the rest of your life, there's going to be people who only see you for who you used to be. You won't be able to change that."

"I know," he said. *That doesn't make me feel any better, though.*

"But I'm sure if you buy that foundation I keep seeing on the infomercials, you can cover your tattoos up every day and everyone will love you."

"You're not drinking your soda," he said, lifting his eyebrows.

"You ordered it without asking me, so you only have yourself to blame." She tossed her spiraling ringlet curls back over her shoulders. "Besides, do you know how many calories are in soda?"

Calories.

Tayshia was worried about calories.

Well, shit.

He had to think of something. He had to think of something to say that wouldn't make anything worse.

"Hey."

"Yes?" she said.

"You know you're beautiful as fuck, right?"

She stared at him as though he'd just sprouted horns. In the silence, his anxiety got the best of him. Had he gone too far? Was that not something he should have said?

"I mean, you don't have to worry about your weight," he said, swallowing against his nerves. His fingers tapped the side of his glass. "Calories, sugar, numbers—none of that shit."

The planes of her face tightened and she averted her eyes. "You say that as if the alternative can't exist at the same time. Like, in your opinion, if I *did* need to worry about my weight, then I wouldn't be beautiful."

"Well, I... I didn't mean—"

Fuck. What the fuck was wrong with him?

"It's not like it's either-or. It's not like I can be *either* beautiful *or* need to watch my weight. You don't have to apply a negative connotation to my body size." Her eyes were as hard as stone. "Beauty has nothing to do with what's on the outside."

"You're right," he said, voice shaking. "Forgive me."

She didn't say anything, instead folding her arms on the table and leaning forward as though she were cold. She glanced toward the door and Ash couldn't help but wonder if she regretted coming with him. He wouldn't be surprised if she did.

"I just worry about you," he added, and then he took another sip of his drink. "But maybe I'm wrong to."

"Why?"

"Why what?"

She scrutinized his face. "Why do you worry about me?"

"I have no idea how to answer that question. I just do. We're friends, aren't we?"

"Or maybe it's just the stars."

Ash felt sobered by that because she was right. If Tayshia's theories were correct, it was entirely possible that they only felt like being in each other's lives because of the fact that the universe had possibly decided that they were two halves of the same whole. Everything he felt towards her could have been fabricated by stardust in his veins.

"And what if it *is*?" he asked, lowering his voice so people at nearby booths didn't hear their conversation. "What if our feelings *are* fake?"

"It could be. Let's say we are soulmates. If we weren't, then would we even be able to stand each other?"

"You're saying you think a star can determine the way we feel?"

"We come from the stars, Ash," she said. "It makes sense that emotions like happiness, sadness, and yes—even love could come from them, too."

He nodded, resting his elbow on the table and his chin in his hand. She was right. If all life on Earth came from the depths of space and emotions were inherent in humanity, then it made sense that with a star connection, the feelings would be real.

The waiter walked up, setting their plates in front of them.

Ash cut his steak and then took a bite. It was delicious, exactly the way he liked it. He took another bite, glancing across the table at Tayshia. Much to his pleasure, she was tucking in with zeal. In fact, she was eating faster than he was.

"Slow down," he joked. "I don't know CPR."

Her chewing abruptly slowed.

"You know," he said after swallowing a mouthful, "I'd think you really liked your food if it weren't for that sour expression on your face."

Her upper lip curled. "Yeah, well, I'm suddenly not in a good mood."

Something in her tone made Ash's head pull back on his shoulders. It was curt and dripping with acid. It wasn't like he'd told her to stop eating altogether. Why was she so pressed?

Could he do *nothing* right?

They ate the rest of their food in complete silence, the air between them frigid. Ash felt a bit sick and it made everything worse. At least before, they were laughing and enjoying each other's company. Now, it just felt like a bad date.

Right as the waiter brought over the check, Tayshia pulled her wallet out of her purse. She dropped a twenty on the table and got up.

"Where are you going?" he asked, both him and the waiter looking at her.

"To the bathroom, if that's okay," she snapped, and then she stormed off.

"Damn, bro," the waiter said, giving Ash a wide-eyed look. "What'd you say to piss her off?"

Ash hadn't the slightest clue.

Ignoring her money, he paid for both meals and both sodas with his own money. He knew he should be a bit more careful with it, given that he wasn't exactly going to be anyone's first choice for employee with a felony on his record. That life insurance money may very well be the only real money he had for his entire life.

But he wasn't going to take Tayshia to lunch and make her pay.

When she came back, she frowned at her twenty dollar bill, which lay untouched where she'd left it.

"You paid?"

"Of course I did. Tipped, too," he said, shrugging back into his coat. "Who do you think I am? Kieran? Your parents cut you off. I wasn't about to make you pay for a meal I told you I'd treat you to."

She didn't reply, her brow still furrowed as she gathered up her money and shoved it back into her purse. Then, she pulled the strap on over her head and arranged it so it crossed her body.

"You ready?" Ash said, standing up.

"Yes."

They walked to the door. When they reached it, Ash fell in-step behind Tayshia right as she stumbled. She let out a gasp as she went flying forward. Quick as a flash, Ash's arm was around her midriff and his other hand was gripping her elbow, holding her up. His heart pounding at how close she'd come to slamming her face into the wood, he dipped his head down near her ear.

This was the ten millionth time she'd fallen over. This time, he had a feeling he knew why it kept happening.

"I'm fine," she said, sounding breathless as she placed her hands on his forearm, beneath her chest. "I just tripped over a — maybe a loose floorboard, or something."

Just then, the door opened and a group of younger students Ash recognized from Christ Rising traipsed in, trailing rainwater behind them. Ash, with his arm still around Tayshia's middle, drew them both to the side so the students could get by. One of the girls looked up at him, in the process of saying something to the group. Her gaze fell, settling upon his arm and the way Tayshia's hands were gripping it.

Fuck, was all he had time to think before the girl was practically shrieking into the restaurant.

"Oh, my God! Are you two *dating*?!" The girl looked revolted. "Didn't his dad *shoot* yours?"

Tayshia pulled herself out of Ash's grasp faster than he could blink and shoved her way out into the light, drizzling rain. Ash followed after her, shaking his head as he pulled his hood on. As soon as it was on, he pulled hers up with one hand and made sure it covered her head.

"With any luck, that'll make it back to Kieran by Monday," he said. "Next, the rest of Crystal Springs."

"Lucky for you, but not for me, hm?" Her tone had returned to its former acidity. "Everyone will think I like playing with guns."

He slowed to a complete halt, coincidentally right next to the alleyway that he and Elijah had seen Kieran and Quinn in all those weeks ago. She turned to look at him with an annoyed expression.

"Aren't you coming?"

"Is this about what I said while we were eating?"

"No."

He narrowed his eyes. "Is it about what I said at the bookstore?"

She averted her eyes and shoved her hands into her pockets. The raindrops were falling around them and the sky was a light grey that made her skin look uncharacteristic in its equally-grey pallor. The water disappeared into in the dips and hollows of the curls that fell out of the safety of her hood. By the look on her face, he could tell that she was angry.

"I told you I didn't want to talk about it," she said in a hiss, and then she took a step toward him so she could lower her volume. There were people everywhere. The passersby kept stepping off of the sidewalk to get around them. "You just keep trying to drop hints and bringing it up again and again. What makes you think you have the right to bring up the memory of my *rape* in casual conversation in public?"

He flinched at the word. He hated hearing it. The reminder of what she'd experienced combined with the fact that he'd felt everything she'd felt made his stomach churn.

"Maybe if you'd talk to me, then I wouldn't be fucking thinking about it all the time," he said, taking a few steps toward her until they were only a yard away from one another. "I was there, too."

"Except that you weren't, you selfish asshole," she hissed, eyes blazing. "You weren't. You may have been there in the memory. You may have felt it. But you will *never* know what it feels like to lose that part of yourself. You will *never* know what it's like to feel yourself being torn apart from the inside out. You will *never* know what I felt — what I *feel*. So don't fucking mention it like it's just a memory. It's not a memory to me, Ash. I have to relive it every damn day."

Her words hurt. They hurt like stones to the flesh or a knife to the heart. He knew why.

Because he liked her.

He liked her and he wanted to take care of her and be there for her and do whatever he could to make her happy. It felt real. It felt like they'd gone from tearing each other's throats out to caring about one another in a matter of hours.

It felt like it had happened overnight.

"I said I was sorry."

"And what, now you deserve a medal? You have the rights to my memory because you saw me get fucked in an alleyway?"

"I felt it, too. I keep bringing it up because *I felt it, too.*"

She scowled. "Don't give me that bullshit. You're twenty years old. You know how to read people's energies. I made it clear that I didn't want to talk about it. But you acted like just because you saw it, you have a right to my thoughts. Like just because you were there, you're in love with me, or something. Am I a woman of worth to you now that another man's had me? Have your dreams come true now that you know what a whore feels like inside?"

Ash fixed her with an accusatory glare that could have turned the water dampening her curls into ice. Her words were so vitriolic, so full of pain and hatred.

They were sickening

He spoke his next words like he was raising a sword.

"You say that like you think I only want to fuck you."

Tayshia didn't shrink back. In fact, she straightened her shoulders and stood up as tall as she could.

"Forgive me for thinking you're all the same."

All the same.

"We're *not* all the same," he growled, walking towards her. Her eyes went wide as she moved backward, her back hitting the corner of the building. She stumbled to her right, into the alley. "And while I get that it's hard for you to see that, it doesn't give you the right to go applying that mentality to me. I'm not like him."

She continued to back away, her feet crunching against gravel and glass on the pavement of the small alleyway. Her expression was acrimonious.

"I have every right to apply whatever mentality I want to any man who looks at me and thinks I in any way, shape, or form belong to him."

"I never said that."

"No, you didn't. You didn't have to."

He stopped walking, but she wasn't done talking.

"I know you were inside my head. You were inside my memory. Inside my body. You felt what I felt." She tilted her head back and to the side as she looked up into his eyes, searching them for whatever it was she was hoping to find. "And I know that's what scares you. The fact that in spite of what you felt having to relive it with me, you still want me."

Tayshia's hand snapped out to grab his jacket, the suddenness of her movement causing him to jump. She yanked and he stumbled forward as she moved. Her back hit the wall. Ash's hands slammed against the stone above her head to keep himself from crushing her. She held his gaze.

"What happened was real, Ash. And it doesn't matter if it was a memory. It doesn't matter if it was a dream. It doesn't matter what the stars say. You felt what I felt. I felt what you felt. I'm in your dreams just like you're inside of mine, and there's nothing you can do about it. So, I know exactly what you want to do to me. You *are* all the same—you're just a man who's too scared to kiss me first."

"Fuck you," he spat.

"No doubt that's *exactly* what you want to do."

Ash couldn't remember ever feeling so angry in his entire life yet so, so alive. Every part of his body felt like it had burst into flames. A storm brewed in his chest, filling him to the brim. It all seemed to pale in comparison to his thoughts.

Because yes, he *did* know what he wanted to do to her.

Ash's lips descended upon her own, his mouth covering hers and pulling her into a kiss that drowned like the tides.

Tayshia gasped into it, maybe from shock or something else, and his tongue delved into her mouth with abandon. He kissed her like he'd never wanted to do anything else, turning his head so he could deepen it into something that stole her breath.

In full view of everyone walking past the alley, he grabbed both sides of her face, pressing his entire body against hers and pinning her to the wall. He felt like he was trying to tell her with his tongue that he would never hurt her. To whisper with his lips that he *did* want her, and that that was the problem.

He felt her hands pushing against his chest, hard. He moved back, their lips coming apart with a loud *smack*, punctuated by their breathless panting. They stared at each other, blue eyes meeting brown, and she looked terrified.

"What's wrong with you?" she breathed, sounding livid. "Have you lost your damn mind? What the *fuck* is wrong with you? Do you not—"

"Oh, shut the fuck up," he said, shaking his head. "Just shut *up*."

Ash grabbed her, palm against her chin and fingers digging into her cheeks, and surged forward. He bent to kiss her lips again, his hand sliding down to squeeze her throat until it forced her lips open to his. He was neither sweet nor slow, finding that his desire was spurned only by passion and possessive need.

Mine.

Mine.

Mine.

The moment his hand braced itself against the wall again, something seemed to shift within her. To break apart, the ice melting into a sigh that entered his mouth from the cavern of her own. She threw her arms around his neck, hoisting herself up on tip-toe as she kissed him back with double the energy he was giving her. The storm in his body retracted to the pit of his stomach, where it condensed into the solid heaviness of fervor.

Kissing her felt right.

She shoved him back again and he felt her hand lifting. She was going to try and slap him. He snatched her wrist out of the air and gave her a glare that sent a shiver rolling through her body.

"If you slap me again, we're gonna have problems."

The fire in her eyes died out in an instant, becoming replaced with the shyness of who she was: a twenty-year-old girl kissing a boy in an alley. Her hand curled into a fist and he felt the muscle in her forearm flex as she did so. She tried to pull her arm out of his grasp, but he held tighter. Her head lowered, chin tucking towards her chest.

He dipped his head, chasing after her and brushing his nose against hers.

"Because if we start having problems," he breathed, trailing kisses along her jawline that caused her to suck in her breath, "then we can't kiss like this." The tip of his tongue traced the shell of her ear, and she jolted, barely managing to stifle a cry in the fabric of his shirt. "And I can't make you feel good."

"Ash," she said, and it was a whimper. Her back arched as he kissed down the side of her neck. "Ash, w-wait, I—"

"And I really, *really* wanna make you feel good."

He found her pulse and laved his tongue against it, the gentleness in direct juxtaposition to the way that he'd devoured her mouth. She buried her face to hide the sound that left her lips. A sound that made Ash's head spin and all of the screws holding his faculties together come loose.

He turned his face. She turned hers to meet him.

Their lips came together again and again, his low murmurs of how soft her skin was and how sweet she sounded crashing against the keening sighs that rose to greet him. In a few moments, it wouldn't matter that it was the middle of the day and this was an alley. He was going to grab her by the back of the thighs and —

This is an alleyway.

We're in a fucking alleyway, and I'm trying to...

Jesus, fuck.

He was in a brick alleyway, shoving his tongue down her throat, practically forcing her to kiss him when she clearly didn't want to.

Ash used his hand on the wall above her to push himself away. He tilted his head back, gasping for breath as he fought with his own body. Fought against the raging torrent that was swirling in his abdomen.

"I'm not scared to kiss you," he said, his voice hoarse. "I'm scared I'll hurt you."

"Is there a difference?"

"Yeah, Tayshia. There's a fucking difference."

CHAPTER THIRTEEN

Sometime mid-November, Ash realized his roots were coming in quicker than he wanted them to.

His hair grew fast, so there was about a half-inch of black hair growing in at the crown of his head. No matter which way he tried to sweep his hair—forward, over the side of his head, back—the new growth showed. It looked ridiculous.

He didn't want to go all the way to the salon when he was already hemorrhaging money paying all of the bills but at the same time, he didn't want to do it himself. He'd absolutely fuck it up.

There was only one other option.

It was Saturday. Tayshia was on the living room floor between the couch and the coffee table. She wore a hoodie and leggings and her curls were pulled up into her favorite two bun style. She had a pint of ice cream balanced on her chest and knees, already almost empty. The spoon hung out of her mouth as she played her handheld game console, humming the music under her breath. The blinds were open on the sliding glass door, spilling grey light in from the cloudy Fall day.

"Hey, what're you doing?"

"Playing pocky monsters," she said in a small voice around the spoon, not tearing her eyes off of the screen.

Ash's lips twitched upward. "Can the baby stop playing pocky monsters and do my hair?"

They hadn't spoken much since the argument in the alleyway but things didn't seem too volatile. Now, she gave him the most revolted look he'd ever seen her level in his direction.

"Can the *what* do *what* now?"

"Can the baby… Stop playing pocky monsters… And do my hair?"

"Um, *ew*. Don't call me that ever again."

"Aw," he said with a smirk, "but you like when I call you baby when we're—"

"*Shut up!*" she yelled, tossing her console onto the couch and scrambling to her feet. "Nope, nope, nope. I'll do it. I'll do your hair."

Ash threw his head back and laughed. "All's I'm sayin' is you never seem to have a problem with it when we—"

"*Shut* your damn mouth!" She pranced into the kitchen, glaring at him before going to the sink to drop the spoon in. "God, you're such an asshole."

"So you'll do it?"

"Yeah, let me just use the bathroom and then get ready."

"Where do we go? The grocery store?"

She tossed the empty pint container into the trash can, giving him a disturbed look.

"Boy, are you crazy? We're going to the beauty supply. *The grocery store.*" She scoffed and passed him in the hallway. "Headass."

"Well, I don't know!" he cried.

The bathroom door swung shut.

Ash rolled his eyes and went to his own room to put his shoes on.

This was what they did.

They got angry, they fought, and then they pretended it never happened. They said hurtful things that were borderline unforgivable, and then they forgave them without saying so. They went back and forth, around and around, and then they feigned indifference.

Anything to keep each other.

It was times like these that confused him the most. Times where they were joking around, teasing, getting along. Where it was easy to pretend that nothing bad had ever happened. To pretend like the ice cream shop never happened. That Paris never happened. That they were just two people who were hooking up.

If things could stay just like this, he'd pretend forever.

✿✿✿

Tayshia put the address of a specific beauty supply store into a navigational app in her phone.

It took them to a shopping center across town that was in an outdoor strip mall with clothing stores, food shops, and a cell phone store. Ash had never been to this particular shopping center so he followed Tayshia into the store with a bit of a bewildered look on his face.

Inside, there was hair everywhere. Hanging on the walls, adorning mannequin heads, stacked in boxes on shelves. There were hair products, too, as well as accessories. It was overwhelming for him but Tayshia seemed to know exactly where to go. She waved and said *hello* to a store employee who knew her name.

"Do you come here a lot?" he asked.

"Is that a joke?" Tayshia grinned at him.

Seeing her smile was so rare that Ash couldn't think of any words to respond with for a solid ten seconds.

"Well, where do we go?"

"This way."

Tayshia led him to the aisle that had the hair bleach. She grabbed a large tub of powder bleach.

"It's just my roots," he said. "You don't need that much."

"It's okay, I'm gonna use it on my next sew-in," she told him, picking up a bottle of developer and reading the label. "What's left, I mean."

"Oh."

Tayshia bit her lower lip around another smile. "You have no idea where you're at, do you?"

"Uh..." It was Ash's turn to give her a bright smile. "Nope."

She laughed, a merry sound. He followed her down some more aisles. They stopped to grab some toner.

"We're gonna go in a sec," she said. "I wanna get a few packs of braiding hair."

"You're gonna braid your hair?" Ash raised one eyebrow.

Tayshia shot him a suspicious look over her shoulder as she walked. "Yeah. And what? You don't like box braids?"

"I think they're sick," he said. "And I think they'd look good on you. I'm surprised you can do them yourself. How long does it take?"

They stopped in front of the braiding hair. The packages all said "yaki", "synthetic blend," or "human hair," on them. Tayshia knelt down in front of the shades of red, hunting through them for one she liked best.

"To do it myself, if I do like, medium-sized braids, then about nine or ten hours."

Ash's jaw dropped. "Nine or ten *hours*?"

"Yep." She grabbed three packs of a wine-red color, then stood up and grabbed three packs of chestnut brown. "When I do sew-ins, it takes me about the same time if I take my time."

"Don't your arms hurt?"

"Beauty is pain, white boy."

She patted him on the cheek, looking up into his eyes. For some reason, she froze in place, gazing so deeply into them that it unsettled him. Ash was standing in the aisle, tall enough that he was able to sling his elbow along the top of the shelf beside him. Though the store was somewhat crowded, it felt like they were there by themselves.

"What?" he murmured, his eyes flickering up and down her face in query. She looked so cute with her hair in buns.

"Nothing," she murmured, her fingers trailing down to the side of his neck. "Let's go."

He stood there for a moment, wondering why his heart was beating so fast. He'd kissed her plenty of times before.

Why did it feel like he had a schoolyard crush?

"Do you prefer my natural hair, or something?" Tayshia asked as they waited in line. "This is absolutely a trap, by the way. I already know what answer I want."

Ash reached up to lift one curl. "Tayshia, you could be bald."

She snapped her fingers. "I could be bald, and…?"

"And what? And nothing." He laughed and tugged on the curl. "I like your face."

She seemed to be hiding a smile behind another suspicious glance. "Mm-hm. You talkin' like you like *me*."

"Yeah," he said under his breath, gazing down at her lips. "I like you."

His heart thudded a stop.

What did he just say?

Someone called them over, signifying that it was their turn, and the spell shattered. Tayshia and the clerk talked for a few moments, laughing and carrying on. Once again, Ash was happy to see her smile. He paid for everything, and then they left with their purchases.

"You didn't have to buy my yaki," Tayshia said in a joking manner once they were in the car. "That was—"

"Shut up."

Tayshia's head whipped to the left, giving him a shocked look.

Ash grabbed her chin with one hand, palm pressed to the underside, and dragged her lips against his in a kiss that seared like sunlight against bare skin. She melted the same way too, falling across the console with her hands gripping the sides of his neck, fingers digging into the hair at the back of his head.

When he pulled back, he said nothing, leaving her to click her seatbelt in with a dazed facial expression. Ash placed one hand on the back of her seat and turned to look out the rear windshield as he pulled out of the parking spot. His palm turned the wheel in a circle. Their eyes met.

"You're just all types of bold today, aren't you?" Tayshia said facing forward.

Ash smirked.

As the car started through the parking lot, they both seemed to catch sight of the door to the ramen shop at the same time. It was opening, two familiar people exiting one right after the other.

The coincidences in this town were astronomical.

Kieran held the door aloft for Quinn to walk past him, the two of them smiling and laughing more in those few seconds than Ash had ever seen Kieran laugh with Tayshia.

That had to hurt.

The air in the car seemed to shift to a more negative plane, like a black hole passing by an unsuspecting star and consuming it. Tayshia's thoughts and her silence were so loud that they felt deafening.

After one hesitant moment, Ash's hand dropped to her lap where his fingers slid between hers. He pressed their palms together and lifted her hand. Without looking away from the road, he kissed her knuckles.

"He's nothing. He's never going to be anything."

Tayshia just watched him, watched him kissing her hand again and again, gentle presses of his lips to soft skin that deserved to be worshipped. The dejected sigh that left her mouth made him tighten his hold on her.

Ash didn't know if he really did *like* her, but he knew that he didn't like it when she was sad. He wished she could forget about Kieran and all the years he'd spent traumatizing her. He wished he could take it all away from her.

Everything that had caused her pain, he wanted to erase it.

✧✧✧

"Sit down on the toilet," Tayshia said as she set the bleach container and developer on the counter. "I have a mixing bowl and a hair dye brush in my room."

"Lid up or down?"

Tayshia short-circuited, staring at him in horror until Ash's raucous laughter had her smacking him on the upper arm.

"Fool, sit your ass down!"

"All right, all right."

Ash sat down on the closed lid of the toilet. He'd changed into an older black tee shirt of a deathcore band he liked and a pair of joggers that he didn't care about. While Tayshia went to her room, Ash searched through his phone to pick some music. In the hallway, he heard the dryer door open and then shut again.

He made a playlist and by the time he was done, Tayshia was back.

She'd changed into one of his tee shirts, colored grey. It dwarfed her frame, the hem falling to mid-thigh on her. Her hair buns looked a bit fuzzy.

"That's my shirt."

"You've literally washed this shirt like, fifteen times. You never take it out of the dryer," she protested. "I've never seen you wear it except for like, one time."

He narrowed his eyes. "You didn't ask me."

"Well, can I wear it? Please?" She whined. "I don't have many clothes and I don't wanna ruin any of my hoodies."

Ash tried not to stare at her legs. They were so long. He wanted to touch them.

"Yeah, you can wear it."

"Thank you," she said, beaming down at him. She turned to the sink, where she began to prepare the bleach and developer in the bowl. "Didn't you just get your hair done? Your hair grows fast."

"Yeah," he said, his voice a bit scratchy from talking in a low tone. He rested his hands on his thighs as he leaned back against the back of the toilet. Around them, the playlist he'd selected played. Tayshia didn't seem to mind the heavy guitars and drums like she used to. "It's like, half an inch a month."

"Your dad's hair is black, right?" She mixed the bleach, the tapping of the brush against the edges of the bowl sounding almost soothing.

Ash nodded. "My mom was blonde."

"That's why you got those blue eyes, huh?" Tayshia said, her lips quirking up.

"I guess."

She reached down beneath the sink, pulling out a pair of rubber gloves that she already had in there. They snapped against her wrists as she tugged them on.

"So… Is it your mom that's mixed?" he asked. His gaze darted up to meet hers. "Sorry, I hope that's not rude. I'm just asking."

"It's not rude," she said, shaking her head. She ran her fingers through his hair, sliding the pointed end of a fine tooth comb along his scalp to create rows. "And I'm not mixed. Both of my parents are Black."

"Oh, okay," he said. "I've only ever met your… Well, your dad."

"I know," she said, moving to stand in front of him. "What about you?"

On instinct, Ash opened his knees so she could stand in-between them. The comb on his skin felt nice, almost like a massage. He closed his eyes, fighting the urge to sway forward until his forehead fell against her abdomen.

"Me?" he said quietly.

"Yeah, what's your ethnicity?"

He could almost laugh. "White."

She rapped him on the head with the comb. "Bruh, I know all that. I'm asking you what your heritage is. Like, your ancestry."

"Uhh… I dunno," he said, reaching up to scratch the side of his nose. "I think my dad's Greek. My mom's Finnish—I know that for sure."

"That's cool," she said, leaning over a bit to grab the mixing bowl and brush. Ash felt the cold product on his skin as she began. "So you're not very connected, then."

"Nah. My parents were both only children and my grandparents' siblings all passed away before I was born. I don't have any family, really."

Ash didn't know how to explain the feeling that wove through him upon saying the words. Speaking aloud his loneliness made it feel real. It reminded him that his family had always been doomed to dwindle. Now, there were only two left.

Him and his father.

"I have a big family," Tayshia said, still making her way through saturating his roots. "Sisters, cousins, aunts, uncles. It's crazy. Christmas is wild. But you know about my sisters."

"Sounds like it would be," Ash said, trying not to think about the fact that his family's Christmases were probably nothing like hers.

"It'll be annoying this year, though," she muttered, the scent of her perfume warring with the pungency of the bleach. "Kieran's family is friends with mine. My parents have informed me that we'll be spending Christmas Eve dinner with them."

Ash remembered her mentioning something about it in the car the day they'd gone job hunting.

He looked up at her as best he could without moving his head. "That really sucks."

"Oh, yeah. If I could stay here for Christmas, I would."

Ash bit his tongue. He'd almost told her she could.

It wasn't like he was going anywhere.

"It's honestly hella weird being in here with you," he said with a laugh, changing the subject. "You're usually in here by yourself for hours."

"Oh, stop," she said, her gaze fixated on his scalp as she painted the bleach onto his roots with practiced ease. She definitely knew what she was doing, since she was separating the layers until they were thin enough to become saturated. "It's not *hours*."

"One time—"

"*Stop*." She lifted the brush and gave him a scathing warning look. "Or I'm bleaching your eyebrows."

He wrinkled his nose.

"You are way too interested in every little thing I do," Tayshia said after she resumed. "Kieran was never this interested in me."

Ash didn't think Tayshia realized what her words had just implied. He tilted his head as she worked on the right side of his hair, sorting through his thoughts.

"I don't know how you stayed with him as long as you did. I doubt he even touched you," he said.

"He didn't."

"Like... At all?"

"Unless we were messing around, no." She shrugged her shoulders. "He didn't like PDA and he got mad when I tried to hold his hand until it was for like, a specific reason. He wasn't affectionate at all."

"*Why?*"

"I dunno? Maybe my skin's ashy. I don't wanna talk about it."

They went quiet.

Ash found that he couldn't stop thinking about the fact that Kieran had made out in a public alleyway with Quinn but couldn't touch Tayshia. It didn't make any sense. Why was one girl worthy of being treated right, yet the other one wasn't? What was wrong with that fucker?

How could he *not* want to touch her?

Without realizing it, Ash's hands had lifted from his thighs. They drifted up the sides of Tayshia's legs, around to the backs of them. She let out a soft cry, her knees buckling. She had to stop herself from falling with the bottoms of her forearms braced on top of his shoulders.

"Hey!" she said, sounding irritated as she stood up straight and got back to work. "If you don't want me to spill bleach all over you, then knock it off."

Ash didn't say anything. His gaze remained trained on her skin, on his fingertips grazing up the backs of her thighs. She squirmed a bit but remained silent as his hands moved up and down in soft, gentle motions.

"Ash," she said, her voice soft. "What are you doing?"

He merely shook his head, finding it difficult to talk when she was this close to him, wearing nothing but his shirt and allowing him to touch her. Trusting him to touch her like this. He didn't deserve it.

"Head forward," she said, breathless. "So I can get the back."

Ash's head pitched forward, his face pressing into her abdomen. She stiffened but didn't move away. He felt the brush painting bleach on the roots through the back of his head. His fingers traced patterns on the backs of her thighs.

She felt so soft.

Ash wished he could take his fist and punch Kieran right in the dead center of his mouth. Tayshia didn't deserve the things he'd done to her. She didn't deserve to feel like there was anything wrong with her. Her skin wasn't dry or ashy—it felt like satin. It always felt like satin.

"Do you like this? Does this feel good?"

"Maybe. Is your scalp burning yet?"

Ash's *no* was muffled against her stomach.

"I'm surprised," Tayshia replied. "Mine's usually burning by now. Anyway, I'm done."

She set the empty mixing bowl and brush in the sink. Ash stood suddenly, causing her to have to move backward so his head didn't hit hers.

"You probably need like, no more than thirty minutes, and then you can wash it out and we'll tone it," she said. "We only used a low volume so it'll take a little longer to lift."

"Okay."

Ash studied, her his lips slowly curling up. "You look so cute today."

"Ew." Tayshia wrinkled her nose. "Stop."

"What? Why? I can't tell you look good?"

"No. I don't like compliments. They make make me feel weird."

"Good weird or bad weird?"

"Like, I think you're lying weird."

They stared at one another, Tayshia leaning back against the door with her bleach-covered, gloved hands held up by her chest.

"Why do you keep doing that?" she asked.

"Doing what?"

"Staring at me like that. Being silent. It's creepy."

He arched one eyebrow as he stood up. "Would it be creepy if I kissed you right now?"

"Yes. Er—no. Not necessarily. I just have bleach on my—"

Ash's hand pressed flat to the door as he dipped his head to capture her lips in a kiss. He wasn't soft and gentle, nor was he hard and bruising. He was determined and passionate and dominant. He cupped the back of her neck with his other hand, holding her head in place as he tasted the inside of her mouth like she was made of candy.

She was always so sweet.

He broke the kiss to move down the side of her throat, laving her pulse so he could feel it fluttering against his tongue. She gasped, her words coming out in a stammer.

"A-Ash, the—your h-hair. And m-my—I have g-gloves—*ah*."

Her head fell to the side as she lost herself to the sensations. Ash kissed his way back up to her mouth and she moaned into it. It was clear she didn't know what to do with her hands.

"You're," she murmured against his lips, "ridiculous. Can't I take off the gloves?"

"Nope." He sucked her earlobe into his mouth and she shivered, moaning so loudly that it almost drowned out the music playing on his phone.

"Why are you doing this then?" She found strength and laced her voice with it. "You're causing problems."

"Mm, what sort of problems?" He wondered why the skin on her throat tasted so good, and why it felt so nice to grip her waist.

"You know what sort."

Ash groaned, his hand sliding around to her lower back so he could hold her flush against him. The hand of his that was against the door slid upward. "Are you wet for me?"

Tayshia was quiet before saying, "Why don't you find out?"

Her words burrowed deep within Ash's psyche, shattering any lingering concerns he had. His hand slid down, reaching beneath the hem of the shirt she'd stolen from him so he could reach around to grip a handful of her backside. He cursed beneath his breath.

His fingers slipped beneath the waistband of her underwear, sliding past curls and sinking through her arousal. He gathered it. Took his time swirling it up to the apex of her core. Each exploratory pass of his fingers had her hips twitching and her face burrowing deeper into his chest. She was exactly as wet as he thought she'd be, and she felt even softer down there than the skin on her legs had felt.

"Oh, please," she breathed, sounding desperate. "Please, Ash. Please."

"Please what? You want me to stop?"

"No. God no." Her hips rocked forward and ground down with a small movement, one that seemed like she was trying to hide it. "Just—please. I want to—"

"Want to what? Want to fuck my fingers?"

She nodded, whimpering against his shirt as his fingers continued their slow dragging. He turned his face towards hers, pressing occasional kisses to her temple. He could see her arms were getting tired from the way they shook.

At a particularly firm drag of his touch, she shivered and cried out.

"Yes. Yes, please. I'm—*please let me take the gloves off.*"

Ash took his time removing his fingers, stepping aside so she could stumble forward to the sink. Hands shaking, she pulled the gloves off, dropped them into the trash can, and turned the tap on. In the mirror, Ash could see her keeping her gaze down. The terracotta of her cheeks had flushed a deeper color. Her chest heaved as she caught her breath.

His mind was starting to fill with the sea.

A vast, endless sea that churned with the storm of lust inside of him, with waves that reached for the moon. Tayshia was in the center of it, being buffeted back and forth by the winds, struggling to stay above the surface.

But Ash wasn't afraid. This ocean was his. It was a sea that belonged to him, that answered *only* to him. He wouldn't drown. Tayshia might, but only if he pulled her down to the depths and held her there. Ash was in control of this angry, moonlit sea.

He was Poseidon.

Ash's hands found her waist, sliding down to her hips as his gaze fixated upon the way she looked in his shirt. His gaze flickered up to meet hers in the mirror.

She looked like a deer in headlights.

"What are you doing?" she said, her voice cracking, water still running over her hands.

"Exactly what you told me you wanted." His fingers trailed down over the swell of her rear. "Unless you want me to stop?"

His hands stilled on her upper thighs, his facial expression calm and brow quirked in challenge.

"But the mirror," she whispered, turning off the tap.

Ash said nothing.

The mirror was the best part.

"And you'd stop if I wanted you to?"

"Of course," he said, his tone of voice impassioned, brows coming together. He pulled her back against him, turned his face toward hers. Their gazes remained locked in the mirror as he turned more, pressing his lips to her throat. "Just say the word. I would never hurt you."

Her eyelids fluttered shut, her chin trembling a bit. "I'm not a whore."

His heart clenched and for a suspended moment, he wanted to get his keys, leave, and drive to Kieran O'Connell's house.

"No, you're not," he said, his fingers digging into her hips with slight pressure. His eyes glinted with a ferocity he hadn't realized he could hold back. "And even if you were, it wouldn't make you any less valuable. You're a human. Humans feel things."

Even with her eyes closed, he could see her thinking deeply on his words.

"I feel things." She said it like he didn't know and she wanted him to.

"What kinds of things?"

"Good things." Her head lolled back against his chest, her wet hands curving around the front edge of the bathroom sink and counter. "With you."

"Do you want me to make you feel good things right now?" he asked, his voice curling around them both like a hissing snake. He wanted her so badly that his muscles ached. He wanted to make her feel so good that she saw stars. That it changed her entire outlook on herself and eradicated the thoughts that told her she wasn't allowed to feel anything.

"Okay."

"Okay what?"

"Okay, touch me. But—But tell me what you're going to do."

Ash's stomach curled into a tight, excited knot as he smoothed one hand down to her hip. He placed his other hand on her shoulder.

"I'm going to play," he murmured, nose brushing her pulse. The moment it touched her skin, his eyes met hers in their reflections once more. He pushed his tongue against her skin and licked a fiery path up to her ear. "And I'm going to make you come. Spread your legs."

She hesitated for a moment before she placed her left leg out further.

"Just say the word," he whispered, repeating his promise like he wanted to seal it in blood.

Because he wanted her so bad that if she let him, he'd bend her over the counter and fuck her, so he could watch her face in the mirror while he made her forget about everything around them.

While he took her to the stars that might connect them.

Tayshia gave him a nod. Across her face, a nervousness flickered that he recognized from the night they'd first hooked up. And as he put one hand on her hip and pressed the other to the center of her upper back so he could push her forward over the sink, he realized that the nerves were not a response to the things other people had told her.

They were a response to the way he made her feel.

Ash's gaze fell to her body as he pulled her panties aside and slipped his fingers between her legs again. A shudder ran through them both simultaneously as he sought out her entrance.

"Your hair looks cute," he said.

She laughed, incredulous. "What? Why are you—"

Ash slammed two fingers inside of her body, pulling a loud moan out of her lips. Her right hand lifted from the counter and slapped against the mirror, her back arching downward and eyes falling shut. Her lips parted and would not close again.

He wouldn't let her catch her breath.

"I'm just thinking." He held her hip, watching his wet fingers disappear into her while he fucked her with them, hard and fast. The veins on his forearm rippled through his tattooed skin. "Maybe you'll accept my compliments when I'm doing this."

Her eyes cracked open, her face twisting in ecstasy as he pulled her back against the thrusts of his hand. She was gasping like he'd just pulled her out of deep, stormy waters. Like she was trying for air but not quite managing enough to fill her lungs.

Ash bit his lip through a grin that was as mischievous as the glint in his eyes. He was twisting his fingers, alternating between thrusting, and sinking in deep while curling and massaging.

Tayshia looked like she was going through an existential crisis.

"Yeah?" He lifted his eyebrows as though he were asking her a simple question. "You like that, don't you? And that?"

She pitched forward over the sink on her tip-toes, her entire body quivering as her head fell.

"Come here," he growled. "Where you goin', huh? Where? Come the fuck back here."

Ash grabbed the back of her neck and pulled her onto three of his fingers with a firm yank. The desperate, wailing sound she made coupled with the way her eyes rolled made him groan.

Once again, Ash couldn't think clearly. His mind was as empty as space, devoid of all life that didn't involve Tayshia. She took his fingers so good, so perfect. She was perfect. Everything he could ever want in a person and more.

"Ash," came her strangled whine. "It—" A gasp. "Feels so good. I need—I have to—I'm sorry."

Ash barely managed to adjust the angle of his hand before she was using her palm against the mirror to push herself backward again and again. She let out a sob with every slam of his fingers inside of her.

He was so hard he thought he might pass out. He wanted her more badly than he'd ever wanted anyone in his entire fucking life. Ash wanted to be inside of her but this moment wasn't about him.

It was about her.

"That's it. Yeah, that's it." His voice was hoarse. Fervent. "Fuck them just like that. You're so good, such a fast learner. Look how good you are."

His fingers slipped around, down into the front of her panties to rub her most sensitive spot in slick, gentle circles. He loved it, loved giving her the contrast she liked so much. Loved getting her off in front of the mirror like this. Loved watching her be so overcome by the things he was making her feel that she couldn't hold back anymore.

Trusting him.

"When someone gives you a compliment, you should say thank you. Come on." Ash looked into her half-closed eyes in the mirror, lifting his chin in silent challenge. The bleach in his hair was white, his hair slicked back like he was going to a fancy gala. The black of his shirt made his tattoos stand out again pale skin. "I said look what a good girl you are for me."

Tayshia's eyelids fluttered open on a gasp.

They stared at one another in the reflective glass. Everything she'd been through—all the horrible things she'd endured—and he could see the guilt brewing like a storm on the horizon in the brown of her eyes.

It wasn't fair to her. Why couldn't she feel things without hating herself?

Why did they have to take that away from her?

"Fuck," Ash said, his stomach curling tight with a sudden whip of yearning that lashed through his sensibilities. His fingers moved faster, with more assured purpose. They dipped inside of her body, pulling back out to touch her where she needed it most, then sinking deep inside of her all over again. His mind was orbiting distant stars, reveling in the way it felt to do this. "You deserve this."

Tayshia's body rocked faster, hips grinding against his fingers like they always did when she was close. He moved the pads of his forefingers back and forth across her, earning himself a whimper and a series of barely intelligible pleas from her sweet lips.

"You deserve to be touched, okay?" he said, desperate for her to know. "You deserve to feel good. You deserve to feel beautiful."

Ash watched her dangling off the precipice, watched her losing herself to the shattering that was hurtling toward her with the speed of a comet.

"And your hair looks cute today."

She shattered, her teeth trapping her bottom lip for a moment before she couldn't hold her words in anymore.

"*Fuck.* Thank you," she whined over and over. "Thank you. Thank you."

Her eyes rolled up into her head as she came with a shudder that made her entire body shake. She fell off the precipice without grace, collapsing forward onto her elbows, words falling from her lips like teardrops.

When she came down from her high, she stood on shaky legs and turned to face him. Ash placed his hands on the counter beside her hips, caging her in. He didn't care where his fingers had just been.

She tilted her face up and he covered her lips with his own, kissing her with more than just the desire he had for her. He kissed her with silent apologies and assurances. Promises that everything would be okay and that if it wasn't, then he'd be there to take care of her. Kisses that told her he didn't care how intense his feelings were for her in such a short time. Kisses that told her he was hers.

"Tayshia." He kissed her a few more times. His heart felt too big for his chest. "Tayshia, I'm sorry. For the alley and for what I said. For all the mistakes. For reminding you —"

It was like throwing a pail of cold water on her.

Tayshia tore her mouth away from his, her entire body going stiff. Her hands pressed flat to his chest and pushed him back. Her eyes looked a bit wild.

"Stop. I'm sorry," she said, sounding almost frantic. "I don't know why I—I'm overwhelmed and I don't want to talk about it. I'm sorry. I'm so sorry, I just—"

"It's okay," Ash said, his guilt weighing him down with despair. "I was too forceful. I'm the one who's sorry. I just keep saying the wrong things."

She looked up at him and for a split second, he could see past the barriers in her eyes. It hurt his heart to see the terror there. The fear that she was making a mistake. The confusion. The guilt that he himself felt.

"I just want to be normal," Tayshia said, her voice sad and face downcast. "I'm sorry I always freeze up."

"You don't have to be normal," Ash said. "You can go at your own pace. I need to stop pushing you."

She frowned. "You *are* pushing me. I want to do these things with you but I just don't know how to feel clean when I do them. And you're pushing me."

"Tayshia, you—oh, *shit*." Ash's scalp burned. It felt like tiny things were digging their claws into his skin, making it itch. "Time to wash it out."

She looked up at him. The happy expression that had once lingered in her eyes was gone, replaced by something bitter. "Is it burning now?"

"Yes. But are you okay?"

"I'll be back to dry your hair so we can tone it."

Tayshia left, walking towards the living room.

CHAPTER FOURTEEN

Andre brought him weed the day before Thanksgiving.

Ash was grateful for it, given the stressful circumstances his life had fallen into. He felt like he'd tripped and toppled headfirst into a pit full of tarlike emotions, like they were pulling him down deeper with every gasp. He was tired of being unable to breathe.

He'd rather suffocate with smoke in his lungs.

The days since the afternoon Tayshia had done his hair had passed by as normally as could be expected. They were friends now, so it was easy to fall into roommate routines that didn't feel as volatile as their living situation had been in September, and as tense as their situationship in October.

Tayshia still used the bathroom for long periods of time and left her dishes everywhere, but instead of letting everything go to Hell, she helped clean. So while Ash was doing the dishes, she cleaned everything else.

She vacuumed the carpets, picked up their things and returned them to their respective rooms, and wiped the kitchen counters and stovetop. At some point, their laundry started to pile up, so she sorted them by color and washed them together. It got to the point where all Ash had to do was put the dishes into the dishwasher and sit down on the couch to play video games.

But he wasn't stupid.

In all that time that Tayshia was cleaning, she wasn't eating.

She hadn't come into his dreams and when he fell asleep, he felt like his consciousness made attempts to go into hers but could never seem to find a way in. It was strange. How could he have been watching her dreams for months yet now, he saw nothing but darkness?

He'd woken several times over the past two weeks in a cold sweat, feeling confused that no one was in his arms. Then, he'd felt stupid because she'd only slept in his bed twice.

Why was he so fucking weak for her?

And he had lay there, staring at the ceiling in the moonlit room, with the ghost of her lips against his own. He felt her absence like a physical wound, a gaping hole in his psyche. When he thought about keeping his distance from her, it felt like he was tearing that hole wider and shoving his heart into its depths.

That wasn't normal.

School was decent for Ash. He wasn't failing any classes and he was focusing well. The teachers weren't having to wake him up during lectures quite as often. So far, the first term was looking to be a good one, which was a good prediction for Winter and Spring terms.

"I'd say thank you, but you owe me a lot more than this," Ash said. He was in the cafeteria eating breakfast that day, having felt too exhausted to cook at the apartment.

Andre stood across the table from him, still bundled in his coat, hat, and scarf. One hand was wrapped around the strap of his backpack. The other was empty, him having just tossed the plastic bag onto the table. It landed in front of Ash's bowl. He had snatched it up quickly, shoving it into the pocket of his leather jacket before any rule-following students saw.

"Don't remind me," Andre said, setting his bag down. He slid into the bench, unlooping his scarf. "I'm tired of owing people things. Wait, what do I owe you for again?"

"For making me wait this long!" Ash scoffed, reaching up to make sure his hood was still on. "I haven't smoked since like, before Halloween."

"I know," Andre said with a sigh, unzipping his coat. He shrugged out of it, ignorant of the eleventh grade boy next to him who appeared disgruntled by the loose rainwater. "And that's why I came straight here."

"Shit—thanks. Where's Ji?" Ash asked around a mouthful of shitty egg scramble. "She didn't come with you?"

Andre rolled his eyes. "She was *nightmare* in Portland this weekend. I'm boutta ask you—"

"If you can smoke with me?" Ash gave him an incredulous look, spluttering a laugh. "Are you dumb? You're sitting here without a bruise around your eye by the grace of *God*, Andre. That's *my* weed."

"If I didn't adore how much of an asshole you can be, I'd be pissed," Andre said, smirking. "Oh well. I got my own."

"Of course you did."

They shared a knowing look and then fell into easy conversation for a few minutes. Andre and Ji Hyun had gone to Portland for the weekend for a nice dinner, some shopping, and a post-hardcore show. Andre had gotten another tattoo—this time on his calf—and had convinced Ji Hyun to get a small one on the back of her shoulder. In spite of the good parts of their weekend date, Ji Hyun had been in a sour mood, their bickering nonstop.

"I just don't think she realizes what she did," Andre said. "I mean, I know she doesn't play video games, but I mean... Come on. She almost broke my console. Damn."

"Yeah." Ash sipped his coffee, which he'd stopped through a drive-thru to get on his way to school. It was black, the way he liked it, and the bitterness was apparent on his tongue. "That shit's like four hundred dollars, bro."

"Yeah, and she doesn't seem to grasp the full effect." Andre waved a dismissive hand. "I tried to explain it to her but she can't see reason when she's like this. I'm over it."

"I don't get it," Ash said. "You guys were late to dinner here in town, and she picked up your console and was gonna throw it? You took her to PDX, but she was still gonna throw it when you got back? If Tayshia did that to me, I swear to *God*, bruh. I swear to *God*."

Andre started to reply, but then his brow furrowed so hard that it put a twitch to his eyebrows. "What does Tayshia have to do with this? You said you didn't like her."

Ash averted his eyes. It was starting to get difficult to keep this all in. The dreams, the sleepless nights, the loneliness. But he didn't want to say anything about it. Opening up to his friends wasn't as easy as opening up to Tayshia.

He felt like Tayshia *knew* him.

"Don't make a big deal out of it." Ash grimaced. "We... We have a thing. That's all I can describe it as. A thing."

"So, you guys *did* get seen at Gianni's!" Andre gasped, holding the side of his fist to his mouth as he bounced up and down. "*Dude. Bro.* For real?" He lowered his voice. "Did you hit that?"

The entire student body was aware of their changed relationship. Especially the high school students. He'd walked into Christ Rising without any idea why a sea of eyes were staring back at him until he sat down at the breakfast table next to an uncharacteristically-quiet Elijah.

An uncharacteristically-quiet Elijah, who ate with the speed of lightning and then left without so much as a word to him.

And when Ash had watched him go with a frown, he'd been stunned to see the majority of the cafeteria glaring directly at him. His gaze had then slid to Tayshia, who was picking at a salad while staring at the tabletop, no one sitting close to her.

It clicked.

Tayshia getting together with Ash was just as bad as Ash getting with Tayshia.

The trial had been so highly publicized in Crystal Springs that the last two people the town would want to see as friends were Ash Robards and Tayshia Cole. Ash was a felon who would forever be seen as the guy who robbed an ice cream shop and stood by while a man bled. And if Tayshia was *with* him, let alone friends with him, that put her on the same level as him, too.

At lunch that same Monday, when he was asked a total of four times by some leery younger students whether Tayshia let him hold a gun to her head, Ash had to leave the cafeteria before he beat the fuck out of a bunch of fifteen-year-olds.

"No, we didn't *fuck*, if that's what you're asking," he hissed to Andre, glaring at him. "Yeah, we've hooked up, but we just messed around. It wasn't like I *knew* it was gonna happen."

"How do you hook up with someone without *knowing* you're gonna hook up with them?!"

"I don't know! You just do. It just happened."

Andre stared at him for a long moment before something shifted in his eyes like the changing wind. A wicked smirk spread across his lips again.

"What did O'Connell say?"

"Nothing," Ash said. "But you can see for yourself what he thinks. Look over there."

Kieran was sitting at a table near the doors, flanked by a couple of other football players and some cheerleaders. No one sat across from them. All of them were glowering in Ash and Andre's general direction. The way they were stabbing their food with the tines of their forks was every bit as threatening as the flames of pure rage that burned in their eyes.

"Shit, we're gonna have to watch your back for a bit," Andre said, turning back around with his eyebrows up. "Because that's... Well, that's something."

Ash wasn't the least bit nervous. They were the equivalent of dust mites floating in the air on a sunny day. He wasn't worried about them. They were more frightened of breaking the rules than he was. The chance that they all attacked him was next to none.

If they came for him, however, he'd handle it.

"If they jump you, don't worry," Andre said, flashing him a grin before he took a large bite of his muffin. "I got your back."

Ash returned his smile with a lopsided one of his own and they resumed eating.

"So, what's up with Elijah?" Andre asked around a mouthful. "You two got beef?"

Ash slowed the pace of his own chewing, his frown returning. He was surprised that whatever was happening between the two of them was noticeable to people who weren't aware of it.

"I'm not sure," he said on a rush of exhaled breath. "He's just not seeing eye-to-eye with me lately."

"Mm," Andre said, nodding slowly. He gave Ash a worried look. "Do you think that maybe the rumors about you and Tayshia got to him a little?"

Ash was silent for a moment as he thought about it. Yes, he supposed it was entirely possible that Elijah was upset at that. With the tension that had existed between them since Tayshia's birthday, he wasn't sure if the issue was because Elijah saw him as a bad guy, or if he liked her.

His throat went dry, the edges rubbing together like sandpaper.

What if Elijah already kissed her before Ash ever did?

"Well," Andre said, "you know he said something to me, right?"

Ash's heart fluttered in his chest, nearly to a stop. His gaze snapped to Andre's, icy and alert.

"What?"

"Yeah. It was last week. Um, no — maybe it was the week before?" Andre shook his head out. "Never mind. It don't matter when it was. Or maybe it does. Okay, basically, I was in the library and I saw Elijah and Tayshia studying together after lunch. I was in there looking for something for an essay, and it looked like they'd been in there a while and weren't leaving. So, shit, I went to sit with them and talk stories. They got along. Like, it was clear they were like, friends, you know, but there was something about the way he looked at her that got me thinking."

As Andre spoke, Ash felt a well of dark emotion starting to grow in his stomach. He'd experienced it multiple times over the course of the year, but it wasn't anything he'd felt envelop him quite like it was doing now. It was like a cavern of molten lava inside of him, starting to boil. Fire licked its way up to his chest.

Andre continued, "Well, she got up to get a different book—fuck, this was... I'm pretty sure this was last Tuesday, now that I think about it. Because they were working on an essay for Sociology, and when I asked them about it, she launched into a tirade against doctors."

Ash set his fork down as though it were going to explode if he moved too fast. In a calm, quiet voice, he said, "What happened after she got up and left?"

"She was gone for like, two minutes. So real quick, I asked Elijah. I said, '*Elijah, what the Hell is going on with you two?*' You know what I mean? I mean, the way he was looking at her, and he had his *hand* on the back of her *chair*. He kept moving her hair out her damn face, cuz. I mean... I was starting to get confused. You know what I—"

"*Andre,*" Ash growled, one anxious hand carding through his hair underneath his hood and tangling there. "*Out with it.*"

"Yeah, yeah. Sorry. I asked Elijah if they were hooking up. He said they weren't but that he's interested in her. So, I asked him if he'd fucked her or something. He said not yet. *Not yet,* dude. But he said that she trusts him more than anyone else, and that he's the only person that she's told things to that she's never even told her parents."

Not yet.

Not yet?

That meant that not only had Ash been right in his suspicion that Elijah liked her, but he'd also been right to feel uncomfortable with the idea. *Not yet* implied that Elijah had intent to fuck her. He *wanted* to fuck her. He had a *plan* to fuck her.

And he had every intention of carrying it out.

In Andre's eyes, recognition dawned like a slow sunrise.

"Oh," he said.

"Oh?"

"Judging by the way you're grinding your teeth and trying to set a fire with your eyes, I'd say you're jealous."

"No, I'm not." Ash bristled. "Just tell me what—"

"Yes, you are. You're jealous."

"No, I—"

"And that's *okay*." Andre held his gaze. "Don't give a fuck what anyone else says—it's okay. Better to focus on the fact that someone else wants her than to focus on keeping yourself and everyone else from knowing you want her, too."

Someone else wants her.

Someone better. Someone safer, who didn't make all the wrong choices. Someone who had a plan to win her over because they knew what they wanted and they were gonna stick to it. Someone who could offer her stability, safety, and the confidence to know he was going to go after what he wanted.

Elijah and Tayshia, holding hands in the halls. Elijah and Tayshia, curling up beside a warm fire. Elijah taking Tayshia to Gianni's. Elijah pushing Tayshia up against the wall to kiss her, to kiss her on the spot beneath her ear that made her cry out, to kiss down the side of her neck the way she liked. Elijah tearing Tayshia's clothes off and sinking into her—

No. We're connected. It's real because I can feel *it.*

That wasn't right because—

She's mine.

It didn't make sense because—

Mine.

That couldn't work *because*—

Tayshia was his.

"Bruh." Andre's voice broke into his turbulent, scorching-hot thoughts. "You good?"

"Did he say what the secret was? Whatever it was that she couldn't tell her parents?"

Andre blinked, taken aback by Ash's sudden vehemence. "No, he didn't. He only said it was something no one else knew."

"Well, pretty soon," Ash bit out through clenched teeth, glaring at Tayshia's distant face, "someone else is going to know it, too."

"Who?"

"Me."

CHAPTER FIFTEEN

"I wanna go back to the bookstore today."

Ash tore his zoned-out gaze off of the TV. He was blazed out of his fucking *mind*.

Tayshia stood behind the far side of the sectional, wearing naught but leggings and an oversized cream knit. Her curls were loose about her shoulders and down her back.

The crystal was not around her neck.

Ash stared at the place where it was supposed to be, a slight delay in his thoughts. Realization crested the top of the wave and slowly settled onto the shore of his psyche. It was the reason, the reason why he hadn't seen her dreams for two weeks. The reason why she hadn't been in his.

She didn't want to see him.

"What happened to *hello*?" he drawled. "Huh? What happened to that?"

Tayshia rolled her eyes. "I said, I wanna go out today and go back to the bookstore. I want to see if maybe she got the book we ordered in, and then I wanna see if we can find a book."

"What?" he said, stifling a laugh as he let his head fall onto the back of the couch. It was Black Friday and he'd been up for an hour after a mid-afternoon nap. He'd immediately smoked and now, he was high as fuck. "You might as well tell me you wanna find *one* loose curl from quadrant four on your scalp. This is *you* we're talking about."

"No, headass. I mean a book that I looked up online. It's about dreams and their meanings. As for the constellation book, I'm just hoping since it's Black Friday today, that she got it in early, and maybe we could pick it up."

"All right," he said with a sigh, rising to his feet. "You wanna drive or walk?"

"It's not raining today, so let's walk. I was too tired to work out today."

Ash cast her a glance as he moved past her to get his coat and shoes out of his room.

Before they left, he stopped her, his hand closing over hers on the doorknob of the front door. She sucked in her breath, but he spoke before she could.

"Where's your necklace?"

She stiffened, her back against his chest. "I took it off."

"Why?"

"Because I needed a break."

All he could think about was Elijah. How he'd said he'd already made a move. Had she taken it off because of him?

"I'm sorry for what I did," he said, his gaze fixated on the floor. His fingers flexed, tightening. "For pressuring you and going too far. Please put it back on for me."

Tayshia was silent for a while. Then, she relaxed.

"Fine," she said. "For now."

He moved aside so she could walk back to her room. When she came back out, the crystal shining against the front of her sweater, he was happy.

It was like she was his again.

After a silent car ride where Tayshia was texting the entire time, they walked across the shopping center together. Ash's thoughts were eclipsed by the things he'd learned from Andre a couple of days back.

He didn't want to imagine anyone's hands all over Tayshia's body. Tayshia wasn't someone who could be scoped out and hooked up with like normal—not with what had happened to her.

Even if Tayshia had told him about Paris, Elijah would never know what it felt like for her. Ash was the only one who knew that. It was the one thing they shared that no one could take away from him.

He slung his arm around her neck. The eight-inch difference in their heights was perfect for it to look careless yet intentional.

"Ash," she said, sounding angry. "What are you doing?"

"Nothing," he said, glancing down at her through his lashes.

Tayshia scowled and reached up to shove his arm off of her. He flexed his muscles a bit, keeping her from being able to do so.

"Did our massive fight in the alley earlier this month not spell it out for you? We're just friends, Ash."

"What, your friends don't put their arms around you?"

"No," she said, tone icy. "Well... They do. But none of them completely disregard respect for me. None of them ignore my vibes and get in my business."

"I told you I was sorry."

"I don't forgive you. And what about it, bitch? What are you gonna do?"

He pulled her closer and leaned down to whisper into her ear.

"Kiss you until you do."

A shiver ran through her body, one that Ash felt against his side. She spun out of his hold, moving away from him. When she glared at him again, it pinned his heart in place mid-beat.

"If you try to kiss me again, I'll get my nails done *specifically* so I can slice your chest open."

Ash opened his mouth to retort, but she was already walking into the crowded shopping center. He sighed and dropped his head back in frustration. This was a nightmare. She hadn't been wearing the crystal, she was studying with Elijah, she was barely interacting with him at home except when they cleaned... What if she didn't want to kiss him because she wanted to be with Elijah?

Had Ash pushed her so hard she didn't want him anymore?

When he entered the shockingly-empty bookstore, he saw someone with short pink hair at the register talking to Tayshia. The two were smiling, talking in amiable tones, so Ash lingered back. He didn't have the energy to deal with seeing the light of good nature leaving the employee's eyes if they recognized him as the kid from the news. He was still waiting for the other shoe to drop with Nurse Pritchard's sudden and unbelievably fake change in personality.

Tayshia walked over to him.

"That worker said the woman we talked to is the manager, who isn't here for the night shift. But they said that the book isn't in yet. I told them we were doing a project on the caverns, crystals, and dreams, though, and they told me which sections to look in. Man, I liked their hair color though. I think I might try a pink sew-in at Christmas."

"Pink is my favorite color," Ash blurted out, and then he felt blood rising to his cheeks. "And blue, too. But I really like pink for some reason."

"Really?" Tayshia studied him. "I think that's cool. Mine's lavender."

"I know."

Fuck.

Would she connect the stars of the skies in his dreams?

Tayshia watched him for a second longer, then wandered away. Ash stood there to recollect his paranoid thoughts, struggling to calm his breath. He followed her, carefully weaving his way through other shelves to cut off her path. When he reached her, she had to slap a hand over her mouth to keep from crying out in alarm.

"You terrified me!" she whispered, smacking him on the arm with a book.

"My bad," he said with a lazy grin. He snatched the book away from her and looked at the title. "*Dreams and Their Meanings.* Seems pretty on-the-nose."

"I know," she said, trying to grab it. He held it out of her way, forcing her to jump up to try and get it back. "Ash, knock it off!"

"Aren't you gonna check the other sections they told you about?"

"No," she said, voice strained as she leapt again. "I feel like — *give it back* — we should just wait on the — *Ash* — constellation book."

Ash laughed as he danced back away from her, still dangling the book high above. "How do you know this book we're waiting on is even worth it?"

"I don't." She caught her breath, one hand over her heart and the other on her hip. "I literally hate you. I despise you right now."

"Jesus, it's not like you just ran a mile, Wheezy. Here." He held the book out to her with a gesture of nonchalance. "But fine, we'll read this book, and then we'll go eat."

"I'm not hungry," she said. "But I'll watch you eat."

"But what will you — wait. Where are you going?"

"There's little alcoves in this store where we can read at enclosed tables, so I'm gonna head over there. It's emptier in here tonight than I thought, but I just wanna sit down."

He followed after her until they found an alcove that was secluded enough. It had a table with two chairs and books on the shelves behind it. It was towards the left side of the large store, far away from the register and doors. The few customers that were in the store were on the other side, wandering the children's and teen's sections.

They were alone.

Tayshia sat down in the left-hand chair, taking off her coat. After placing it over the back of the chair, she opened the book. Ash pulled his coat off and tossed it onto the table. He pulled the hood of his black pullover onto his head, pushed his sleeves up to his elbows, and sat down in the chair beside hers. She stared at him with her upper lip curled.

"What're you looking at?" he said, eyes half-shut. His head swam with a pleasant buzzing.

"You're wearing a hood," she said with a perturbed expression. "It's so extra."

"Oh, my God. Whatever." His eyelids fluttered as he rolled his eyes. "It's not that weird."

"Yes, it is. We're inside. It didn't even rain today."

"Get over it. What're you gonna do? Rip it off my head?"

"I might."

He grinned. "Then come here."

"Leave me alone, freak of nature," Tayshia said, cracking open the book. She scanned the Table of Contents. "I'm reading."

Ash sat in silence while she turned pages, sliding down so far in his seat that if he'd done it in church as a kid, his mother would have smacked the back of his head for poor posture. Legs outstretched, hood on, tattooed arms crossed. He couldn't help but feel a laugh spinning in his chest.

"Okay, I think..." Tayshia said, and then she stopped herself. She held up one finger, eyes still scanning the pages. "I think I've got something interesting."

"Oh, yeah?" He leaned forward, placing his elbows on the table and cracking his right-hand knuckles absentmindedly with his left hand. Her scent was faint but he was so close to her that he could smell her perfume. "Whacha got?"

"This book says something interesting about dreams," she said, turning the page. "Most people dream a lot at night, but they can't remember them. It's like, a series of images flashing that are forgotten when they wake up. But it says that if the dream you're having is a memory of something, then it's related to how we process our emotions about it. However, if you're having a dream that keeps coming back, it can be related to your real life, whether it's a memory or not."

They exchanged glances.

"So a recurring dream," Ash said, thinking both of his dream world and her memory, "can be covering up something about the way you feel?"

"I think so," she said, pushing her curls behind her ears with one hand so the book didn't fall shut. She turned a few more pages, skimming the passages. "Ah! Right here, this section talks about how recurring dreams are like messages from your subconscious. How if you find yourself having the same dream over and over again, it's usually trying to tell you something about yourself or the world around you. It can be a dream or a nightmare but in either case, it's you wanting yourself to know something."

Ash nodded, giving her a slow blink through the hair that fell into his eyes. He was barely following along. Listening to her talk while high was a feat in and of itself. She was so pretty, he just kept staring at the wideness of her nose.

It was the cutest nose he'd ever seen.

Tayshia sighed, pulling her curls to one side of her head. "I don't know how it applies to us, though. Like for your dreams, it's a place you go to. A place we can change by simply closing our eyes and wishing. But mine are... Different. I dream but you can't get in. You only see my memories."

Fuck, she had the longest, most slender neck. He hadn't left bruises on it yet. Perhaps he should, if she ever let him kiss her again.

What would Elijah think of that?

"So, if all I can do is replay memories about my life, then what is it that *I'm* trying to tell *me*? It doesn't make any sense."

Ash looked over at her, frowning. He didn't know how to respond to that. He didn't know how to help her.

"Anyway," she said with a sigh, "this book seems like it's more focused on dreams themselves. Not that I thought we'd find a book called *Dreamwalking,* or anything. I mean, we know that it's the crystals that are making this happen. We know the hot springs have something to do with it. We know the stars are involved, and possibly the constellation Centaurus. There's things we do know. Maybe the nature of the dreams have nothing to do with any of this. Maybe it's something we can't read about—something that we have to figure out ourselves."

"Maybe," he said softly, "it's not about how often you dream, but what specifically you're dreaming about."

He saw the pulse in her throat jump. "Yeah, maybe."

"And maybe we have to face some things before we can hear the message."

She gazed at the table.

Ash rested his temple against his fist. He was so high he was floating in that limbic space between tired and way too energetic. "I think whatever your subconscious is trying to tell you, you'll find out eventually."

"What if we *are* soulmates?" The words came out of nowhere, shocking Ash into lifting his gaze to meet hers. She looked frightened. Nervous. "What if it's all real and you and I were always meant to... To wander eternity looking for each other? What if it's really this coincidental that we ended up at the same school, the same state, the same town? What if you're mine... And I'm yours?"

Ash knew a little bit about stars. He knew how they formed, how they lived, and how they died. He knew that they existed in the frozen, black expanse that pervaded the entire universe, consisting of fire and flame. They would burn for all of eternity, until there was nothing left to fuel them.

He wasn't too out of his mind to understand that whatever connected him to Tayshia was as old and as eternal as the stars that joined together to form the constellations.

Eternity was an awfully long time.

Silence stretched between them like worn, thin linen.

"What do you want the answer to be?" Ash asked, scratching his head before returning to rest his temple against his fist again. "If we research this—if we dive in and find an answer that we can accept as valid—then what do you want it to be?"

Tayshia chewed on her lower lip for a moment, propping her chin in her hand while she thought. The more time passed, the more her facial expression changed. She grew less relaxed, more fidgety. She worried her lip between her teeth, shifting in her seat.

"Come on," he said with a sigh. "We have to be as honest as possible. Otherwise, we're not gonna be able to figure this out. Even if this shit is real, it doesn't mean we're gonna get *married*."

"I don't know," she mumbled, her words as quick as flitting sparrows. "It scares me, the way I feel sometimes. I'm used to using anger to deal with everything. It's quick, easy. But what I feel for you isn't quick or easy or simple."

Conflicted emotions arose within him. Part of him wanted to

reach for her immediately. Another part — the part that was dripping with shame — didn't want to trap her in any alleyways or bathrooms ever again.

"Okay," Ash said, moving to rest his cheek against his fist instead. "So, what you feel is intense?"

"Yes."

He laughed a little. "I'm not the worst person you could be connected to. It could be Kieran."

She wrinkled her nose. Her hands rested in her lap, where he saw her toying with her acrylics. They sparkled light purple and black.

"I *am* terrified. It's overwhelming. A lot of things are overwhelming for me. Because we're being honest — " Her voice was thick, snagged on a deep sadness. " — I struggle with feeling like I deserve certain things. And after what happened to me in August, I was never able to like, *do* anything with Kieran. For some reason, you were the first person I — that I *wanted* to let touch me. At least, for a little while. I felt safe with you, and I didn't know why."

Her words sunk into the ink of his subconscious, jolting him forward through the weed haze. He laughed, incredulous and confused.

"Wait... What? Like, *what*?"

Tayshia's mouth tilted down at the corners. "I said that I felt safe with you when we hooked up those few times, and that I never felt that way with Kieran. Even before August, I was never comfortable touching him, even when we hooked up. But with you, I was."

He rubbed his right eye with the heel of his palm, still laughing. It was absurd. It sounded like she was trying to lead the conversation down a dangerous path. But he was so high that he wasn't able to register how deep she was attempting to go.

"What's wrong with you?" she said.

"What?" He dragged his eyes up to meet hers. "Nothing."

"Yes, there is. There's something wrong with you."

"There's literally nothing." He breathed another laugh. "Fuck, you're perceptive."

She narrowed her eyes, studying him like a puzzle. Her gaze flitted about his face, moving the pieces around until the picture was clear.

"Ash, are you *high*?"

"No." He felt his stomach flopping with a sudden burst of nerves.

"Yes, you are," she said, and then she gestured to her throat. "Your voice is... It's different. It's rougher and scratchier. Hoarser than normal."

"What are you even *talking* about?"

She gave him a searing glare and hissed, "What is it? What did you take? Did you smoke it or is it something else?"

"What the fuck?" he said through a burst of laughter that rolled through his belly. "What the *fuck*, dude?!"

"Stop making fun of me!" She leapt to her feet, causing him to laugh harder. "I need to make sure you're okay! You aren't normally this weird when you're high!"

"Jesus, fuck!" He shook his head, unable to stop laughing. "No, no—shh. It's not a big deal!"

"What did you take?"

"It's just weed!" he cried, laughter attacking him like a full-frontal war assault. He held up his hands, reaching for the fabric of her sweater to try to pull her back down. "No, seriously—it's *just* weed. I smoked before we left. Andre always gets me the good shit."

"Oh." The color of her rage faded from her face, leaving suspicion in its wake. "Just weed?"

"Yes. Now, quit acting like a mother hen and sit down. Fuck." He tugged on the hem of her sweater and she stumbled, collapsing back into her seat. "And stop pouting."

"I know it's legal, but I'm pretty sure you're not allowed to smoke outside of your house."

"First of all, that is not true. Second, since when are the words *not* and *allowed* ever in the same sentence for me? Whose vocabulary do you think I live by?"

"Clearly, your own," she muttered, looking down at the book again. "You act like a child."

"No, I don't," he said, tsking. "I'm twenty. I act twenty."

"Yes, a twenty-year-old boy. A child."

"That makes you a child, too. You're twenty."

"Barely."

"I'm older than you, so don't run your mouth."

"Stop snipping at me, Ash."

"No."

"I mean it!" Her head whipped in his direction with a glare that would have unsettled anyone who wasn't him.

Ash merely smirked and kept looking at her from beneath eyes that were almost completely closed. "No."

Tayshia scowled and said nothing more, returning to her reading. Ash watched her for a minute, wondering to himself the only thing his mind seemed clear enough to worry about.

Did she go up on tip-toe when she kissed Elijah, too?

His mood darkened for a moment and something stirred within him. Something dark and viscous that felt like it seared his skin from the inside out. Something possessive.

"Tayshia."

Like lightning, her gaze snapped to meet his. "What do you want?"

"You pay attention to my *voice*?"

He saw her shoulders jump as though he'd scared her. She turned a page in the book rather quick, nearly tearing it. He saw her cheeks reddening again, the expression on her face one of indifference. She didn't say anything.

But her hands trembled.

That dark, possessive thing inside of him curled and uncurled, reaching for her. Calling to her. It twisted low in his abdomen, alive and dying all at once.

He didn't care if Elijah wanted her.

She was his.

Ash reached out with his free hand and slid it behind Tayshia's back, his fingers tickling her spine. She went stiff as he grabbed her right hip and dragged her to the edge of her chair. The side of her left leg pressed against the side of his right. If he were to move, she might topple over.

"What're you—"

"Tell me," he murmured, his hand sliding up to her waist. He felt it through the thick knit of her sweater. "You like my voice? Is that it?"

Tayshia turned her head to look at him. She was so close he could see the flecks of brown smattered amongst the lighter hazel of her irises. She started to speak, but it was choked off by a small laugh. A laugh of nervousness, of incredulity. Of trepidation.

The demon in Ash devoured it.

"When do you like it best?" he murmured, his thumb twitching, pressing into her back. "When I'm here, talking to you like this?"

The golden light of the store cast shadows across Tayshia's face.

Her words were trapped in her throat behind a cage that he wanted to unlock.

Ash's hand moved again, smoothing down to her hip. He pulled—fought the urge to yank—and she gasped. She lifted from the chair with ease, falling into his lap with her hands flat against his chest. Her cloudlike curls filled the lower half of his face, soft as satin as he inhaled the scent of her conditioner. Something floral, he noted. She shifted, perhaps to try and get more comfortable, what with her sitting astride his thighs the way she was. It brought her ear right to his mouth, which tipped up into half of a smirk.

"Or do you like it best when I'm whispering sweet things into your ear?"

He ended the sentence with a nip of his teeth to her earlobe. Her back arched and a shudder rolled through her body like an ocean wave. Her finger wrapped around the right drawstring of his hoodie, twisting it around and around like it felt good to do so. Like the repetitive motions distracted her or kept her grounded.

Ash lifted his right hand and used it to brush her hair back. He swept the curls behind her ear little-by-little, until he had a perfect view of the left side of her throat. The pads of his fingers brushed along the backside of her earlobe, a barely-there touch, and he saw her eyelids flutter. Her head tilted ever-so-slightly to the right, away from him. Like she was trying to encourage him without saying it.

Like she was too scared to ruin the moment, lest she panic and change her mind.

"Maybe it's not *how* I say things," he said, his gaze swallowing the sight of her pounding pulse leaping towards him. His fingers delved deep into her curls and clenched tight enough to make his desire known. Tight enough for her to know how he felt. "Maybe it's *what* I say."

He leaned forward, his lips moving slow and sure to meet the sharp line of her jaw. As he began to kiss down to that fluttering pulse point, his left hand found its way to her outer thigh, pulling her closer.

By the time his tongue was darting out to lap at her trembling skin, she was limp in his arms and sighing. Her chest heaved. Her fingers were clenched around both drawstrings. Her thighs were pressing against one another like disrupted parts of the Earth's surface.

Neither of them seemed to care that they were in a public

bookstore, tucked away in an alcove that wouldn't be hidden to anyone if they simply walked by.

That dark, possessive thing inside of him forced a gasp of his own from his throat. It intensified his kiss, turning it from gentle to sensual, tentative to scorching. His teeth scraped, biting as though he wanted to taste her blood, and his tongue swept over the indentations in her skin to soothe the sting.

She let out a soft, strangled cry.

Ash felt whatever walls were holding him upright come crashing down at the erotic noise. His mind went as dark as the pit of his stomach. He gripped her curls as tight as he could without hurting her. He kissed his way back up to her ear, his other hand cupping the untouched side of her throat.

"Is that it?" he growled into her ear, causing her to lean closer to him and her shoulder to lift as though it tickled. "You like the things I say to you? You like it when I tell you how soft you are, how sweet you sound?"

"*Ash*," she gasped, her head falling back. She sounded dazed. Shocked. As though what he was saying was every bit as scandalous as it was. As though she wanted to hear more of it. "You're—it's— that's too much."

He gave the skin beneath her earlobe a lewd, targeted lick and she moaned so loud that he slammed his hand over her mouth. It stifled her cry and made him want to groan.

Ash's mind reeled with how high the heat of his body had risen. All of the blood in his veins was flowing South, hurtling to where he could feel her bottom nestled in his lap.

His hand slid down to her jaw, turning her face toward his. He kissed every bit of skin on her throat that he could get to and then his lips brushed hers. They shared each other's breath.

Her eyes were as bright as stars.

"How would you like it if I told you that you were mine?" His nose nuzzled hers. "Huh? How would you like it if I told you that's the answer we're going to find? That you're mine to kiss, to hold, to touch, to fuck?"

Something broke in her eyes, something that made his heart wrench into a tiny knot in his chest. It coiled so tight that it hurt him. Behind those broken pieces, he saw her imagining it. Tasting it. Thinking of what it would be like to give in and accept it.

"Would you hurt me?" Tayshia whispered, her voice trembling the way it always did before she cried. "Would you hurt me, like they did?"

He didn't want to think about it, but he knew that's all she got to do was think about it. It was in her dreams and in her nightmares and in her thoughts. That pain was woven amongst every part of her life. There was no reprieve from it.

"Fuck. No, Tayshia. Never."

The last broken piece disintegrated.

Tayshia wrapped one arm around his neck, placed her hand on his cheek, and slanted her lips over his. She kissed him with fervent need, her lips moving against his with desperation that he knew mirrored his own. She curled inward toward him as though she were trying to make herself as small as possible on his lap.

All he needed to do was grab her thighs and lift her, turn her and pull her close. Their hips would slot together, a perfect fit. Because that's the one thing that their dreams had been trying to tell them — the connection that they'd had all along. Two halves of the same whole. She was perfect for him, and she would fill all of his empty spaces.

He wanted her so badly.

Tayshia's tongue slipped into his mouth, pressing past the seam of his lips with a determination he hadn't thought she possessed. It coaxed his own tongue up to greet hers, where they caressed each other like meeting for the first time after millennia.

It made Ash moan, a bolt of desire reverberating from his loins.

His hands moved along the outside of her sweater, up her back, along her shoulders, and up to cup the sides of her face. Ash tilted his head to the side and kissed her back with all of the need he felt in his body. Every time their lips parted, he heard her whimper like she needed this kiss more than he did. Like *she* was the one consuming *him*.

He would let her devour him.

Ash felt her fingers slide into his hair, fingernails scraping along his scalp. It was good — so good. Everything about her was good. His eyes rolled behind his closed eyelids. His voice was breathy, high-pitched.

"Did you like that?" Tayshia whispered against his mouth, and then she scratched wide circles on both sides of his scalp.

"Yes," Ash said, his head falling back. "*Fuck* yes."

"And this?"

He felt her rock her hips without stopping the gentle scraping of her nails. With her sitting sideways on him, the sensation going from left to right instead of back to front was enough to drag another sound out of him. A sound akin to a quiet keening noise that he knew he'd never made before with anyone else. His fingers shifted up into her curls, twisting them around his hand as he fought the urge to buck his hips upward.

She dipped her head down and ran her tongue along the chains tattooed at the base of his neck. Just licked them, like he was made of sugar. From one side to the other.

Stars burst behind his eyelids.

"God *fucking* damn it," he whined, the words pinned down beneath his breath as he battled every fiber in his being that wanted him to grind up into her. His fingers twitched in her hair and on her thigh. "Shit – I – *Please*. Fuck. *Fuck*."

He didn't want to hurt her or scare her. If she wanted the control, he would give it to her. But sweet fuck, he was as hard as a rock. She kissed his lips again, her mouth open as he moaned into it. He tugged on her hair, pulling her closer, increasing the pressure. His toes curled in his shoes. He wanted her so bad. So, so bad.

She jerked backward, a small sound of confusion coming out. His eyes snapped open as worry bled through his lust and he lifted his head.

"Sorry," she said, closing her eyes. She shook her head a bit and then pulled her hand from his hair, holding it to her temple. "I'm sorry. I just... I haven't eaten since breakfast. I got dizzy."

That was a lie. He had woken to no dishes in the sink.

"You haven't eaten all day." Ash's hands went to her hips. He placed her back in her own seat. The blood in his pelvis began to return to the rest of his body at the alarming news. "Why are you lying?"

She gave him a sharp look, looking windswept by the tousled state of her curls and the swelling in her lips. "Why are you keeping track of what I eat?"

"I'm not." His heart dropped a bit, and he twisted the truth. "I just happened to notice today."

"Well, it's none of your business what I'm eating."

"It *is* my business," he said, raising his eyebrows in silent challenge. "If you die, I'm the one who has to find you. We live together."

For a split second, she looked enraged. Angrier than he'd ever thought her capable of being. She clenched her hands into fists on her lap, appearing as though she were about to blow up on him. Almost like she were going to throw a tantrum.

He leaned back in his seat, taken aback at the level of ire he saw there on her face.

Then, it faded.

"You're being dramatic," she said. "I was busy today and I missed lunch. I just need to eat a snack. Come on."

Before he could say anything else, she got up and walked out of the alcove.

CHAPTER SIXTEEN

Ash was too agitated to sleep.

After feeling Tayshia's lips against his own and her hips rolling in his lap, he wasn't sure how he was going to be able to sleep at all for the rest of forever. He didn't think he'd ever wanted another human being as badly as he wanted her, and he knew he never would again.

Once they got done at the bookstore, they'd gone to a fast food restaurant in the shopping center across the street. They'd eaten burgers while Tayshia looked at her food like it tasted bad.

Ash looked at her.

When they walked back to the car, he kept his distance from her. He wanted to touch her. To put his arm around her. To take her by the hand.

To kiss her.

Now, they were home, watching *anime* in the living room. He wasn't high anymore and after the way their Black Friday bookstore outing had gone, he was tempted to smoke again. But that was a bit difficult with Tayshia sitting on the floor with her back against his legs.

Ash had changed into what he always wore to bed, choosing a random blue tee shirt. Tayshia had changed into an oversized tee shirt that fell to mid-thigh and a pair of fuzzy socks. Her legs were bare and her curly hair was pulled up into two buns once again.

She sat on the floor with her knees pulled up to her chest while her hand sifted through a package of cheesy puffs. The weight of her leaning against his calves was welcome, something he knew he could get used to.

He'd asked her what she was eating. She'd said they were her current favorite and explained in an irritable voice how her favorite foods rotated every few weeks. When he'd laughed and asked her what that even meant, she'd said, *I don't really eat when I'm hungry. I eat what I'm craving.*

"When do you want to do the tree?" he asked. "You said you loved Christmas, so I bet you're one of those early decorators."

"I don't know," she said with a shrug. "Next week? Or the 1st?"

"Fine with me. What exactly are you doing for Christmas?"

Tayshia snorted and chomped on a puff loudly. Her hand dove back into the bag before she'd even finished chewing. "I told you."

"I know. I want details."

She scowled as she licked orange dust off of her fingers and then grabbed more. "My family is friends with Kieran's. We spend every Christmas together and have for years. Just because we broke up doesn't mean the families did. My parents made it clear that Christmas is going to be *exactly* the same as it's always been."

"That's lame," Ash said, pulling a face as he stared at the colorful characters on the television screen. "Don't they care what you want at all?"

"No." *Chomp. Chomp. Chomp.* "My parents don't understand anything that seems like it's not *of* God. Like I told you before — they think Kieran and I are meant to be married. So do his parents. They're gonna push us on each other."

"I know he's got a sister," Ash said, being careful with his words. He only knew about Rory because of Tayshia's memory. "Do you have any siblings?"

"Yes." *Chomp. Chomp.* Pause. *Chomp.* "I have three sisters. Naveah, Imani, and Shay."

"Oh, yeah?"

"Yep. All younger. Naveah is five. She just started kindergarten this year but I heard she wasn't doing well. My mom said she screams every time they drop her off because she's so attached to her. Shay's nine and for some God-awful reason, my parents decided to give her a phone. You should see the ridiculous text messages she sends me."

She went silent. Ash waited until it seemed like she really wasn't going to say anything else, and then he spoke.

"Wasn't there one more?" He yawned and reached up, bending his elbows to tangle his fingers in his hair. "Imani?"

Chomp. Chomp. Chomp. Chomp. Chomp. Chomp.

"Yo." He jostled his leg to nudge her. "You hear me?"

"Yes. She passed away."

"I'm so sorry," he said, his voice gentle.

"She was two, and she got sick," she said. "She was really sweet. And quiet, too. I was thirteen, so it was before I ever came to Christ Rising."

"I know how it feels," Ash said. "Trust me. And I mean it when I say I'm sorry."

Tayshia ducked her head down, saying nothing as she stuffed a large handful of puffs into her mouth. Her cheeks filled to the brim — so full that it took her a bit longer to chew and swallow them all.

Her hand was in the bag immediately after.

Ash sensed that she needed some peace and quiet, so he went back to watching the show. They hadn't turned any lights on, so the only illumination came from the flickering of the *anime*, and a light rain had started outside. He could hear it like a steady droning as it came down. The steady *chomp, chomp, chomp* of Tayshia's eating began to fade in with all the other background noise.

The subtitles on the screen blurred.

Sometimes, Ash was so wrapped up in his own loss that he forgot he wasn't the only one who could possibly know what it was like to have a hole in his heart that would never be filled.

After ten minutes or so, Tayshia cleared her throat.

"I'm off to the bathroom," she said.

Ash watched her go, heard the door click shut, and then he looked at the coffee table with an absentminded gaze. She'd left the bag there. Since she had been eating them so heartily, he was sure they had to be delicious. He leaned forward and grabbed the bag.

It was empty.

Fuck, she ate those fast.

He sighed, stood up, and went to throw the bag in the trash. It never failed to surprise him when his mother had eaten entire packages of food after first opening them. Ash had always been the type to graze, eating small meals whenever he was hungry, so eating an entire bag of chips in one sitting would be unlikely for him. But for his mother, she could eat them in five minutes flat and then go to the —

Wait.

Ash looked down the hall, a deep frown on his face. His heart began to beat faster as once again, reality slammed into him like a stray lightning bolt. Because all the facts were staring him down, waiting for him to put them together.

The alternating eating habits.

The frequent trips to the bathroom.

The buffet.

The swooning spells.

The irritability and borderline temper tantrums.

The baggy clothing she always wore.

The counting he heard her doing when she worked out.

The fact that the cheese puffs weren't the first thing she'd eaten when they got back to the apartment—they were the third. She'd eaten a meal from the refrigerator and a package of chocolates she'd fished from her bedroom.

He remembered the orange flecks under the rim of the toilet.

Orange flecks. Cheese puffs.

"I eat what I'm craving."

He sat on the couch and stared at the TV, his heart racing a million miles per hour as he fought with his panic and lingering anxiety. Thirty minutes later, the bathroom door came open again. Slowly, he leaned forward to place his forearms on his thighs and lace his fingers together. Then, he turned his head to look in the direction of the hallway.

Tayshia padded into the room, wearing only the giant tee shirt. Her curly hair was damp, hanging in wet strips to her elbows that dripped onto the floor. It was clear she'd showered. With her eyes half-shut like that, she looked like she'd never felt more tired. She swayed slightly on her feet.

The crystal was still around her neck.

"Tayshia," he said, stretching her name out. "Are you okay?"

She hung her head, wringing her hands beneath her chest. Her shoulders rose, like she was more uncomfortable than she'd ever been before. He sat up straight, watching her chin quiver and her brows come together on her forehead. She stood before him, carrying herself like she was falling apart, crumbling like a wall made of clay.

His heart squeezed in a vice.

"Come here," he said, the words simple and necessary as he held one hand out. "Come to me."

Tayshia crumpled, dissolving into uncontrollable sobs. Shrinking in on herself, she climbed into his lap, immediately soaking his shirt with the shower water. She curled up there, resting her head against his chest and his shoulder.

And she wept.

His eyes swept her body—her bare arms and legs—and he saw her for the first time. Saw her for the person she used to be. Saw what the ignorance of her friends and family had wrought.

Saw the results of the harm she'd been doing to herself.

Ash knew why she was crying. He knew and even though he didn't want it to be true, he was glad he was the one who did. He was the only person who could possibly understand. The only person who could help her.

The only person who could fix it.

Ash's arm wrapped around her shoulders to show her that he wasn't going to let her fall. His other hand sifted through her curls, getting tangled, and his thumb wiped her tears away in spite of the futility.

"Shh," he murmured, pressing a kiss to the top of her head. "You're okay."

"I'm not," she sobbed. "I'm not okay."

He tightened his hold on her. "But you're strong. You're the strongest person I know."

"Stop."

"No," he whispered, his thumb slick with her tears. "I need you to know that you're not alone."

"*Stop.*" Her weeping began anew, wracking her body and causing her to pull her legs up closer to him. She burrowed her face into his chest. "Please stop. Please, please."

"*No*," he said and he used her hair to tilt her face upward. He looked down, directly into her eyes as they overflowed. "I need you to listen to me, Tayshia."

She started to close her eyes. Ash tugged on her curls to get her to open them again.

"I'm here," he said. "Not Kieran. Not the man in Paris. Me."

"No," she said, choking on her sobs. "I don't want you here. I don't want anyone—"

"I don't care. I'm here."

Silence like a star nearing nova.

"Ash, I need you."

And when she looked up again, lifting her eyes and her sorrows to him, he gathered her closer and kissed her.

Their lips fell together like the covers of a book closing, his tongue pressing against hers in a silent narrative. As the show played in the background, Ash turned Tayshia so she was pressed beneath him on the couch. Her thighs spread apart to cradle him as he crushed himself against her body and kissed her without allowing her to breathe.

Because he didn't want her to breathe. He wanted her to suffocate like he was suffocating. He wanted her to know what it felt like to be so utterly consumed by someone that it devoured every last ounce of air in her body.

He wanted her to know what it felt like to be devoured.

Tayshia clutched at him, fingers digging as though she couldn't get him close enough. He could feel her tears against his cheeks as a sob swelled in her chest, trapped by the sheer intensity of the situation. Ash's fingers slipped beneath her shirt, stroking the soft skin on her sides.

"You smell so good," he breathed against her lips before moving hot kisses along her jaw and to her neck. "Everything about you is so, so fucking good for me."

She gasped and turned her face toward the back of the couch, hiding it in shadows to try and quiet her moans when his tongue laved at her pulse. He could feel it stuttering beneath his mouth, like her heart reached for him.

"Ash," she whimpered. "I want you to touch me. Do it now. Do it—"

He cut her off with a searing kiss. Then, he shoved her shirt up, revealing her bare chest illuminated by the TV's glow. One palm caressed her left breast, massaging in sensual, circular motions. His mouth found the peak of the other breast, lips soft and teeth grazing. She cried out, her spine arching upward and her legs squeezing his sides. When he sucked, she sobbed for another reason.

Ash's fingers reached between them, seeking out her hips and slipping between her thighs. He felt her heat, felt her panties and how soaked they already were. Her pelvis bucked upward, her hand snapping to wrap around his wrist.

He lifted his mouth from her breast, preparing to apologize and comfort her.

But then he saw it.

Her scar.

It lay amongst the ridges of her chest bone, like a dark reminder of her nightmares that she could never wake from. A physical blemish that she couldn't wash away like she'd washed herself five times in the shower that night in Paris.

"Stop, Ash. Please." Her hand squeezed his wrist, and there was terror in her eyes. "Stop looking at it. It's—"

"Beautiful," he whispered in a ragged voice, and then he placed his lips against the mottled, ridged flesh. "You're so beautiful to me."

Tayshia closed her eyes, holding onto his wrist with one hand like it was a lifeline. Her other hand crept toward her scar, like she couldn't decide whether or not to hide it from him.

"You survived," Ash said. He felt her shaking as he kissed the burn again. "Say it."

"I survived," she whispered.

He kissed toward the swell of her breast. "And you're safe."

"I'm safe."

"And you're here with me."

"I'm—" Her breath caught as she sucked in a moan. "—here with you."

Ash covered the tip of her left breast with his mouth again, his gaze snapping up to meet hers as he did so. She let out a keening wail when his tongue brushed against it, slow and soft, and her spine lifted from the couch cushions. Her hand went to the back of his head, sinking into his hair and holding him in place.

He sucked.

"Oh, my God," she groaned, thrashing beneath him. It caused her wet panties to brush against his waiting fingertips, her heat and flesh grinding. "Please. Oh, my *God*."

Ash pinned her down by one hip and began to touch her with purpose, desperately wishing he could feel her bare skin and show her how good it would be with him. How he would take care of her. How he wouldn't hurt her.

But then she began to grind her hips upward against the press of his fingers. Her hand tightened around his wrist and the other moved to cover the back of his hand, pressing it closer to her core. Her back arched even higher, pushing her chest into his mouth, and she whined. Her exhalations came out as *please, please, please.*

"Let go of my hand. I got it. *I got it, all right?*" he growled, wrenching her hand away and moving his fingers to the part of her body that felt the most acute pleasure. They sunk inside and pulled out for only a moment before slamming back in again. Her hips found his rhythm. "Fuck. That's it."

One of her arms reached above her head, sliding beneath the couch pillows as her back arched again. Her entire body shook as he continued to play with her, to awaken feelings in her body that had her near delirium. Feelings that had him growing hard with just the knowledge of her euphoria.

"Wait," she whined. "Wait, wait, I'm gonna — Ash, I'm gonna c-come."

"For who?"

"For..." She paused. "For you."

"Good girl," he whispered into her ear, his voice rough.

"Harder. Please. *Harder.*"

"Fuck," he groaned, his other hand pinning her thigh to the couch cushion as he thrust his fingers as hard as he dared. "*Fuck*, you're so sweet to let me touch you. You're so fucking sweet. Can I taste you? Please?"

Tayshia turned her face into his throat to muffle a scream. Her hips rolled again and again, trapped by his hands, and her head fell back.

"Tayshia, did you hear me?"

"Yes." Her voice shook on another moan. "You can — You can taste me."

Ash was on his elbows between her legs in seconds, his tongue sweeping over her core, tasting her arousal like it was candy. She tasted every bit as sweet as it.

"Oh, my *fucking* God," Tayshia pushed out through clenched teeth, her fingers clenching so hard in his hair that it almost hurt.

He groaned into her core, his fingers still working her from below as his tongue brushed against her again and again. His entire body felt like it was on fire.

Lifting his gaze to meet hers, he grazed her gently with his teeth. Her face seemed to collapse into euphoria.

"Ash, I'm gonna come. God. Oh, *God* — I'm so close."

"Yeah?" He cooed his words at her, his heart slamming against his chest. Alternating between speaking and licking, his fingers never stopped their relentless pace. "You're gonna fucking come for me, aren't you, baby? You deserve it, you know that? You taste so fucking good. Tell me when you're close."

"I'm c-close," she said in halting breaths, as though she'd been waiting for permission. "Please d-don't stop d-doing that."

As the rigidity of her body intensified, Ash took it upon himself to reach for her breast again. He swirled and swirled and swirled his fingers around her nipple. Fucked her with his hand. Tasted her with the flat of his tongue.

Her thighs quivered as she closed them around his head, holding him in place. It hurt, placing too much pressure on his skull. He pulled back.

"Legs."

"Ash."

"*Legs*, Tayshia," he growled. "Spread them. You're hurting me."

"Please." Tayshia took several choking, gasping breaths. "Please let me — let me —"

Ash removed his hand from her breast, grabbed her knee, and wrenched it away from him. He pinned her, opening her wider as he brought his mouth back to her again. Right as his tongue touched her, he turned his fingers inside of her and curled them.

She fell apart.

Her orgasm washed over her, rendering her a convulsing, shuddering mess beneath him. He hovered over her, kissing her lips and touching her through it. Swallowing the sounds of her whimpers as her hips bucked against his fingers. Her hair moved against the couch pillow as the back of her head slid down, baring her throat in a groan.

Then, like a tidal wave crashing against the shore, she took a tremulous breath and burst into tears.

"Ash, stop," she wailed. "I'm sorry. I'm so sorry. Please stop. I'm so sorry, but please, please stop."

Ash immediately withdrew his hands and laid down beside her, sliding his arms around her body and holding her tight against him. Enveloped by him, she buried her face in his chest, her hands twisting in his shirt.

He hated himself so fucking much.

Pushing her. Always pushing her.

"I'm sorry," she kept whispering through strangled sobs. "It was too fast. I'm so sorry."

"Stop apologizing," he murmured, his guilt weighing his chest so heavy that he felt like he couldn't breathe. He should have known this would happen. It happened the last time, so why would now be any different? They'd gotten caught up and carried away. "It's okay. Everything is okay."

Tayshia only cried.

"I've got you now," he whispered into her damp hair, one hand sinking deep within the curls and the other arm curled tight around her back. "I've still got you."

He held her until they drifted off and he wondered.

What was she begging him to let her do?

CHAPTER SEVENTEEN

The Eiffel Tower.

Ash felt his heart sinking as his gaze washed over the tower, the mountains, and the buildings he recognized. He was standing at a window overlooking a Paris that basked underneath the setting sun.

That meant that it was August 17th, 2018.

Again.

The first thing he did was lift his arms, hoping they weren't Tayshia's. Relief flooded his body when he saw the familiar black, grey, and color tattoos littering his hands, forearms, and biceps. He was in his own body.

He looked to the left and then the right, seeing the familiar blue décor of the hotel room. The wallpaper. The carpet. The bed, the bathroom, the mirror.

Tayshia, standing in front of said mirror.

She stared at his reflection, her eyes wide. Her body was wrapped in the short, red dress he recognized, with the low neckline and the ruched sides. The nylons, the strappy heels, the crimson lipstick — he recognized it all.

He took a step toward her, acutely aware of the fact that his feet were bare and he was in the pajamas he'd fallen asleep in.

"Can you — " He stopped when she began to nod. "Okay, good. It's different this time. More like a dream; less like a memory."

"But why here?" she asked, her eyes wide. "Why this again?"

"I don't know. Maybe things are different now that we're figuring things out? Maybe the connection is getting stronger. Or maybe it's because you were so upset. Have you tried to wake up?"

"Yes. But it didn't work. I'm stuck here."

Tayshia looked at herself in the mirror again, appearing crestfallen. She patted her sleek bun, smoothing her fingers along her edges. Ash saw her take a deep breath that shook on its way out as she pressed her hands anxiously down the front of her dress.

"Ash, I can't do this again. I can't."

"Maybe you don't have to." Ash took another step toward her, having every intention of putting his hand on her shoulder. "This is a dream of a memory. Maybe we can make changes?"

"It won't change anything that happened," she said, frowning. He could see her trying to fortify herself, mentally preparing for what was to come.

"Try to close your eyes and change it," Ash said.

"I already tried." She gulped. "I don't think I have a choice. I think it's gonna force me to — "

Then, they both gasped.

"Kieran's going to walk in," she said, speaking the exact words he was thinking. "And this is a dream — I think he'll be able to see you and even in a dream, I don't want to deal with it."

Ash looked around, frantic. Heart pounding, he barreled across the room, ripped open the closet door, and threw himself inside.

"Are you really going to wear that?"

Ash's mind whirled in the darkness as he tried to get his bearings. He knew where he was, and he knew what was going to happen. Whether or not he was going to be able to fix things this time was up to the will of the dream.

"Kieran, I've told you multiple times that all of us girls agreed to dress up. It's our last night in the city, and we want to have fun with it."

Okay, so she was saying the same things she'd said before. Did she have control over what she said? Was it the memory, or was she saying it because she remembered it?

He closed his eyes and allowed himself a steadying breath.

No matter what, he needed to remain calm. The last time he'd been here, he'd been inside of Tayshia's mind and hadn't needed to think about where and when. Now that he was in his own body, he could make his own choices about where to go.

Ash was going to help her. He wasn't going to stand there like he had in the shop the day his father almost ruined his life. He wasn't going to let the man hurt her.

He had to make the right choices this time.

"Okay, but don't come crying to me when someone says you look like a whore."

Oh, fantastic. Now his desire to beat the fuck out of Kieran was refreshed.

Ash waited in the closet until he heard the door click shut. He exited and went to sit on the end of the bed, cursing under his breath.

How many other times had she had this nightmare? How many times had he gone to sleep and not walked her dreams, thinking it was a fluke or anomaly? Had every time he'd closed his eyes and not seen her been a night where she had to relive it?

Maybe their connection hadn't caused the memory.

Maybe it had just unlocked the cell in which Tayshia had imprisoned it.

But there was a big difference this time. Ash was here, in his own body, and she could see him and interact with him. That meant the environment could interact with him, too. Tayshia seemed to be forced to follow the original track the memory ran on. Did that mean Ash was forced to, too?

Could he fix this?

After imagining himself into some clothes, he knew it was time to go. Ash went over the memory in his mind, trying to remember the directions to the bar. Perhaps if he could make it there in time, he could stop the assault from happening.

Perhaps he could fix it after all.

☼☼☼

Ash walked into the bar like he was meant to be there the entire time.

Tayshia, Kieran, Jamal, Rory, and the other youth group members who had been there in the original memory were there. Kieran was still sending surreptitious glances in the blonde girl's direction, souring Ash's mood even more as he recalled Tayshia saying that he'd kissed another girl before they'd even gone on this trip.

As he neared the table, he could hear that they were coming to the end of their interrogation about Tayshia's future.

Ash didn't have to ask her in real life or in a dream to know that she had no idea what she wanted to do after the pre-req program was complete, and that it was stressing her out. He didn't know how he could help her with that.

His own future hung in the balance.

"What about taking some Science courses?" Jamal said, just like Ash remembered.

Tayshia's back was to him and none of the table members seemed to notice him walking by as quick as he could, trying to stay hidden in the crowded bar. He was six-foot-four, but if he ducked a bit, he blended. He took a table against the wall diagonal from theirs, where he had a perfect view of Tayshia's face. He could hear their conversation if he focused.

"That's an option, Jamal," Tayshia said, and Ash couldn't help but notice her voice was a bit monotone. Like she was being forced to follow the track of the memory, but she was aware that it was a dream. "I thought about it. But I can't really make any decisions until I finish the pre-requisite program."

"Are you sure you want to do that? University classes are so much harder than junior college courses. What if you get there and it's too hard to keep up with the homework?"

"I know." Now that Ash knew her so well, he could hear the strain in

her voice. "I have some ideas for time management. Don't worry."

Ash stared at her as hard as he could, willing her to look in his direction. She did.

He jerked his head toward the bathroom hallway. She gave him a small nod of her head. He got up and made his way over there.

Click-clack, click-clack, click-clack.

Tayshia crashed into Ash's back right as he entered the single bathroom. She reached past him urging him inside, and then slammed the door shut behind them. Panting and breathless, she turned the lock and whirled around to face him.

"It lets me make different choices to an extent," she said, voice tremulous. "Like, it lets me make different movements with my body, but it forces me to do and say the same things I originally did. It wouldn't let me order a different drink but it let me choose not to drink it."

Ash looked at her, studying her face. The flush to her cheeks, the light in her eyes that never seemed to be there when they were awake. The way her chest rose up and down. The gentle slope of her neck into her shoulders. The red of her lips playing off the red satin of her dress.

Then, he frowned.

Her body looked different than it had in the last shared dream. She looked fuller, healthier. The dark circles underneath her eyes were gone, and her lips weren't chapped. He couldn't see the parts of her body he shouldn't anymore. And when his eyes swept down to her legs, the only way he could describe the way they looked was supple.

His heart sank.

When it was her choice, her vision was skewed. When her subconscious made the decision, she appeared healthy and well.

It was the nail in the coffin.

"It seems like I'm on some sort of... Preconceived track of events. When you're around, I can speak my mind and do what I want. Before you got here, it felt like I was reciting a script from a play. My body moved, but I wasn't able to make it turn, or stop, or anything like that. And then I saw you, and it was like — " She snapped her fingers. "I was in control."

Determination threaded its way through him, fortifying his resolve. He was strong enough.

He would fix this.

"So," he said, "it makes sense that as long as you stick near me, we can get you through this."

"I don't know. Something doesn't feel right about it. The last time, it was a memory. This time, it doesn't even feel like a dream. It feels like a nightmare. There's something... Sinister about it. It feels like it's not going to be as easy as we think. It doesn't feel like the times I went into your dreams."

"Do you think it has something to do with the crystals?"

"I don't know. Maybe? Or maybe it's a reflection of how we feel."

"About the hot springs and everything?"

"No. About each other."

They locked eyes and then quickly looked away. The bathroom felt cramped, small.

"Whatever happens," he said, "let's just go with the flow."

She sighed and uncrossed her arms, stepping closer to him. Ash felt his breath go still in his chest when she reached out and brushed her fingers across the front of his shirt.

"What are you doing?"

"You're covered in dust," she said. "And hairs. Why would you imagine yourself into this fabric?"

He laughed. "That's what you're worried about?"

"No. That's not what I'm worried about."

She stopped sweeping the imaginary hairs off of his shirt and let her hand rest flat against his sternum. He knew she could feel the way his heart was beating, and he wondered if she knew how nervous he was. There was so much that could go wrong.

"It's gonna be okay," he murmured as he covered her hand with his own, pinning it. "You're not gonna have to relive this again."

"I don't know," she whispered. He could tell she was trying to be emotionless about it. "I don't want to get my hopes up. I've tried to wake up but it feels like I'm trapped."

"Well, I'm not even going to try and open my eyes," he said, pulling her hand away from his chest so he could hold it in both of his. "We're getting through this together, just like last time."

"Do you promise you'll come find me?"

"I promise."

Tayshia turned her head, her cheeks reddening. He knew she was still ashamed. She had to be. How often could someone say they'd had to relive an assault and experience having a man in their head, feeling it all with them?

It was horrific.

"Whatever this is," she said, "this has to be the last time. I absolutely cannot ever relive this night again."

"I know."

"Ash..."

"I'm telling you, I know." He tugged on her hand, her heels clacking against the linoleum as she stumbled closer. "We'll go into my dreams every night, if we can."

"Ash?"

"What?"

"I have an idea."

She extricated herself from his arms, chewing her lip as indecision flickered across her face.

"What is it?" he asked.

"If you being near me is enough to change things like this — for me to be able to come into the bathroom instead of staying out by the table — what if we could change it altogether? What if... What if we slept together here in the dream, and it was enough?"

Wait... What?

Ash wasn't sure about that. It made his stomach twist in a way that wasn't pleasant. Why would she want to try to erase a traumatic event with her body?

She wasn't collateral.

"I mean, it's just a dream, right?" Her voice shook. "It doesn't have to mean anything. It's not exactly real, even if we can feel it. Maybe if I paint over it with something else, then it won't happen again. Maybe I'll never have to relive it again."

That didn't make any sense. If Ash was enough to make the course of events change, then they could just stay right here in this bathroom. There was no need to erase anything using their bodies.

"No."

"Ash, please. I think this could work." Then, she drew back. "Is it me? Do you not want to...?"

"It's not that," he said, his voice lowering to a rougher tone. "I just don't know if you're thinking clearly. Yeah, it's just a dream, but what happens when we wake up?"

"Do you want to sleep with me?"

"It's not that simple."

"Just answer the question. Ash, do you want me?"

"Yes," he breathed out, feeling his cheeks warming. "But that's not — "

Tayshia's hands snapped up to grab the sides of Ash's face. His arms flew out to his sides as she yanked him down to her level, a surprised sound leaving his mouth.

And then she was kissing him.

She was standing between his legs and kissing him with the full force of *a woman on an angry mission. He tasted a toxic cocktail of ire, desperation, and stress in her mouth, reflected in the way her tongue lashed against his. She dominated that kiss, from the tips of her fingers slowly scraping their way into his hair, to the way she leaned her entire body against his.*

He gasped into her mouth and clutched her hips for some sort of anchor as he tried to keep up with her, his mind and heart racing.

Tayshia pulled back a bit, her back arching to fit the curve of his torso.

"Wait," he said. "You —"

Her lips met his again, searing in how hot they were. It pulled him under, keeping him from breaching the surface and getting a breath of fresh air. The bathroom felt even smaller than it had before, the walls seeming to be their entire world.

Ash tilted his head and kissed her back, trying to gain some sort of footing on solid ground so he could dominate. He didn't like being the one caught off guard. He didn't like that they were making out right now.

He didn't want to disappoint her but he didn't think this would work. He didn't think having sex in a bathroom for her metaphorical first time would be the best way to help her forget what happened to her.

Pushing her back, his hands cradled her cheeks and jaw.

"Wait a fucking second," he said. "What —"

She pushed herself up onto the tips of her toes with a forceful jerk, her face slipping through his hold. Her lips smashed against his yet again and her arms wrapped so tight around his neck that it would be impossible for him to extract himself from her hold.

He could feel his feet slipping on ice, the dips and crevices in his resolve melting beneath him.

Tayshia's lips broke from his, ghosting along his jawline and sending shivers rippling throughout his body. Her fingers gripped his hair, pulling him down again so she could stand on her heels.

"It's only a dream," she whispered into his ear, her voice sending chills down his spine. "It's only a dream, and I can't relive it again."

She was right. It was only a dream.

"Ah, Hell. Fuck it."

Ash tossed his faculties aside, turned his head, and captured her lips. The moment he did, he consumed her like flames devouring flesh. His hands stroked down her sides, sliding around to grip her rear, and he lifted her.

Tayshia let out a cry against his lips as he spun her around and set her down on the front edge of the counter surrounding the sink. Her thighs bracketed his hips as they kissed, the heat in the room rising to almost unbearable levels. Her back pressed to the mirror, one of her hands reaching up to touch the glass while the other tangled so deep in his hair that it actually hurt. She gasped.

"You know what you're doing," he growled against her lips. Desperation to be close to her urged him to wrap his hands around her thighs and pull the lower half of her body against his. His eyes opened, darting up and down her face. "You manipulative little brat."

He kissed her again, moaning when he felt her moving her hips against his. His heart pounded even harder. The way she was arching into him, the sensuality in the sounds she was making. It was clear she really wanted to do this. She really wanted him to fuck her, right here in the bathroom of a bar in her dream. And they were going to because at this point, Ash felt like he'd do anything for her.

Tayshia pushed against his chest.

"I have to go out there," she said, looking terrified. "I think Rory's about to go outside to smoke, like last time. The dream wants me to go out there. Ash, don't forget —"

"I got you. I told you. I'll be out soon." He felt relieved.

With a pinched facial expression, Tayshia slid back to the floor and headed for the door. She cast him one last look, the dead soul of her failed plot lingering there.

"Please come," she whispered. "Don't leave me there."

"I'll be there. I swear."

Tayshia left the bathroom.

Ash watched her go, trying not to drown in the helplessness. What if his presence wasn't enough?

What if he wasn't going to be able to keep his promise?

He turned to the sink and the mirror above it. His hair was a disaster, sticking up in all directions. His skin was flushed red. Splashing water against his face, he halted his train of thought.

No. He wasn't going to do this.

He wasn't going to let his fears get the best of him. He was going to set his shoulders back, march out there, and stand by Tayshia's side for as long as the dream would let him.

Ash left the bathroom, his gaze falling upon the table.

They were gone.

Confusion etched lines into Ash's face. The table was empty, completely cleared of drinks and napkins. For all intents and purposes, it looked as though no one had been there at all.

No.

This couldn't be happening.

Ash walked outside. He combed the fingers of both hands through his hair and looked down the sidewalk. He couldn't see them in the distance, and he was definitely tall enough to be able to. From what he recalled, they went left when they exited the bar, traveled a couple of blocks, and then Tayshia and Kieran had argued.

"Where the fuck is she?" he muttered under his breath as he walked, glancing down the side streets in the hopes that she'd somehow managed to get them off the main road. "Where are they?"

He came to a stop underneath a streetlight that was exactly where they were supposed to be having their fight. No one was there.

A small part of him hoped that perhaps his presence in the bar was enough to redirect the dream. He hoped she'd already woken up, because then —

Well, that wasn't possible. If she was awake, why was he still here? No, she was still sleeping.

But where was she?

Ash waited there, crossing his arms and shouldering the lamppost as he did so. His best bet was to wait the same amount of time that Tayshia had waited for Kieran to come back. Maybe she'd show up?

He only had forty-five minutes.

So, he waited.

And waited.

And waited.

Neither Tayshia nor Kieran ever came.

There's no time, *he thought, a burst of panic bleeding into his chest.* I have to follow where she went last time.

I have to find her.

He started running.

☼☼☼

Ash walked up and down the alleyway three times.

She wasn't there. The man wasn't there.

The alley was empty.

This was his worst fear. That he wouldn't make it on time, or that he wouldn't be able to help her. And he was trying — he had tried *— but something had gone wrong. He didn't know if it was the dream or if it was Tayshia herself, but something had kicked him out. She was going to stay on the same track and experience the memory in its entirety.*

And this time, she'd be alone.

Again.

Ash felt the icy claws of fear sinking into his heart, pulling him down into a crouch on the ground. He let out a heavy, despairing sigh. Scrubbing at his face with his hands, he steepled his fingers in front of his mouth and let himself wallow.

He remembered what she'd endured. Remembered what it was like to be trapped inside of her mind while it was happening. The pain and the fear and the desperation.

Ash glanced behind him, at the alley wall right where she should be standing. His gaze scoured over the spot. Over the red brick and the grey grooves between each stone, recalling the feeling of her nearly tearing her fingernails out from clawing against them. Remembered her telling the man she couldn't breathe. Remembered what it felt like to feel that suffocation.

Anger rose up like a fiery dragon inside of him, vengeful and fierce.

That man had his hands on her. Again.

Ash had failed to help her. Again.

He was living down to her expectations. Again.

This was just like that day in the ice cream shop. All of the pressure of the world on his shoulders but none of the strength to carry it.

"Fuck!" he screamed, drawing the gazes of several of the people walking by. The emotion overwhelmed him and he hung his head, speaking again in a broken whisper. "I have to figure this out. Why can't I just fucking figure this out?"

Within seconds, Ash was on his feet again and lunging toward the wall. He drew his fist back and slammed it into the brick. It was agonizing, lightning bolts of pain shooting up and down his arm from shoulder to knuckle.

He wished he were awake so he could feel it for real.

She didn't deserve this. She did not deserve this.

No one did.

Ash tilted his head back and closed his eyes, trying to settle his spirit. He was still in the dream, which meant she was still sleeping. If she was still sleeping, then it wasn't over. He had a chance to do something good.

He had a chance to make the right choice.

☼☼☼

Ash gasped for air.

Hands braced against either side of the hotel room doorframe, he panted as he caught his breath. His heart was beating so fast that he was seeing spots. He'd never run that far, that fast in his entire life. He hoped he never had to again.

But he would if she needed him.

Taking another breath, he knocked on the door.

No answer.

Agitated and terrified that something worse had somehow taken place, *he began to pace. He ran his hand through his hair, rubbed his chin, and resisted his very distinct desire to punch another wall. His knuckles had stopped bleeding, but they were as sore as the immense guilt that ached through him.*

He hoped they were sore when he woke up.

Ash slammed his fist against the door a second series of times.

"Tayshia, it's me!" he hollered. "Come on and open the door, all right?"

When she still didn't answer, he knew that it was because she was about to break down. He remembered these moments well — perhaps more vividly than any other moment in this horrific memory. She'd walked all the way back to the hotel in a dazed stupor. The moment she'd broken down was the moment that had shattered Ash's heart.

If there was one thing he'd learned from his mother, it was that the people who seemed the strongest were the ones who were the least likely to ask for help when they needed it the most. They'd let their despair poison them if only to keep their armor from cracking.

Gabriel had done it. Lizette had done it. So had Ash.

Their family had perished.

Something possessed him to reach for the door handle. Something unexplainable that told him it was the right thing for him to do. And when his hand closed around it and turned, his heart stopped.

It was unlocked.

The last of his panic ebbed away like the gentle pull of the tide's end. With a steady arm, he pushed the door open enough for him to sidle into the room. He shut it behind him and locked it without looking.

Tayshia stood at the end of the bed in her torn dress, her body covered in scrapes and newly-forming bruises. Blood trickled down the insides of her legs — legs which trembled and shook with growing weakness. The sight of it was almost enough to make him lose himself to his rage again.

His heart sank to the depths. It had happened anyway. The dream hadn't let him save her. Even though he wanted to know why, it wasn't time for that. She didn't realize he was there yet.

There it was.

The inhuman sound that had haunted his mind for weeks. The high-pitched, keening, guttural wail that left her lips as though it were trying to escape the cage her pain created.

She collapsed.

Ash darted forward and threw his arms around her from the side, one hand gripping the elbow of her outer arm and the other wrapped around the front of her abdomen.

"No, come on," he breathed. "Come here, baby. Come here."

"I can't," she sobbed, her body leaning against him like a limp rag doll. She was shaking so violently that he was terrified she was going to splinter into pieces. "I can't, I can't, I – "

"You can," he whispered, using his determination to keep his voice strong. "You can because I'm here now. I've got you. And you're strong. You can."

Either she didn't hear him or she was too emotionally broken to listen. She kept whispering the words, wailing them as her body continued to pull downward. Ash gave in and sank to the floor with her, knowing that this was what she needed. This – holding her – was the very thing he'd wanted to do.

And she needed it.

Her head lolled against his shoulder and she wept, and wept, and wept. She wept tears of grief and shame. Anguish and horror. The tears of having to experience it the first time, and the tears of having to experience it again.

It was just a dream but Ash cried, too.

Tayshia tilted her head back to look up at him, her face devoid of feeling. Without speaking, she reached up to wipe the silent tears from his face with her thumbs. Her touch was achingly gentle.

"Shower?" he said.

She nodded.

Getting to his feet, Ash took her by the elbows and guided her to hers. She wobbled on two trembling legs, just like she had the first time, and allowed him to escort her into the bathroom. Tayshia stood swaying, catatonic and quiet as Ash handled the water.

Last time, she'd made the water ice-cold. This time, it would be warm and comforting.

He turned to face her right as she pulled the ripped straps of her dress down. Her fingers quivered so badly that he had to help her. She reached behind herself to undo the zipper, leaning her forehead against his chest with a dejected sigh. He helped her with that, too.

"Come here," he said in a soft voice, gentle as he batted her hands away. "Let me help."

The zipper slid down and the sides of the dress came open in the back.

"Wait," he said. "Should I leave?"

She shook her head, her chin trembling again. There were tears clinging to her lashes. When she spoke, her voice was cracked, barely much more than a whisper.

"It's just a dream," she said.

Ash felt his brow furrowing as he realized that she was about to reveal *herself in her entirety to him. This was a gift that he did not deserve. He didn't deserve it.*

He would not take advantage of it.

The dress fell to the floor at the same speed as the tear that traveled down her cheek.

Ash didn't look. He simply wiped her tear with his finger and helped her with her undergarments. Holding her hand, he assisted her into the shower, steadying her as she wobbled. He kept his eyes respectfully on her face as he reached up and began to take her hair down.

After grabbing a washcloth and handing it to her, he took a step back, preparing to shut the curtain.

She didn't move.

When it became clear that she wasn't going to wash herself like last time, he drew his shoulders back. Tayshia didn't need him standing there, acting like a child. She needed someone who was going to be there for her. If they were connected, then he needed to step up and show her that he was going to be able to take care of her.

She was strong but she didn't have to be.

Fully clothed, he got into the shower.

The water was hot. It scalded as it seeped into his clothes. It felt odd to be in the shower with them on.

He could completely envelop her if he wanted to. Which he did want to, if only to protect her from being hurt again.

Ash looked down at them both, at the crystals around their necks and for the first time, he hated the sight of them. He wanted to snap the silver chain and rip the black leather cord so they could wake up. Then, he wanted to go back to the caverns and stick the rocks back into the wall. Or drive to the coast so they could throw them in the sea. Or bury them deep in the ground.

He'd never before felt so violently protective over someone and whether it was the crystals or not, he wasn't going to ignore the urge. Not right now.

Tayshia dragged her gaze up to meet his. He didn't look away, even as he lathered up the washcloth with soap. Not even when he began to wash her neck and shoulders. Not when he smoothed the cloth down her arms. Not when he washed her breasts and abdomen. Not when he reached around behind her to wash her back.

He rinsed the cloth and lathered it again.

This was the part he dreaded.

Ash spoke over the sound of the pounding water, his hair dripping into his eyes. "Do you want me to turn around?"

Tayshia shook her head. Then, with a shaking hand, she took the cloth from him. Her left hand went to his shoulder, light and barely-there as she used him for support. Her eyes squeezed shut as she reached between her legs.

He didn't know if it was because he was there this time or not but last time, he remembered her being so robotic about it. So closed off, as hard as stone to protect herself. Now, she was allowing herself to feel the pain.

Which meant that he was helping.

"I can't do this again," she whispered, and he could hear her falling apart. "Not again."

"It's okay, it's okay," he said, words rushing out as he took the cloth from her again. He wrapped his right arm around her, his fingers trailing up the vertebrae of her spine. "Shh. It's all right. I'll help you."

"I'm sorry."

"No, don't be sorry."

He just wanted her to be okay.

Taking a deep breath and steeling himself, he placed his hand on her hip and then crouched down in front of her.

"Okay?" he said, looking up at her.

Tayshia placed her hands on his shoulders and nodded, her curly brown hair falling in wet strips to her upper arms. She looked worried and terrified.

"I have to look to be able to make sure I get all the blood," he said, keeping his voice low to mask his discomfort, anger, and sadness. Trying to stay strong. Trying to be what she needed. "Is that all right?"

Another nod.

He forced himself to feel and think nothing as he very clinically and thoroughly washed between her legs. She whimpered from the pain, and it made him want to cry all over again. He knew exactly how much pain she was in — it wrenched his heart into a knot. Watching the blood run crimson down the drain was as nauseating as it was infuriating.

When he put the cloth in the water stream to rinse it out, he heard her whispering.

"One."

For a brief moment, his eyes closed. He remembered. It was one part he'd never forget.

More soap, and then he washed her again.

"Two."

Yet more soap. More gentle scrubbing. His heart hurt almost as bad as the day his mother died.

"Th-Three." Her voice broke. She wrangled it back under her control. "Three."

He did as she wanted. When he looked up, her eyes were shut and he

couldn't tell if she was crying or if it was just the water.

"Four."

Even though she was clean, he washed her again.

"Five."

He started to stand, but she pushed on his shoulders.

"Again," she said, voice pleading.

"You're clean," he said, standing anyway and dropping the soiled cloth to the floor of the tub.

"No." She shook her head. "No. I'm not clean. I always regretted not washing again. I should have — I should have kept washing."

"You're clean," he said, smoothing his hands over her hair in tender motions.

"I'm not. I'm not, and I haven't been, and I know it's just a dream. It's just a dream but I'm not clean. I need you to — "

"Tayshia. You are clean."

A couple of beats passed — a couple of beats of time where Ash wasn't sure what to do. Because he knew. He knew that if she asked him again to wash her, he would do it. At this point, he'd do anything for her.

Her face fell as she dissolved into tears, covering her eyes with her hands. Ash hurried to wrap his arms around her shoulders, cupping the back of her head. He held her while she cried again, feeling the shaking of her shoulders as the sobs wracked her body.

He'd do anything for her.

Ash was the first to step out. His clothes were absolutely soaked, so he peeled them off and dropped them to the floor. Guilt rendered him forlorn as he closed his eyes and imagined himself in his pajamas again.

The dream let it happen.

Why couldn't it let him save her?

"Come here." He grabbed one of the white hotel towels and held it open for her, knowing full well that they could dream themselves dry. "I'll take care of you. Let's go to bed."

Tayshia held her arm over her breasts, modest as she stepped into the circle of his arms. She even let out a soft laugh as he mussed her hair with the fabric, shaking her back and forth. It felt important to hear it.

It sounded like music.

She told him where her suitcase was and he helped her dress in her pajamas. They climbed into bed together as though it weren't a dream. As though they were on vacation in Paris in a hotel together, surrounded by the color blue and lying on a mattress that felt like a cloud.

Tayshia checked her phone. Ash felt the way she trembled when she read her father's heartfelt message again.

208

The moment she burrowed her head into the crevice of Ash's throat and shoulder, he didn't care about anything else.

"Where were you?" she whispered. He heard it there — betrayal, sadness, and the unspoken I called for you.

Because she had to have called for him and that was what made him hate himself the most.

"I walked out into the bar," he said, his voice hoarse from disuse. One of his arms was around her back; the other hand traced up and down her forearm, which banded his waist. "You guys were gone. Then, I went to the place where you and Kieran were supposed to be. I waited forever but didn't see you. I went to the alley and it was empty. I don't think the dream wanted me there."

"You promised."

His heart clenched. "I know."

"The other night," she said slowly. Carefully. "The other night on the couch. I didn't want to stop. I wanted to keep going."

"You weren't ready."

"Yeah, but I want to be. It's not fair, Ash. It's not fair that I feel like this. I keep trying with you because I have this stupid idea that every time will be the last time I feel dirty afterward."

Ash turned to face her, looking into her eyes, feeling the ache expanding in his chest.

"I'll wait," he said. "You're all I have. You're the only person I've ever felt this close to, and the only person that knows me better than anyone else. I can wait for you. I want to wait for you."

Her stare was blank, like she was gazing at the physical manifestation of her despair.

"You might wait forever."

He gave her a small smile and reached for her crystal, picking it up and touching its jagged faces. "Good thing we have eternity."

Tayshia let out a laugh that faded into sadness and silence.

"I'm scared that this isn't a dream or a nightmare," she breathed. "I feel like this is a punishment."

His guilt seeped into every inch of his body. "What were you asking me to let you do?"

It took Tayshia a long time to reply. When she did, it didn't sound like news to him. Ash was just less prepared to hear it than he thought.

"I wasn't asking you for anything. I was asking God to let me have something good for once. To let me be with you without being afraid of the way I'd feel after. I was asking him to let me be happy. It's the only thing I

want, and I want it with you. I'll try again and again and again until He lets me have it."

Ash cupped the side of her face that was turned toward the ceiling, his thumb swiping through the tear track that painted her face. Every time he touched her, he felt like he was going to fall into thousands of broken pieces.

Why did he feel this way for her?

"You make me feel beautiful," she continued, "and it's not fair that it feels like He doesn't want me to feel that way."

Ash's heart had cracked.

"I've got you now," he whispered, crushing her against him as she cried. "You're gonna feel all those things with me. You're gonna have everything. Whatever you want, I'm going to give it to you. You understand?"

Whatever she believed. Whatever he didn't. Tayshia deserved to feel beautiful. She deserved to feel beautiful and wanted and happy.

She deserved to feel loved.

CHAPTER EIGHTEEN

Tayshia wasn't in his bed when he woke for class on Monday.

Ash felt her absence almost as acutely as he felt the guilt, still coursing like a river through his heart. He hadn't meant for things to get so carried away that weekend. Maybe if he hadn't, she wouldn't have gotten triggered, and they never would have gone into the memory again.

If she blamed him for having to relive it yet again, he would understand.

When he went into the bathroom to shower, he checked the toilet just like when he was younger. Something he should have been doing the moment he first noticed something was off with Tayshia's eating habits.

Lizette's illness had been something that was hidden in plain sight. Gabriel was too self-absorbed to notice anything, but Ash was attached to his mother. When he was a kid, he'd realized she was sneaking off to the kitchen for late night meals. He would sneak after her just to be near her and sit on the stairs for as long as he could.

She would eat two, three, sometimes as many as five or six meals, use the bathroom between each one, and then make her way slowly back up the stairs. Ash made sure he was back in his room before she did, so that he wouldn't get in trouble. But it was less about getting in trouble and more about saving her the mortification.

Ash didn't connect the meals to the bathroom usage until he was thirteen and they learned about it in Health class. He wasn't an idiot—he knew his mother wasn't sick in the physical sense. She was *making* herself sick and even though he had no idea why, he knew that it wasn't something she was proud of.

Lizette was ashamed.

Sitting on the stairs and then rushing up to his room before she came out of the bathroom was the best way he could help her feel less alone. She wouldn't know he was there, but her heart would.

At least, that's what he liked to tell himself.

It was better than trying to figure out why his chest hurt whenever he heard the stairs creak on her way back up to bed. Much better than thinking about the fact that she never cleaned up after herself. Much better than Ash realizing that the messiness was part of it, part of her rebellion against herself.

Much better than thinking about how hard the floor was under his knees when he cleaned underneath the rim of the toilet himself.

So when he lifted the lid after Tayshia had been in the bathroom, he wasn't thinking about his hurting heart, how messy she might be, or how hard the bathroom floor would be in the apartment. He was thinking about how he was going to fix it all. He was thinking about how he could do better this time.

He was thinking about how he hadn't tried hard enough before.

But Ash couldn't save her. It wasn't what she wanted. It was wrong. If he saved her against her will, it would infantilize her.

"It's a bad thing to act like a white savior for a Black woman who didn't ask you to save her."

"I don't need pity, sympathy, and a knight. I need you to listen, learn, and reject the privilege you have."

She was her own person. She didn't need him to swoop in on a horse with a sword and shield and save her from every little thing that happened to her, even if he wanted to be the one to do it. Tayshia didn't *want* him to do that.

Neither had his mother.

Deep down, Ash knew it. That was why she never brought it up with him and why Ash never brought it up with her. They both knew that he was present on the stairs during her nightly episodes. His mother knew he was the one cleaning the toilet. Lizette could clean it herself but she let him do it.

As long as he didn't try to make her stop.

What if that was what Tayshia wanted, too? If he confronted her, would she maintain innocence? Or would she want to sweep it under the rug like his mother had?

But how could he step back and just let her kill herself? How could he take away pity, remove sympathy, and not be a fucking knight to protect her if *she* was the one who was hurting herself? He was listening, he was learning, he was rejecting the privilege he had to just exist, but she was *hurting* herself.

Ash wanted to fix it. He was *going* to fix it.

Because she didn't deserve to die just because some piece of shit stole away a part of herself that was supposed to be hers to give.

Because it wasn't fair that Tayshia should have to suffer for the rest of her life, burning alone and in pain while people like Kieran fanned the flames.

Because it killed his fucking mother.

In the bathroom of their shared apartment, there were no orange flecks under the rim. It was as clean and white as porcelain should be. Either he was entirely wrong about Tayshia's secret, or she was covering her tracks.

Ash wasn't exactly sure how to help her, but he knew he wasn't going to do anything in secret, behind closed doors like he did for his mother. If he was going to get involved, she was going to know it, and he wasn't going to stop until she was better.

He wasn't going to watch another person he cared about die.

After his shower, he dressed for the day in a light grey pullover that was a bit big on him, a pair of black skinny jeans with rips in the knees, and combat boots. He ruffled his damp blond hair in the hopes that it would dry in some semblance of a style. Ash looked at himself in the mirror for a second—at his rugged appearance and pale tattooed skin—and wondered when he'd become so fucking wrecked.

Tayshia had *wrecked* him.

Ash wanted to cry at the thought that he not only hadn't been there for her last night but had been standing idle while she destroyed herself for the past two months. He was such a fucking failure. Why could he never do anything the right way, even when he was trying to do the right thing?

He couldn't stop his father. He couldn't save his mother. He couldn't save his friendship with Elijah.

How the fuck am I supposed to save Tayshia?

Ash had a vicious desire to destroy himself, too. To feel the pain of glass shattering and his skin splitting, blood leaking down his knuckles and over the tips of his fingers.

Fist clenched, he raised it, his face contorting with a combination of the anger and self-hatred that he felt burning within him. He pulled his arm back, hesitating. Ready to destroy the reflection so he could destroy himself.

No.

That was the old Ash.

The new Ash had a lot to think about and a lot to take care of. Just like in the dream the night before, he had to keep in mind that the probability of him being connected to her was higher than maybe. It was almost fact. That meant that no matter what course their futures took, they'd be walking their paths together. He had a responsibility to her now.

Much calmer and more determined, Ash entered the kitchen to get some water and saw that the sink was empty. Frowning, he placed his hands on the edge of the counter and hung his head. He'd woken up late. It was already lunchtime and if the sink was empty, there were three possibilities.

Either she had washed her dishes this morning, she'd gone to the cafeteria, or she hadn't eaten at all.

☼☼☼

Well, this was a good start.

Tayshia was in the cafeteria for lunch. She sat at her usual table with a plate of food in front of her. When he entered the cafeteria halfway into the period—which was about one-quarter full, as not everyone had finished eating yet—Ash felt hesitant. Should he go to the table he always sat at, where there were only a few other students and Elijah? Or should he take the risk and go to her table?

Choices, choices.

After getting his food, he headed to the right of the food line, striding towards Tayshia.

Schooling his facial expression to be as indifferent and aloof as possible, he scoped it out. He saw Tayshia's friends, but they seemed to have gathered away from her. The football team was at the far end of the long table, and Kieran was amongst them. There were other students there, most everyone watching Ash walk up with a sourness to the downward pull of their lips. Tayshia sat on the end with her back to the rest of the room.

Ash slid in on her right, staring off at the other tables to try and make it seem like he was more interested in them than the fact that he was sitting down with her.

He began to eat.

Tayshia, who had her phone on the table beside her very full plate, turned to stare at him. The silence was so total and absolute that he felt like he was alone in the large room.

"What?" he said around a mouthful of bread, meat, and cheese.

"Did someone dare you, or are you lost?"

At this, Ash rolled his head back and gave her a deadpan look. "I wasn't dared to ask you out, if that's what you mean. And no, I'm not lost. I'm exactly where I want to be."

She narrowed her eyes, searching his face for whatever it was she was suspicious of, and then she frowned.

"You never sit with me."

"I can't try new things once in a while? I mean, come on."

"What if I don't *want* to sit with you?"

"Sounds like a 'you' problem."

He took another bite of his sandwich. A sting afflicted his heart. He knew things were bound to be awkward after reliving the memory again, but he didn't think she'd be this revolted by being around him.

Maybe this was a bad idea.

He dropped the sandwich and wiped his hands free of crumbs, the frown on his face so deep that he could feel his forehead wrinkling.

"What?" Tayshia said. "I'm just surprised, is all."

"If you don't want me around you, it's fine," he said. "Just make sure you eat."

She didn't respond. He picked up his plate and stood.

"Wait."

He stopped and looked over his shoulder, down at her. "Yeah?"

"Why?" She was looking at him strangely, with a mixture of irritation and wariness dancing across her features. "Why are you telling me to make sure I—why are you saying that?"

"Because I am," he said, his gaze washing over the other people around them. They were watching, but Ash didn't care.

"Why?"

"Does it matter?"

"Yes," she said, lowering her voice as her brows came together on her forehead. "Since when do you care what I eat or when I do it?"

"Since I decided I did," he snapped. He ran his fingers through his hair and looked down at her again, hoping she could see the sincerity in his eyes when he did. For good measure, he leaned down. "I *want* you to eat, all right?"

She opened her mouth, her words dying in her throat. The wariness and irritation faded to something akin to confusion.

Without saying anything further, she turned back to face her plate and phone.

Ash walked to his normal table, keeping his distance from Elijah and refusing to look at him. Instead, he sat down and set back into his sandwich, watching Tayshia from his place with the eyes of a hawk. Watching as she tried to go back to scrolling through her apps and not touching her food. Watching as she stared at the plate for three minutes, her leg bouncing as though she had too much energy and nowhere to expend it.

Tayshia picked up her burger. He saw her shoulders lift as she took a deep breath.

Ash trapped his own breath in his chest, his food forgotten for the moment. It was as anticipatory a moment as when he'd gathered up those wallets for his father, knowing that not only his future, but the future of everyone in that shop's lives rested upon his shoulders. And now, it was the same. If he and Tayshia were truly connected to one another, then his destiny was intertwined with hers. He had to take care of her if she couldn't take care of herself.

Perhaps that wasn't the only reason he cared.

Ash's heart raced in his chest. Would she go through with it?

Tayshia took a bite of her sandwich.

He didn't think he'd ever felt so fucking relieved in his entire life. As he watched her scarf down the food, he wondered if he'd been overreacting the entire time. The emptiness left by his mother's death could have caused him to see things that weren't there.

He thought she might be okay.

But then she got up and went back through the food line.

This time, she paid the lunch lady for a few sandwiches and two cans of soda. She carried them all back to the table, no one looking in her direction as she did. She sat down, practically inhaling the sandwiches as though they were liquid. He watched her finish the first, then move on to the second and third without stopping for more than the occasional drink out of her sodas.

When she got up to leave, Tayshia glanced in his direction. The expression she wore was one that surprised him.

Guilt.

Ash ran his hands down his face, trying to decide what to do. If nothing was wrong, he had no idea where she was headed to. If something *was* wrong? She was going straight to the bathroom.

And he had no idea what to do next.

He sat there until students began to trickle out to go to class. Elijah was one of the first to go, leaving right after Tayshia, and he didn't look in Ash's direction. Ash felt hollow emptiness in his chest where his best friend used to exist.

☼☼☼

Later, when Ash was home and Tayshia still wasn't, his cell phone rang.

He leaned forward on the couch, elbows on thighs and a hand rubbing his chin. His phone held idle in his right hand, he stared down at the screen. Stared at the name. Stared at his past knocking on the door to his present.

Ryo was calling.

It wasn't a text. It was a phone call. It was a phone call, and it was ringing, and ringing, and ringing, and —

Ash's thumb hovered over the red button. He closed his eyes, feeling the phone buzzing in his hand. Having lost count of how many times Ryo had tried to contact him, the fact that he was calling now was proof enough for Ash to know that he wasn't going to give up.

He felt the anxiety clawing at his chest, ripping the already gaping hole wider.

The phone continued to buzz.

Fuck. I just need to suck it up and do it. Just suck it the Hell up and answer.

Ash pressed the green button.

"Hi." Ash cleared his throat. "I mean, hello?"

"Hey there!" came Ryo's boisterous, ever-chipper voice. "Long time no talk, kid!"

"Yeah. Uh, yeah, I..." Ash trailed off, leaning on his elbows over his thighs again, staring down at the carpet. "It's my bad. I just haven't—I wasn't ready, I guess."

"Well, we miss you, you know," Ryo said, and there was a slight hitch to his rowdy tone. It smoothed out a moment later. "How are you settling in since getting out? You find a place to be, food to eat, water to drink...?"

"Yeah, I—" Ash cleared his throat. His right leg began to bounce. "I signed up for the pre-requisite program this year, so I'm living at the school-owned apartment complex over on Birch. You know, near the—"

"Near Gianni's, yeah. Oh, well that's nice. That area's quiet, right at the foot of the mountain. So, how is school going for you? Good grades and everything?"

"Sure. I mean, yeah. They're decent," Ash said, voice shaking as he forced a quiet laugh. His hair fell into his eyes as he dropped his forehead into his free hand. "I passed all my classes when I was locked up, and then I'm passing this year. So I'll be able to go to a university if I want."

"Ah, okay. And is that something you want?"

"Yes. Er—well... I do, but I don't at the same time." Another feigned chuckle. "I'm not sure what I want to do, or if I can even get in anywhere."

"Oh, you'll be able to get into a university. Don't you even worry about it, kid. They love a good rags-to-riches story. If they hear you went to jail and still managed to continue your education, they'll eat that shit up."

"Yeah, maybe."

"I believe in you. You're smart. You can whip up a damn good essay in two seconds flat, I know it. But don't stress. You're twenty now, so you got your whole life ahead of you. I didn't even start college until I was twenty-seven."

He remembered his birthday. Ryo remembered his birthday and knew how old he was.

For a second, Ash felt like he was talking to his father. The father he'd never had. The father he'd always wanted. Someone who cared about his future and his dreams and the things he wanted.

In that moment, Ash wanted to tell him everything. He wanted to tell him about the caverns and the crystals. The hot springs and Tayshia. The dreams and the nightmare that was Paris. How it felt like he was standing right at the edge of a cliff. He felt like he was going to fall headfirst into a ravine that ached deeper and darker than anything he'd ever experienced with his mother's secrets. He just wanted to tell someone but it felt like the chains tattooed on his neck were slithering down to wrap around his lungs.

He couldn't trust anyone.

It hurt.

"Ash?" Ryo's voice was soft. "You still there?"

Ash tilted his head back, tears blurring his vision and his throat aching. Panic wrestled with his breath, rendering him suspended and breathless.

"Yeah," he whispered, his voice choked with emotion. "I'm here."

"Why don't you come see us for Christmas?" he said.

"I'll—I'll think about it," Ash said. "Is that like, okay? For me to—to think about it?"

"Of course it's okay, Ash. Of course." Ryo's voice sounded impassioned. "We care about you, Steven and I. We just want to have you in our life. If you can't do Christmas, we'll wait until you're ready. But keep in touch, okay? Don't shut out the people who care. You aren't alone. I love you, son."

Ash's chest spasmed. The words tried to come forth, but they terrified him so badly that he almost burst out crying. He dragged them back inside of himself, back into the cage around his chest to imprison them in the areas where it was safe.

"I'll talk to you later, Ryo."

They hung up, and then Ash was alone with his thoughts and the black screen of the TV. He laid down on his back with his fingers interlocked behind his head on a pillow in the corner of the sectional. Exhaustion settled over his bones, the situation with Tayshia and the conversation with Ryo having drained him.

Sleep claimed him within minutes.

CHAPTER NINETEEN

"I knew I'd find you here."

That was Tayshia's voice.

Was she waking him from his nap? Why did she sound so chipper? Earlier that day at lunch, she'd sounded so flat, so monotone. Ash's eyelids fluttered open to see a sky he knew as well as he knew the blue one in the real world.

It was lavender.

Tayshia stood over him, swathed in white chiffon that floated around her thighs and fell off of her shoulders. Her hair was plaited in what looked like hundreds of long, boxy braids that swung at her hips. Her crystal hung around her neck, nestled against her sternum. She smiled at him, and it was the most genuine smile he'd seen from her in months.

It reached her eyes.

"Took you long enough to wake up," she said with a slight laugh. She clasped her hands behind her back and bit her lower lip, studying him. "I got home and you were napping. I was so tired that I took a nap, too."

"Shit," he said, rubbing the back of his neck as he sat up. He looked down and saw that he wore black skinny jeans and a pink button-up with black-and-red bats printed on it. "What time was it?"

"Like six when I got home." Then, she said, "Want to go play in the water?"

Ash sat up, feeling a light breeze coming from the west, ruffling his hair and her short skirt. He tried not to focus on the painful body size she'd imagined for herself, wishing there were some way he could imagine her differently. Healthier.

Why was she so fucking happy like that?

"In the water?" He grimaced. "Nah, that's not me."

"But it could be," she said, voice bright as she held her hand out to him. "Come on, it'll be fun. Have you never done it before?"

He eyed her, wanting so badly to sit and wallow in his troubles. His troubles that were also hers. Wanting to sit right there on the hill and talk about Paris. To talk about Paris and the things they'd felt in the shower. To *tell her about his mother.*

But she looked so happy.

"Come on," she said again, holding her hand out to him. "Take my hand."

With a begrudging sigh, he reached up and took her hand. Her skin was warm to the touch, in direct contrast to how cold it was in the waking world. It made his heart ache.

She pulled him to his feet, grinning up at him.

And then they were running.

Tayshia let out a high-pitched laugh and pulled him down the hill, running faster than he expected her to go. They headed across the field, crushing the gardenias underfoot as they made their way towards the beach. The closer they got, the easier it became for Ash to leave the hurt behind — the consternation and the worries and the negative feelings — and let go.

Right as they reached the sand, a wicked grin spread across his face. Ash let go of her hand and wrapped his arms around her waist from behind. Tayshia shrieked his name when he dragged her into the air, her feet clearing the divide between grass and sand, hands clutching his forearm. He heard her playful voice pleading with him to put her down, and he did.

Another shriek and she was running again.

This time, he chased her and it was easy. It was easy to pretend like they weren't Ash Robards and Tayshia Cole. To imagine for a second that he hadn't stood and watched her father's blood stain her hands after his father shot him. To act like they were just two twenty-year-olds on the beach. To let go and live in the dream. To forget about everything else and just go flying after those braids and that beautiful girl.

When he caught up with her, they went careening into the water, falling into the crashing waves and laughing as they were both soaked to the bone. Every time they tried to get up, another wave would come, knocking them down again. It was even easier to laugh and smile at that point, especially when he grabbed her around the waist again. He held her close as they tumbled beneath the surface of the salty water.

Fuck.

Even here, it ached to hold her.

They came up for air, hair dripping and chests heaving, and beamed at one another.

"See?" she said, panting. "Told you it would be fun."

"Yeah, well." He brushed his wet hair out of his eyes. "You owe me for this."

"What could I possibly owe Ash Robards, with his bougie ass?" she said,

leaning forward to gather her braids to one side of her head and twist the water out of them. He watched her, watched the way the moonlight glanced off of her cheekbones, watched her lashes dusting her skin and the gentle curve of her smile.

She was beautiful.

"Nothing I could afford if it weren't owed," he murmured, looking down into her eyes.

"What's that mean?"

"Nothing. Come on."

He took her by the hand again and they headed for the piece of driftwood that was always there. Droplets of water clung to their skin and sand stuck to the soles of their feet.

They sat down on the wood, each of them wrapping their arms around their knees and gazing out to where the water kissed the lavender sky. The stars were silver, just as they always were, and they sparkled around the pale moon above them.

"Where are you?" Ash asked.

"Huh?" Out of the corner of his eye, he saw her glance in his direction. "I'm here."

"No, I mean out there. Where are you?"

"Oh." She averted her gaze, back out to the sea. "I'm in my bed."

"You were really tired, you said?"

"Mm-hm," she said, nodding. "I went to an early dinner with my friend. To the buffet again."

The buffet. The one that Tayshia had gone to so many times the past month. The one she claimed tasted good.

What if it wasn't just about the taste for her?

Either she wasn't making herself sick and he was fucking insane, or she was and she'd used the buffet to do it in plain sight. But how had she gotten away with that without anyone saying anything? Wasn't she embarrassed? He supposed that it didn't matter if she was never going to see someone from a public restroom again, but it seemed like a lot of trouble to go through when she could just use the bathroom at home.

But perhaps she had used the bathroom at home. Maybe she'd waited to do it until she returned. Or perhaps it didn't matter.

Maybe she was fine doing it anywhere.

Ash remembered his mother falling asleep at the kitchen table one night when he was fifteen. It was the Summer and he remembered it being especially warm that night. The sort of warm that made the skin underneath his arms prickle with sweat — the kind of heat that buzzed. It was late and Lizette had been in the kitchen almost as soon as the clock struck midnight.

After her fourth trip to the bathroom to get rid of her nightly meals, she had seemed lethargic and droopy-eyed. Ash had watched from the shadows on the stairs as she folded her arms to use as a pillow by her empty plate. She'd slept there for an hour while Ash stood in fear and confusion, waiting. She'd awoken, of course, and hadn't caught him because he was so quick on his feet.

Lizette swayed like a willow branch in the wind on her way back to bed.

Was that what had happened to Tayshia today? Had she gone to the buffet, came home, made herself sick, and then grown so tired that she simply could not keep her eyes open? Was this like Halloween, when Tayshia used the bathroom and then fell asleep on the couch within moments of lying down?

He looked down at Tayshia, his legs shaking from the intensity of his emotions. Gritting his teeth against the depth, he scrutinized her and tried not to imagine what it would be like to have two women he cared for die in front of him.

"Tayshia."

It took her a languorous moment to tear her eyes away from the sea. When they lifted to meet his, they were sparkling.

"Hm?" she said.

"If your heart feels tired... Will you promise to tell me?"

She appeared confused. "Okay."

He closed his eyes for a moment. It didn't feel any better.

"Ash."

"What?"

"What do you see when you look at me?"

His heart skipped a beat, stuttering in his chest as it caught up with his mind. Something about the way she said the words — fear draped in innocent delivery — made him think she was looking for a specific answer.

"I see..." He shrugged his shoulders. "I don't know. Earlier this year, I would have said I saw a bitch with a superiority complex."

"And now?"

"I see..." He met her eyes, searching deep down into them as he tried to sense what he could possibly say to assuage her. She wanted an answer. She wanted to know what he thought of her.

Did his opinion matter?

"Ah, actually never mind," Tayshia said, the sudden irritation in her voice shattering the spell. She dropped her chin to her folded arms. "It was a silly question."

"Silly? No — I was just thinking of what to say." He rubbed the back of

223

his neck with one hand.

"It was silly."

"It really —"

"It was stupid, all right?" she cried, glaring at the empty air in front of her. "I shouldn't be asking you questions like that. It's too much." She looked crestfallen as she tilted her head up to the starlight. "We don't need to be getting familiar when without these crystals, we're so... Unfamiliar."

"Tayshia," he said, voice sharp enough to draw her gaze to his. He placed his hand on her shoulder, pretending not to notice the fact that he could feel her bones jutting into his skin when he did. "There's nothing wrong with making the best of things. We wouldn't be able to walk each other's dreams if we didn't have the crystals and you know that, so you might as well accept it. Accept what your life is. Accept that you're connected to me in some way, shape, or form, and accept that it's okay for us to be familiar."

"Easy for you to say." She was stiff beneath his touch, her jaw tight.

"What is? Thinking it's okay?"

"Practicing acceptance," she spat. "You accept what you've got and it doesn't overwhelm you. It doesn't feel like this giant ball of darkness, constantly hovering in the back of your mind." She reached up to touch the amethyst, her frown so deep that it looked carved. "If I accept any part of my life — including this connection — I'm afraid I'll completely..."

She trailed off and if it weren't for the way her voice shook, he would have thought she hated the sand from how intently she glared at it.

"Afraid you'll what?"

"I'm afraid I'll fall apart."

"Why? You know who you are. You've always known who you were, which is more than I can say for myself. I didn't know who I was until I went to jail. I went through some tough shit there, especially in that part of my life. Why pretend like it's hard for you to figure it out now?"

"Because you're wrong. You're wrong about me. I don't know who I am and I never have. I know who I am to the world — my mother and father's daughter, a sister, Kieran's ex-girlfriend, everyone's friend, Christ Rising's resident Good Girl." The bitterness in her tone dripped like molten rock. "I know what everyone sees when they look at me, and —"

"How do you know that?"

She appeared taken aback, like his interruption of her rant had thrown her for a loop.

"How do you know what everyone sees when they look at you?" Ash put his hands on the large driftwood surface beneath them, leaning back. He stretched his legs out and crossed his ankles. "Unless you're psychic, you don't know what they think."

"Yes, I do. They're my friends and my family. I know exactly what they think about me."

"No, you don't." He raised his eyebrows. "You think you do because they're your friends and your family, and you're asking me what I think of you because you don't know me as well. You can't read me like a book — not the way you can read the people you know."

"And you know me?" Her breathing hitched, and he knew he'd hit a nerve. She jumped up. "I guess that's why I said it was stupid of me to ask you that question, especially since I already know the answer!"

She turned and started walking.

Ash scrambled to his feet, turning to watch as she slipped and stumbled across the loose grains of sand underfoot.

"You don't know the answer, and that's the point, Tayshia!" he shouted, feeling his temper snap like a brittle, charred branch. "You can't know everything about everything. You can't know what other people think of you. You — "

He cut himself off. Realization dawned so suddenly that it nearly bowled him over. Tayshia kept stomping off, yelling things back at him that he could hardly hear due to the crashing of the waves against the beach.

Ash took off after her, catching her right as she stepped onto the grass.

"That's the problem, isn't it?" he asked, turning her to face him. "You like to tell yourself that you know what everyone's thinking of you because it gives you some sort of control over your life. But you know deep down that you can't know everything — that any idea you have could be completely wrong at its foundation. They're your friends. They're your family. They'll lie to you."

"That's not — "

"But I won't." He smiled, but it was out of sheer incredulity. Keeping his fingers wrapped tight around her upper arm, he pressed on. "I won't lie to you, because you actually think I despise you so much that I have no reason to lie to you. You want to know what I see when I look at you because you think I'll tell you I see someone repulsive."

The silence felt thick within his ears. But he could see it there — could see her faltering. Could see her resolve beginning to crumble and shatter and fold in on itself. Her chin tilted down toward her chest as the guard she worked so hard to keep up came down for him.

Again.

"I know you do," she said, voice soft. "And I want to hear you say it so I can feel right."

"Why?"

"*Because I want to hear it.*"

"*Hear what?!*" he said, eyebrows shooting upward. "*That you're repulsive?!*"

"*Aren't I?*" she cried, and then she ripped her arm away from him. "*Aren't I? I'm messy and I'm rude and I'm conceited. Oh, I'm so conceited. I completely and utterly think that I'm God's gift to the Earth, and I've always lived my life that way. I have* always *walked the halls at school thinking I'm the best. When I would go home, I was the good girl. I wanted to be good because I am good, and I—I—*"

"*And you've been trying to prove to everyone that you're not bad.*"

She looked up at him, her face pinched. She tried again and again to say something but had been rendered speechless. Her chin quivered.

So he spoke for her, his hand sliding down to hold her elbow gently. He ducked his head to hold her gaze before it fell to the ground again.

"*You've been trying to prove it to everyone, because you don't really think you're the best, do you? You think you're the worst. You think you're the fucking worst. And you think if anyone found out how awful a person you really were, that no one would want to talk to you or be your friend. Because if you really were the best person you could possibly be, then you wouldn't have gotten attacked in that alley. You would have been able to handle it.*"

She turned her face away as he continued.

"*And you want to hear me say you're repulsive because that satisfaction hurts in the best kind of way—knowing that you were right, even when being right means you hate yourself.*"

Tayshia squeezed her eyes shut.

"*Sound about right?*"

She opened her eyes again, tears swimming in them, and then she turned her back on him.

"*I'm tired of crying, Ash. I can't. Not here. Not here. It's supposed to be safe.*"

Ash gripped her other elbow and pulled. Her head fell back against his chest as she looked up at him. A tear slid down her cheek.

"*It* is *safe, Tayshia. With me, you're always gonna be safe.*"

Her face screwed up as she fought with herself for another moment. Then, like a volcano, she erupted. The tears fell out of her the way they always seemed to do, and she buried her face in her hands. Her body, so frail in the dream world, was easy for him to pull against his chest. He wrapped his arms around her, pain coursing through him at the touch.

Why was she imagining this for herself?

Ash held Tayshia while she wept. Again. And he would continue to do *it again, and again, and again. As many times as it took her to cry all of the tears. Because now, as he stood here underneath a pale lavender sky studded with the silver stars of his dreams, he knew that he wanted to be there the moment she ran out of tears.*

He wanted to be the first one to see her when the smile finally reached her eyes.

"I'm sorry," she said after a few minutes, extricating herself from his arms. "Can we just sit down?"

"All right. Back on the driftwood?"

She looked around, her gaze settling on the vast field with its flowers and shifting grass. "Let's lie in the flowers. I don't want to wake up yet."

☼☼☼

Ash followed her for a while, until she came to a place she seemed to like.

Tayshia laid on her back, so he followed suit, lying beside her. It was soft beneath his back, like lying on a cloud. He felt the flowers around him tickling his face, almost like the soft brush of a mother's fingers against her child's cheeks. Ash rested his hands behind his head to provide himself something to lay on.

Above them stretched the stars for miles. Lying here, trapped in a dream with the person who might be his soulmate, it felt like they were the only two people in the entire universe. They were small and insignificant. Their trials and tribulations meant nothing compared to the black holes that ate the cosmos and the galaxies that swirled for eternity.

Eternity was a long, long time.

"I've always liked looking at the stars," Tayshia said in a muted tone. Her braids fanned out like a halo around her head and her hands rested on her stomach. One curved over her ribcage while the other was positioned over her belly. "I never wanted to study Astronomy in school or anything, but I've always loved the way the skies look when there's nothing else around. Nothing to pollute the light with shadows. It makes me think of when I was kid."

"Oh, yeah?"

"Yes, my dad used to open the curtains in my room for me at night so I could fall asleep while I like, looked at them you know." She turned her head to look at him. "I memorized Orion's Belt the fastest."

Ash turned his head to look at her, too. "Of course you did. It's the easiest one to spot."

"I know."

Half of his mouth curved upward. They both looked up at the sky again.

"What about you?" she asked with a sigh. "What's Ash's favorite

constellation? I'm guessing Cassiopeia, since she was just as conceited as you are."

"Shut up," he said, cracking another half-smile. "You like the most basic constellation. What does that say about you?"

"So, I was right! Cassiopeia is your favorite constellation. How boring."

"No," he snapped, resisting the urge to elbow her in the side. He didn't want to hurt her. "My favorite constellation is Sagittarius."

"Hmm. Why?"

"Because it's at the center of the Milky Way, and I like to be the center of everyone's attention."

They burst out laughing, sharing the joke amongst one another like old friends. Her laughter sounded musical, a unique song he felt like he was hearing for the first time. One that only he would ever know the lyrics and melody to.

"I've never liked being the center of attention," she said, her amusement slow to fade. "I remember winning prom queen was a nightmare for me. All that make-up, the fluffy fabrics. And the dancing. God damn. It was a 'no' for me."

"You don't like dancing?"

"Oh, Hell nah," she said with a groan. "It's decrepit. Kieran was terrible at it and it felt like all anyone wanted to do was bump and grind like it was the 2000s. And I felt like everyone was watching me."

"They were."

"They were what?"

Their eyes met again, as if on cue.

"Watching you," he said. "Everyone was."

She arched one eyebrow, giving his face a once-over. "Even you?"

"I wouldn't know. I wasn't at prom. I was probably fucked up on addies, or something."

"Mm-hm." Her lips twisted. "You probably would have been mean to me, anyway."

"Bruh, shut up. No, I — "

"You were a sarcastic jerk when we were younger — don't play. You always liked riling me up and breaking the rules on purpose."

"It was because you were pretty."

"Miss me with that patriarchal bullshit," she said with a laugh. "Well, I'd say those were my peak moments, then. The entire student body, watching me. Ash Roburds, thinking I was pretty enough to be rude to. Now, I've lost my looks. Whatever is a girl to do?"

Ash breathed a laugh. "Lost your looks? Oh, yeah, because you were fourteen-going-on-seventy-five. Wrinkling already."

"I don't look seventy," she muttered, "but I've certainly lost whatever looks I may have had back then."

"Wait, what?"

"I mean, I was never really that **pretty**, per se, but whatever I did have is — " She waved a hand across the air above her, as though wiping the sky free of stars. " — gone."

"Are you serious?" He lifted himself onto his elbows. "Are you being serious right now?"

"Yes," she said. "I'm not blind, Ash. I know how ugly I am."

"Tayshia," he spluttered. "You're not ugly."

"Yes, I am!" she cried, moving her hands up to feel different parts of her face. "My forehead is too big. My nose is horrific with how wide it is. My skin looks awful; it's so dry and patchy. My lips are too — too pouty. Like, they turn down when I'm not smiling and it makes me look unapproachable. And my — around my jaw right here — is so puffy. And the underside of my chin is bloated and it — " She massaged the flesh underneath her jaw. " — is too much. There's too much of it. It's like I don't even have a chin at all." She held both hands over her stomach. "I feel like it's crawling inside of me."

"Whoa, whoa, whoa — " He tangled the fingers of one hand in his hair and sat up fully. "What the fuck? What the actual fuck?"

"What?"

Of all the things he thought Tayshia might think of herself, all of that bullshit? Definitely not something he could have predicted. And it made him angry. Was she absolutely blind?

"Tayshia, you'd better not ever let me hear you say that shit again. I'm serious."

"Huh?" She pushed herself up onto her elbows, her braids falling back. "What?"

"All of that?" He sliced an enraged hand through the air. "Stupidest shit I have ever heard you say."

"Stupid." Tayshia let out a mirthless laugh. "Right."

"You're not ugly. And it's ridiculous that you think that about yourself. First of all, your forehead is balanced for your face shape. Your nose is unique and it's cute as fuck to me. Your skin being dry has nothing to do with the way you look. It's just skin. I happen to like the way your lips pout. And you know what?"

He darted forward, slamming his lips against hers to prove a point. They smacked as he gave her a peck.

"They serve their purpose, so shut your fucking mouth unless it's to say good things about yourself, or to kiss me back."

In her face, he saw an openness that he hadn't seen before. Like he'd cracked a seal and spread her open. Now that she was sitting here, susceptible to his opinions, he felt like words he'd been holding in were spilling out of him.

"And another thing. I'm not gonna tell you that you repulse me just to satisfy some sick, twisted voice in your head that's telling you that you do. Does it tell you that you're ugly? Well, you're not. Does it say your forehead is too big, or your nose is weird? It's wrong. You're fucking beautiful, Tayshia. Do you get that? You're fucking beautiful to me, and I won't let you use me to convince yourself otherwise.

"So, to answer your stupid question: I see you. When I look at you, I just see you. And I always have." He felt like he was sinking into the flowers but it was the most honest he'd ever been in his entire life. "After the caverns, you meant something to me, I just didn't know what."

"Just stop," she said, ripping out a clump of white gardenias and tossing them aside. Her expression had soured. "Stop lying. I get that things are different now, but you don't need to lie."

Ash's head was on its way to implosion. He was so sure in that moment that he was going to throttle her that it scared him. His head snapped to look down at her and she flinched, perhaps terrified of the same thing.

"Have you gone absolutely fucking nuts?!"

Tayshia's eyes flashed in the purplish glow from the sky. "I can recognize that you think that I'm beautiful, but I don't see it! When I look in the mirror, I don't see anything I like, so why should I pretend I do just to make a man feel comfortable? Why do I have to care about everyone else's comfort all the time?!"

Her voice rose higher, growing into more of a whine as she went. "What about me? Why's it so bad when I admit that I'm not comfortable with who I am or the way I look? Why can't I just say I think I'm ugly to the person I trust without him getting angry with me?!"

Wait.

"You trust me?"

"Yes, so why don't you just let me think I'm ugly and get over it!"

A silence stretched thick and electric between them. The absurdity of her words hit them at the same time.

They began to laugh. Their laughter intensified every time their eyes met, until there were tears streaming down Tayshia's face again. Until Ash's stomach hurt from laughing so hard. Until Tayshia was fanning herself from howling.

Until Ash's heart wanted to burst from how much he liked to hear her laugh.

"You're not ugly," he said, a bit breathless. "You can think it all you want, but I won't."

Her eyes twinkled and her smile was small. It was small, but it was present. That mattered to him.

It was there.

Suddenly, she perked up with a gasp.

"Do you want to roll down one of the hills?"

"Huh?"

"Did you do nothing fun growing up? Come on!"

She got up and took off like a cheetah, dashing towards the nearest hill. He sighed and followed her, no longer sure if he entirely liked Tayshia when she was happy. She was too fond of exercise.

When they got to the top of the hill, she laid down horizontally, gesturing for him to follow suit. After she explained to him what to do, he laid down, stretching out with his head near her feet. Like she'd told him to, he crossed his arms over his chest.

"Ready?" she said, excitement woven through her voice like golden thread. "On the count of three. One... Two... Go!"

Ash and Tayshia rolled at the same time, letting gravity pull them down the hill like wayward logs. Over and over and over, Ash's stomach flipped and his head spun. It felt like he was floating. He heard Tayshia shrieking with delight, felt his own heart leaping up towards the stars that flickered in his vision every time he rolled upright, and he laughed again.

When they finally came to a stop in a thick smattering of gardenias, they laid there to catch their breath. He was too exhausted to move. Once again, they looked up at the stars.

"So, what do you think this is?" she asked.

"What do you mean?"

"The dreamwalking. The reason why you were able to come to my dreams without me being able to come to yours. The reason why it suddenly changed and let me in. What's your verdict?"

Ash was silent for a moment.

He didn't know why things had changed. He didn't know why she let him in before he did, when she didn't know she was doing it. And the more he thought about it, the more he realized that he didn't care.

It felt like he was just happy to have her.

"I don't know," he said. "But I'm sure we'll figure it out. We've got time. What about you?"

She was quiet for a drawn-out moment.

"I think my theories are right. I think we're two halves of the same soul, and I think that the reason why I'm here is because your heart knows it. That's why I never took the crystal off. It felt like the only thing holding us together. And the way I feel when I'm with you is... Safety. I just feel safe. And I think that's why I let you in."

"Yeah?"

"Yes. I always liked you. I liked you but I had a boyfriend and you were the antithesis of the type of guy my parents wanted for me."

Ash smirked. "So, what? You just start fights with me all the time for the Hell of it?"

"To push you away? Yep." She laughed. "I think my heart recognized you first. Yours just took a little extra time. And when it realized, you let me in."

"You think?"

"I hope."

They watched the stars again.

Ash took them all in, splattered bursts of silver light across a canvas of lavender. They were beautiful, the way they each represented billions of years of existence without ever apologizing for it. If the stars had brought Ash to Tayshia, he'd rather be the one to apologize to them for him having taken so long to see her.

"Ash," Tayshia said, "do you remember our dreams together?"

"Yeah."

"You never say anything about it when we wake up. I'm worried it doesn't mean anything to you."

"I could never forget anything I do with you."

And he meant that.

"But does it mean anything to you?" she said. "Do I mean anything to you?"

Ash's brow furrowed and he closed his eyes. His mind erased itself as he lost himself to the feeling of his heart pounding back to a normal rate. His chest rose and fell, ribcage expanding with the circumference of his lungs.

It was because he could lie beside her and just breathe that he knew she meant something to him.

"Are you listening to me?" she said, her voice sounding far away. "It feels like you're not listening to me. What I'm saying is really — "

"Tayshia."

"What, Ash?"

Ash pushed himself to sit up, looking at her over his shoulder. His gaze washed over her braids splayed out across the white petals, his lips parted as she continued to catch her breath. Her eyes were half-lidded from this vantage point, and the way her hands rested beside her head.

He was stricken.

Rolling so he was on all fours, he reached for her. Without removing his gaze from hers, he grabbed her by the thighs and dragged her downward with her hands still by her head. She gasped but didn't move to stop him. Her eyes tracked his movements as he hesitantly placed his left hand beside her right hand in the grass. His left knee brushed her waist as he hovered over her.

"What?" she repeated.

He grabbed her chin with his right hand, holding her head in place. Slowly, gaze flickering up and down from her eyes to her lips — those pouting lips he liked so much — he lowered his head. The fingers of his left hand curled into the grass right as their lips touched. He heard her sucking her breath in as his lips parted to try and steal it back.

When he pulled away, she looked like she'd forgotten how to breathe. Her chest remained unmoving as he spoke into the tense, charged silence.

"I'd dream forever if you were here with me."

He kissed her again, igniting a flame between them.

Ash felt his heart lurching forward, rising to meet hers as her hands gripped his shoulders and pulled him closer. She kissed him with a tentative mouth, in direct juxtaposition to the hungry way her hands grasped for him. Swinging his knee over until he was straddling her, he loomed above her in a way that felt protective due to the sheer difference in their sizes. His stomach looped, twisting into a tight, desperate knot. His hand drifted from her chin down to the column of her throat, resting there with a light touch and a finger tapping a silent tune against her pulse.

Tayshia's back arched.

He turned his head and deepened a kiss that already felt as deep as his dreams would allow him to go. His tongue slipped between her pliant lips, tasting the inside of her mouth like it was the first time. Sensuality drove him onward, urging him to kiss her harder.

Faster.

Until their bodies were pressed together in the grass, undulating like the waves of the sea. He heard a small sound lingering in the back of her throat and it sent his mind whirling through celestial spaces.

Fuck. The noises she made.

Ash's hands drifted down the sides of her waist, one gripping her hip and pinning her down while the other hand curved around the back of her bare thigh. Even in dreams, her skin was as soft as the gardenia petals they were now laying in. He pulled her leg up against his side and ground against her center. It was bold and it was unnecessary and it felt good.

After what they'd just had to endure again in her nightmare, it was selfish and it was wrong.

But she moaned.

She moaned into his mouth, where he devoured the sound and renewed the vigor of his kiss. His fingers dug into the flesh of her thigh as his lips trailed across her cheek to the spot that made her cry out the loudest. They grazed her earlobe and he felt her shuddering beneath him, her hands twisting in the fabric of his printed button-up. Her face fell to the side, exposing her neck to him.

He attacked her there with teeth and tongue, his heart pounding as desire pulsed through his veins. Her panting grew heavier, punctuated by more small moans, and then he sucked at the skin beneath her earlobe.

Hard.

She cried out, strangled and echoing. Her hips jerked and then began to rock, canting up to press harder against his. Ash wrapped some of her braids around his hand, letting go of her thigh so he could keep her right where he wanted her.

Because this was his dream and here, she was his.

"That feel good?" he murmured, nose brushing her jaw. "Huh? Does it feel good when I kiss you?"

"Yes," she gasped when his tongue and his lips pressed to the wet skin. "It's so good. It's —"

She broke off with another choked noise when he paid more attention to her pulse than either of them could handle. Her body writhed beneath him, her hands seeming confused — like they couldn't decide between pulling against his chest and curling into the hair at the base of his head. And when she gave that hair a sharp tug, a chill rippled down his spine and caused his eyes to roll.

"Fuck," he half-breathed, half-laughed. It felt good, to feel her heat rising to meet him where he wanted her the most. It felt like they were dancing the only sort of dance he liked to do. "You're so fucking beautiful. You feel like you're mine."

"I am."

He froze. "What?"

"I am yours."

"You are?"

She nodded, her brows pulling together as though she were afraid. "Is that — I mean, is that okay?"

Ash couldn't think about anything else.

"You're mine," he whispered before his lips descended upon hers again. He pulled back to whisper it again and again, kissing her between each one. "Mine. Just mine."

"Ash?"

He looked down at her. Her eyes wide, lower lip worrying between her teeth, she looked nervous.

"Let's try again."

His heart skipped a beat. "Are you sure?"

She nodded.

"I told you I'd wait."

"But," she said, her tone lilting a bit, "this is your dream. It's safe here. I'm me here."

His resolve cracked.

Ash's hips moved to meet hers, as though they weren't completely clothed, lying in a flower field beneath a sky made of dreams. He covered her throat with his hand again, squeezing slightly as he kissed along her shoulder. The strap of her dress fell down further, nearly exposing her breast to the starlight. The taste of the skin that stretched across her collarbone was divine.

Tayshia hooked her leg around the back of his thigh, her foot dragging down to the crease of his knee and using it to anchor herself as she drove her hips up harder. It distracted him from kissing her, and he tore the grass out in his haste to put his left hand on her hip. Ash was going to stop her — to slow her down before things got too out of hand, even here.

"It feels so real, Ash. How can it feel like this?"

The words fell from her lips like pleas.

His stomach twisted tight, clenching so hard that he thought he might cry. He had to hold himself back. No matter what, he couldn't go too far with her. He couldn't. It would hurt her. It was too soon. She wasn't thinking clearly, and neither was he.

It was the crystals. It had to be the crystals.

He felt her core through the fabric of her knickers and his trousers. He felt it as though it were wrapped around him. A jolt of something unexplainable rocketed through him as she tightened her leg around his, practically holding him in place while she ground against the same spot over, and over, and over, and over.

"So good." She was breathing the words out, the whispers falling from her lips as though the stars themselves were raining down around them. "Feels so good with you."

He looked at her face for a brief moment — at her beautiful face — and saw the desperation there. Like something from another universe altogether.

Nothing existed outside of this place.

His lips claimed hers again. They kissed as though they were just two teenagers with way too many hormones. Bodies writhing and rolling, *holding each other tight enough to meld their bones together. He was so hard it ached. She was so close she was keening. It was absurd and it was nonsensical.*

It was everything.

"Tayshia, look at me," *he groaned, hovering above her with his forearm flat on the ground to put enough distance between their faces. The rocking of her lower body stuttered as she cracked her eyes open and took a shaky breath.* "No — don't stop. Just look at me."

She resumed the movements of her hips but now that he could see into her eyes, he could feel her trepidation. It floated around them, heavy as fog.

"It's just a dream," *he murmured, voice gentle.* "Okay? It's just a dream."

Her hips found the spot again — the one that made her whine — and she relocated her earlier rhythm. Her breathing grew heavier, causing their chests to meet when she inhaled.

"You want me to touch you the way you like?"

He saw her gaze flit over the tattoos on his arms and hands. "Yes."

"Yeah?"

"Yes. It's just a dream."

He kissed her pulse, tasting her heartbeat as his fingers crept underneath the hem of her white dress. Her breathing hitched once again and stayed suspended. The closer he drew to her, the more her back arched toward him. She exhaled a groan the moment his touch found her center, caressing her over her panties.

They were soaked through.

"Fuck," *he cursed again, and then he pressed more firmly against her softness.* "Fuck, you're always so wet for me, you know that?"

Her answer was a sweet, stammering moan.

Ash found the apex of her core through the fabric, feeling her nerves as easily as though they called to him. Her leg, which was still by his right hip, fell open and laid flat on the grass. Her body went limp beneath him as he played with her, never once straying beneath her underwear. He didn't want her to panic again like she had last night.

"You like it slower or faster?" *he whispered, voice hoarse as he looked down to watch what he was doing to her.* "Huh? Tell me. Tell me so I can make you come."

"Faster," *she replied, her fingers digging into the back of his neck.* "But gentler."

"Like this?"

"I — oh — " *She bit her lip and whined.* "Mm-hm. Yes. Like that."

As Ash fell into a pattern that had worked to get her off before, he noticed that the way her hips were rolling were encouraging his fingers to slide downward. Closer and closer to her depths.

When she reached for his hand and pulled it towards the edge of the center of her panties, he knew what she wanted.

"Are you sure?" he whispered, his voice hoarse and husky from kissing her. "Because we can stop – "

"I can take it." Tayshia looked him directly in the eyes. "If it's here with you, I can take it. I want it."

Lifting his chin and holding her gaze, Ash slid two fingers past the cotton barrier. He didn't stop to explore the soft curls he felt, didn't want to go slow when his passions were burning so bright. He simply slipped them inside of her body. She let her eyes fall shut as they sank within her and pulled out again.

And he lost it.

"Oh, fuck," he groaned, his lips pressing kisses to her throat that were as hot as she was inside. His fingers moved faster, his mind traversing empty expanses as he forgot who he'd become and reverted back to the guy who knew how to make a girl come multiple times before he ever fucked her. "I'm gonna make you fucking come... Right here... For me."

Tayshia threw her head back, her spine arching off of the ground as Ash touched her exactly the way she liked. She was so wet. Beyond wet. Fucking Hell, did he want her. He wanted all of her for the rest of eternity, right here, right beneath the stars. And holy shit, if he could make her come undone just like this – just fucking like this – he would lose it.

"You're so fucking perfect like this," he growled as he moved his fingers faster and faster, until they were slamming in and out of her body. "You look like an angel when I'm fucking you with my fingers, baby."

Her face screwed up and her body went rigid. He looked up at her through his lashes as she moved her hips to meet the thrusts of his hands. He paid attention to her – she liked contrast. No matter how hard his movements. He knew better than to switch anything up now.

Not when she was so close.

"Ash," she squeaked out, her trembling fingers wrapping around his forearm. They squeezed involuntarily, almost to the tune of a heartbeat. Like she wanted his fingers out of her because it was too intense, too relentless, but closer because it felt so good. "Ash – I can't – I'm going to – "

"Yeah?"

"Please," she groaned, her head so far back that he could hardly see her face anymore. "Please, please, please, please. I'm right there. I just – "

"Look at me."

She did, through hooded eyelids as she bit her lip, her entire body shuddering on the edge.

"It's just us." His other hand disappeared into her panties, where he used those fingers to work her from the outside while he continued to work her from the inside as well. "Just you... And me. And I'm gonna keep you safe, okay?"

Tayshia inhaled a stuttering gasp, her eyelids fluttering like she wanted to close them. Ash leaned forward to kiss her, and it changed the angle. His fingers hit deeper and he swallowed her screaming moan. She tore gardenias out of the grass as he maintained his pace. Slow outside, fast inside. Gentle, hard. Affectionate, punishing.

He heard her groan, saw her nodding and her brows coming together. She was concentrating. She was scared. But he could see it in her eyes — there was no stopping it.

There was no stopping the way they felt about each other.

Tayshia shattered for him a few moments and two wet swipes of his fingertips later, her muscles convulsing and a series of tapered moans singing out into the night air when she did.

"That's right," he whispered between kisses to her jaw. "Good girl. That's it, come for me just like that."

Her legs closed around his body as the sensations overwhelmed her, but he kept touching her until she couldn't take it anymore. Tayshia opened her eyes and the moment he looked into them, he broke. Ash covered her lips with his own in a kiss that was ten times more frenzied than the last. Dream or otherwise, he would never be able to get the image of her face when she came out of his mind. He would never stop cherishing that sort of trust. After everything that had happened to her, she'd felt safe enough with him to let him touch part of her like that.

But then, as their tongues pressed together, something shifted in the dream.

It felt off, like the sky was lavender bleeding blue, and the stars were fading from silver to white. Reality was crashing back down, like a curtain made of constellations being drawn.

What was going on?

He heard something — a new sound. Was it coming from the beach?

Ash lifted his head and glanced behind him, placing his hands on either side of her in the flowers to keep himself upright. He felt her fingers slipping beneath his shirt, feeling the bare skin on his abdomen.

Nothing but the waves crashing.

"Ash."

He turned back to her, seeing the way the stars burned in her eyes. They kissed again, just as frenetic with need as before, but this time, it didn't feel right.

It didn't feel real anymore.

"It's just a dream."

There it was again. The sound.

He pulled away and looked behind him.

The sea was there, a tidal wave hundreds of miles high rearing up over them. Panic exploded in his chest as the ocean began to arch downwards. He looked down, not knowing how to protect her.

But she was gone.

The water crashed over him, alone.

CHAPTER TWENTY

Ash woke.

He could hear a scraping sound in the kitchen, could smell something cooking. There was an ache in his neck from having fallen asleep on the couch. It was dark outside and the only light came from the stove light spilling a warm glow outward. He felt so tired that he was contemplating drifting off again.

The sound came again. His eyes snapped back open.

"Is that you?" he called.

"Yes," Tayshia said. "I'm making a snack."

He groaned and stretched. Getting to his feet, he ambled over to the light.

Sure enough, it was Tayshia. She was standing at the stove. There was a pot of noodles in some sort of red sauce on the burner, and she was stirring it with a spatula. She'd changed into the oversized sweater he'd gotten her on her birthday, and she wore the hood up over her unruly curls. Her legs were clad in pink leggings. Her eyes looked hollow the way they stared at the food.

"This is your version of a snack?" he asked, leaning against the wall. "You know, you could just make a normal dinner and then have a real snack later."

"It's okay," she mumbled. "I'm only craving this right now. Did you sleep well?"

"I guess. Did you?"

"I napped," she said, and he saw her cast him a sidelong glance.

He wondered if she was avoiding it on purpose.

"What time is it?"

"Almost eleven. I slept for longer than I wanted to."

"Ah."

What if it really was just a dream? What if all the heartfelt things they'd shared, the things they'd talked about, weren't real? What if it was all a figment of his imagination?

A yawn escaped him.

"Well, it appears I'm still fucking tired."

"So, go back to sleep," she said, her tone somewhat clipped. "We got school tomorrow."

"All right."

Ash pushed away from the wall, eyeing her for a second more. Tayshia looked up at him from under the hood, lips pouty and eyes wide.

"What?"

"Nothing. You just look beautiful."

She stared at him like a doe for a second and then she ducked her head down to focus on stirring the boiling noodles. "Is that the crystal talking, or is it you?"

"Does it matter?"

"Yes."

Ash turned to go. "If I tell you I think you look beautiful, don't question where it comes from. Just accept the compliment."

He heard her scoff and start to speak, but he interrupted her.

"Even if you think I'm lying."

He went to his room and collapsed in bed. Whatever happened in the dream, he'd deal with it all later.

Right now, he just wanted to sleep.

☼☼☼

Ash woke for the third time that day.

His bedroom was even darker than before he fell back to sleep, and he was groggier than Hell. His head pounded, throbbing with a dull ache. His stomach rumbled, curling in response to his hunger. He sat up, swinging his feet around to place them flat on the floor.

He hadn't dreamt of anything at all, which was surprising for him. Even before Tayshia could enter his dreams, he always dreamed of something. Of *her*.

And he'd been hoping for a glimpse of her smile again.

Ash glanced at the clock. It was midnight and fuck, was he hungry. He felt the same dismay he felt when he woke up too early for his school alarm, but not early enough to go back to sleep. He was exhausted after so many nights of such vivid dreams. If it weren't for how starved he was, he'd just go back to sleep.

He was going to sit with Tayshia at breakfast, he'd decided. Even if they couldn't talk frankly about the dream or Paris at the table, he was hoping she'd let her guard down further if she spent more time with him. They needed to discuss it so they could figure out how to avoid having to endure that nightmare again next time.

Ash crossed the hallway. His jaw stretched as he released one final yawn of sleepiness on his way to use the bathroom. He combed his fingers through his hair and opened the door. His heart leapt up into his throat.

It was occupied by someone who'd forgotten to lock the door.

"Oh, fuck," he said. "I didn't know you were..."

He trailed off.

She should have remembered to lock it.

Tayshia was in the bathroom, on the linoleum floor worshipping a god made of porcelain. She was on her knees with her forearm braced along the seat. The fore, middle, and ring fingers of her right hand were sliding out of her mouth.

Covered in vomit.

It was on her chin, smeared across her lips and the lower halves of her cheeks. It had clumped beneath her nails. It riddled her fingers and the back of her hand. Red sauce and chunks of noodles dripped down her bare arm—which was exposed because she'd rolled her sleeve up—and into a toilet full of her sick. The entire room reeked of acid and pasta.

One hour.

He'd only been asleep for one hour.

Ash's mind flashed to the fear that had plagued him for years. The fear that had kept him staying up night after night on the stairs when he was a kid. The fear that pushed him to clean up after his mother because he thought if he were supportive and helped her, that she'd get better on her own. That she'd see how much he loved her and stop doing it.

Tears of panic stung at his eyes, thousands of pins pricking and stabbing.

Was this what his mother had looked like when she was worshipping that same god?

"I'm sorry," Tayshia gasped out, coughing. Appearing mortified, she drew the back of her clean hand across her mouth. "I'm sorry, Ash. I'm sorry. Please don't be mad at me."

Ash's hands trembled at his sides as he took in the heartbreaking, revolting sight. Inside, he felt as cold as eternity.

It hurt.

It fucking *hurt* to look at her and see someone who was supposed to be strong look so damn broken. Ash couldn't bear it. It was like tearing a black hole open in the center of his chest and letting it devour him alive. He could feel it ripping him to shreds, turning the memories of his mother to nothing.

He couldn't look at her. It was because he couldn't look at her that he turned around, took what remained of those torn memories, and walked down the hallway.

"Ash, wait. *Wait!*"

He could hear the tap water running, no doubt as she tried to clean herself up as fast as possible. Ash didn't look behind him as he went to his room to tug his shoes on.

Tayshia appeared in his doorway, the moonlight illuminating her silhouette like a night ship at sea. "I'm really sorry, okay? Can't we talk about this?"

Ash tied his boots one after the other, then went to stand in front of her. He couldn't look at her. If he did, he'd break down. She always broke him down.

"Move."

"Come on," she said, her voice high-pitched and needy. Panicked. "Come on. Just go back to your bed and we can talk."

"I'm getting my keys… And I'm leaving." He glowered into the hallway over the top of her head, sending his ire to the darkness. "*Move.*"

Tayshia's hands pressed to his chest, smoothing over it like she could quell the flames that blazed inside of him. "Let's talk first, okay? It's fine. Everything is fine, so let's just talk."

Ash's hands shook with the sudden burst of rage that overcame him. He wanted to shove her away. Tayshia disgusted him. She wasn't his girlfriend or his hook-up. She wasn't his anything.

She was just a reminder.

"If you don't get out of my fucking way, I'll move you myself," he whispered, bending until his lips were beside her ear. He continued to look past her so he wouldn't have to see her face. "I said *move.*"

Tayshia ducked her head down, her shoulders curling inward as she wordlessly stepped aside.

Ash moved past her, an iceberg passing by in the night.

He'd made it five steps before she dashed after him. Her fingers wrapped around his, continually grabbing at his hand even though he kept wrenching himself out of her grasp. Panic and rage were expanding in his body, shredding him apart. He was gonna lose his shit.

Tayshia didn't get it.

"Ash, *please*—"

"*Get the fuck off of me!*" he roared, yelling at her louder than he'd ever yelled before. He glared down at her, pointing with two angry fingers. "You get the fuck away from me *now*."

Her face fell, puffy and streaming with tears. "I'm sorry. I'm really, really sorry. I wanted to tell you but I didn't know how!"

"That's your mistake. Thinking I care what the Hell you do to lose weight. But if you *had* told me?" He hissed his words, looming over her as she cowered back towards the couch. "I would have told you to keep that shit out of my fucking house."

Tayshia sank to sit on the armchair, her curls limp and damp around her face where she'd gotten them wet.

"Please just stay," she said, sobbing with her hands clasped before her. Begging. Desperate. "Just stay and we can talk about everything. We can talk about it, and I can explain."

"What is there to *explain*, Tayshia?!" he shouted, his fingers at his temples. "Are you delusional? There's nothing that can explain this! You eat all the fucking food I buy and then you make yourself throw it up. Sounds pretty *fucking* self-explanatory!"

"Please stop yelling." Her voice was meek. She was carrying herself small, a lioness tamed by chagrin. "I'm sorry. I'll eat something for you if you just stay."

"No."

"You promised!" she wailed, tears pouring down her cheeks and dripping off of her jaw. "You promised you would give me everything, so stay. I want you to *stay*!"

Fury.

How dare she use that against him?

Ash spun and stormed toward her. Her eyes popped open and she started to stand but she was too slow. Ash's hand wrapped around the underside of her chin, forcing her to look up at him by a bruising grip on her cheeks.

"The girl I promised that to is not the girl I just saw on her knees in that bathroom. The girl I promised that to is strong and fights for herself. She fights to be happy. The girl I saw in there? Weak. As good as dead." His mouth twisted as he debated holding his vitriol in. Then, he let it loose. "This girl smells like vomit."

Ash tore his fingers away from her skin, went to the kitchen counter to grab his car keys, and wrenched the front door open.

"I'll do anything if you just stay," Tayshia said through her gut-wrenching weeping. "Please. Just stay."

The slam of the front door echoed louder than the sounds of her sobs, which he could hear through the thin apartment walls. He paused, twirling his keys around his forefinger as he debated. His crystal felt heavy around his neck, connecting them even though he felt like she was very, very far away.

He could turn around and go back inside. Pull her into his arms and lay with her on the couch. Apologize until she felt safe again.

Hold her and fix everything.

Glancing over his shoulder, his heart reached for the door. Reached for her. Like she was his favorite star and he'd wished on her.

He'd hurt her. He'd told her in that alleyway outside the restaurant that he was afraid of hurting her. Yet here he stood, listening to her weep so loud it was probably going to wake their classmates in the neighboring apartments. He knew he should turn around and march back in there to handle this the right way.

But what was the point?

It wouldn't bring his mother back.

Standing there outside the apartment that was theirs, he could feel it. The sea. The waters, deep and pressing, spreading for miles. Stretching to the horizon, where the waves disappeared into the sky. That sea with the bright days and the starlit nights.

And he was drowning in it.

It was pulling him under, erasing him. Leaving nothing behind. His lungs were full of Tayshia, and he was drowning. That was why he couldn't go back inside. Because if he went back inside and drowned in her, he'd never forgive himself.

Ash no longer feared the sea.

And now, an exclusive excerpt
from Book Three in the *Apricity* series:

THE APRICITY SERIES

SUNLIGHT
through the Shadows

Ash drove for a long time.

For over an hour, he drove into the darkness of the freeway out of the mountains and West towards the coast. He didn't know where he was going to stop. He simply put on his favorite band, blasted the music, and drove. There were plenty of other cars and trucks on the road so he didn't feel lonely.

He felt stressed out. He felt stressed out, angry, and lied to. Like every time she'd ever eaten and then gone to the bathroom, she'd lied to get him to turn a blind eye. Everything was built on lies.

So he drove fast.

He drove faster than the speed limit, pushing seventy so he could feel like he had control over *something*. Because he couldn't control her and he knew he couldn't, but he *could* control his car. He could put the pedal down to the floor and weave in and out of lanes, zooming around bends that brought him as close to the cliffs overlooking the ocean as possible. He could play cards with Death to see who folded first. To see who *did* win.

And he may have cried.

It was overwhelming because in order to be angry with Tayshia, he'd have to admit that his mother was a liar, too.

Ash didn't want to be angry with his mother.

He stopped at a gas station in Nehalem, completely uncaring of the fact that tears were streaming down his face even as he handed his debit card to the attendant. The attendant gave him a strange look before walking over to swipe his card.

Ash was going to drive to Brookings.

No.

He was going to go further. To California. He was going to drive and keep driving, until Oregon faded into California and California faded into Mexico, and he was never going to come back. He had the money. He could do it.

What was the point in doing his prerequisites if he didn't care enough about his future to go on to finish his last two years at a university? After college, he was looking down the barrel of a gun that his time in jail had created. He was going to have to fight for every opportunity that he could have had given to him if he hadn't made the wrong choices.

What was stopping him from going to another country and never coming home?

Ash took a deep, shuddering breath. He needed to stop crying. The fucking tears in his eyes were making the road blurry. Going seventy miles per hour in the middle of the night on the freeway while playing tag with semi-trucks everywhere wasn't exactly going to get him a royal flush with Death.

His engine revved as he crossed behind a sedan to the left lane, shot past it and the semi-truck in front of it, and then shifted into the right lane again. Before the truck driver on the left could realize what he was doing, Ash was speeding past him and shooting into the left lane again. The driver honked angrily but he ignored it.

He was running away from home.

Home.

If he went back to the apartment, back to Tayshia, it *would* be like coming home. And aside from Andre, Ji Hyun, and Ryo, she was the closest thing he had to family right now. She knew him.

As he sped in and out of the left and right lanes, passing cars and causing more people to have to hit the brakes to avoid his eternal assholery, he knew.

He needed to go home.

As Ash glanced across the windshield, over at a large sign that marked the next exit, he saw them in his rearview mirror.

The flashing blue-and-red lights.

"Ah, fuck," he said, slamming the heel of his palm against the edge of the wheel. "*Fuckin'* Hell."

The siren sounded right as he was turning his blinker on.

Ash wiped his clammy palms on his before he rolled the window down. The cars on the freeway zoomed past like giant buzzing bees as the officer came sauntering up to the window.

"Evening, son," he said from beneath a bushy grey mustache and a hat with a wide brim. He peered down at him almost curiously. "How you doin' tonight?"

"Fine," Ash said, flashing a nervous smile. "Uh… You?"

"Just fine, just fine. You realize you were going seventy-two in a sixty-five, right?"

"No. I-I mean, yes." Ash cleared his throat, keeping his hands on the wheel at ten and two to ensure he was following any possible rules. His entire body shook as the December air wafted into his cold car. "Yes, I know I was."

He was glad he'd managed to stop crying, else he'd probably get forced to take a breathalyzer test. He hadn't been drinking but he was terrified of what would happen if the officer decided to be a stickler tonight.

Ash was on probation.

The officer pursed his lips and watched him, then glanced off into the distance down the highway. When he turned back, Ash was so scared he thought he might pass out.

He never should have gone driving. He should have just gone home.

"Have you had any drinks tonight? How old are you?"

"I'm twenty," Ash said, his voice cracking. "And no, sir. I was just going too fast. "Being—"

"Being reckless."

"Y-Yeah. Yeah, being…" Ash hung his head for a second. He felt sick. "Being reckless."

"Why don't you show me your license and registration?"

"I have to reach for my back pocket. My license is in my wallet."

"Go ahead."

Ash swallowed, remembering what it was like in jail to move his hands too fast and have a correctional officer hit him with his baton. He lifted his rear from the seat so he could pull his wallet out. After handing the officer his license, he reached over to the glove compartment.

God, this was fucking terrifying.

"And this is my dad's car, is that okay?" he asked, even though he knew that the only problems would be if he was under the influence, or if the car had been reported stolen.

"Just go on and get me that registration, son," the officer said, glancing off into the distance again.

Ash pulled the compartment open, feeling mildly irritated at the fact that the light in the box was out. He couldn't see anything. He reached into the darkness, knowing the registration was there. He really hoped that—

His hand came in contact with something hard and cold.

Something he'd forgotten his father had in the glove compartment of both cars.

His other gun.

His second gun, which no one had any reason to know of because Lizette was dead and Gabriel was in prison. The police officers had only searched the car that had been used in the robbery—not the second car.

Fuck.

The officer couldn't have seen. There was no way. It was dark, the light in the box was out, and Ash had slid the registration out from under it faster than it took him to take another breath. As the officer accepted the registration from him, he felt his heart pounding faster with every step the officer took away from his car and back to his own vehicle.

Ash closed his eyes while he waited.

What was he supposed to do if he got arrested? He'd be fucked. He'd be absolutely fucked. He didn't want to go back to jail. The loss of freedom. The loss of any chance of a future. The loss of his friends.

Losing Tayshia.

Ash glanced at his phone. He needed to go *home*.

The officer returned. This time, Ash saw that his nametag read Officer Holloway.

Officer Holloway handed the license and registration back to him, then adjusted his pants by the belt. "Why don't you step outside the car, Mr. Robards?"

Well, shit.

He fought back the urge to burst out into tears as he unbuckled his seatbelt. Without a word, he stepped out of the car and stood up. He towered over the short, squat officer by at least an entire child but he felt smaller than dust.

Officer Holloway told him in a matter-of-fact tone that because he was on probation, he was going to run all of the necessary tests to make sure he hadn't been drinking and wasn't under the influence.

Luckily, Ash hadn't smoked any weed that day. It was legal but he didn't want to take any chances.

He was compliant as he did the tests and answered the questions. He knew his voice was trembling and that he was having a hard time maintaining eye contact out of shame but he knew that the officer wasn't going to arrest him. He could tell by his tone and the banality of the requests. The officer knew he wasn't drinking. He wouldn't be arrested.

He was just fucking with him.

Since Ash looked like he was on the verge of breaking down, Officer Holloway declined to write him a ticket. He told him to report the traffic stop to his probation officer, giving him a hollow warning that *he'd be calling to check*. Before he left, he warned him to go the speed limit.

Ash was really, *really* fortunate.

He sat there in his car, waiting for the officer to be long gone. The imminent plan would be heading to the next exit and turning around.

He was going the fuck home.

Ash's gaze slid to the glove compartment.

What if it wasn't what he thought it was? What if it was something else, like a—a walkie talkie, or something? It could be anything. There was no guarantee it was a gun.

He reached into the glove box again. His fingers closed around the metal object. The familiar shape pulled his heart to the depths. With slow, careful movements, he pulled it out and held it in his lap.

It was his father's second gun.

Ash stared at it for a long time, remembering that day. That day that everything fell apart for their family. Remembered how terrified he'd been, seeing his father waving the gun around at him, at all those people, at Mr. Cole. At Tayshia.

Sometimes, with all the things he and Tayshia had been through together, it was easy to forget where he came from. It was easy to forget the horrible things he had done. The horrible things his father had done.

But here, sitting in his father's car with his father's gun in his hands, he realized that if he shot himself with it, it wouldn't make up for the pain he'd caused the Cole family. That was how insignificant he felt. That he could die — his existence could cease — and it wouldn't matter because he was a criminal.

That terrified him.

Bzzt. Bzzt. Bzzt.

In the cup holder, Ash's phone was going off. He had a text. From Tayshia.

Please come home, it read. ***I'm sorry you had to see that but please come home so we can talk about it.***

Ash held the gun in one hand and the phone in the other. His past in his left hand and his present in his right.

He was scared of which one he'd choose in the future.

AVAILABLE NOW

ACKNOWLEDGMENTS

To all of my Tiktok followers who support this book, me, and my future.

I would be nothing and nowhere without you.

This book is dedicated to you.

I love you.

LOVED THE BOOK?

If you enjoyed this novel, if it spoke to you on an emotional level, or if you feel compelled to tell me your thoughts, please don't hesitate to leave me a review when you've completed it. I want to hear your opinions and most of all: I want to hear your stories. Every review means the world to me. I read each and every single one that I get.

To leave a review, you need only go to your Amazon orders, scroll to the purchase of this book, and click: *Write a Product Review.*

Alternatively, you can review on Goodreads.

www.goodreads.com/author/show/20655146.Mariah_L_Stevens

Thank you so much!

Mariah L. Stevens is a half-Black Autistic author and artist who lives in the PNW. She is a survivor of eating disorders, abuse, and sexual assault. She advocates for recovery and a life worth living. As someone diagnosed with BiPolar 1, she supports mental health awareness, as well as eating disorder awareness in Black individuals, and weaves all of these elements into her work with the sole purpose of helping others seek recovery.

Mariah has been writing since she was 13 years old, and she plans to use her passion and life experience to help other survivors through the power of prose. She loves Japanese fashion, *Kingdom Hearts*, Disneyland, and her cat.

Website: **www.starlightwriting.com**
Tiktok: **@theapricityseries**
Instagram: **@starlight.writing**
Facebook: **Starlight Readers**

Amelia Louise Carter (Meialoue) is a full time graphic designer and freelance illustrator from the UK. She's massively inspired by manga and anime, but also has a unique style all of her own. Completely self-taught, she's incredibly passionate about creating artwork and strives to be better one step at a time, every day.

"If you can't see the end of the tunnel right now, or you feel like everything is just hopeless, please don't give up. Get help, keep going, because if you keep trying and fight for your dreams, whether they're small or large I promise you, if you fight, you'll accomplish them."
✧✧✧ Meialoue, ever the imperfectionist.

Website: **www.meialoue.com**
Tiktok: **@meialoue**
Instagram: **@meialoue**
Etsy: **www.etsy.com/uk/shop/Meialoue**

Printed in Great Britain
by Amazon